Nobody writes mysteries better than the Queen of Suspense!
After thrilling readers for forty years,
#1 *New York Times* bestselling author

MARY HIGGINS CLARK

is still "a flawless storyteller"
(*The Washington Post Book World*).

Praise for *I'VE GOT MY EYES ON YOU*

"Clark—as always—ratchets up the suspense before the big reveal.... Superior storytelling."

—*Richmond-Times Dispatch*

Praise for *EVERY BREATH YOU TAKE*

"Mary Higgins Clark and Alafair Burke take the reader on another gripping journey.... Powerful."

—*New York Journal of Books*

Praise for *ALL BY MYSELF, ALONE*

"Murders and men missing at sea provide Alvirah and Willy dangerous excitement and ample opportunities to further test their amateur sleuthing skills. The tried-and-true whodunit formula benefits from Alvirah and Willy's down-home charm."

—*Booklist*

Praise for *THE SLEEPING BEAUTY KILLER*

"A clever plot and a cast of intriguing characters, whose actions and agendas are easily misconstrued.... The authors keep Laurie and the reader grasping for answers till the end."

—*Publishers Weekly*

Praise for *AS TIME GOES BY*

"Once again, Mary Higgins Clark validates her title as 'Queen of Suspense.'"

—*New York Journal of Books*

MARY HIGGINS CLARK

& ALAFAIR BURKE

EVERY BREATH YOU TAKE

Pocket Books

New York   London   Toronto   Sydney   New Delhi

Pocket Books
An Imprint of Simon & Schuster, Inc.
1230 Avenue of the Americas
New York, NY 10020

This book is a work of fiction. Any references to historical events, real people, or real places are used fictitiously. Other names, characters, places, and events are products of the author's imagination, and any resemblance to actual events or places or persons, living or dead, is entirely coincidental.

First Pocket Books paperback edition November 2018

POCKET and colophon are registered trademarks of Simon & Schuster, Inc.

For information about special discounts for bulk purchases, please contact Simon & Schuster Special Sales at 1-866-506-1949 or business@simonandschuster.com.

The Simon & Schuster Speakers Bureau can bring authors to your live event. For more information or to book an event, contact the Simon & Schuster Speakers Bureau at 1-866-248-3049 or visit our website at www.simonspeakers.com.

Manufactured in the United States of America

10 9 8 7 6 5 4 3 2 1

ISBN 978-1-5011-7173-4
ISBN 978-1-5011-7165-9 (ebook)

For Lee and Philip Reap
With love
—Mary

For Danielle Holley-Walker
With appreciation and admiration
—Alafair

Acknowledgments

Once again it has been my joy to cowrite with my fellow novelist, Alafair Burke. Two minds with but a single crime to solve.

Marysue Rucci, editor-in-chief of Simon & Schuster, is again our mentor on this journey. A thousand thanks for your encouragement and sage advice.

My home team is still solidly in place. They are my spouse extraordinaire, John Conheeney, my children, and my right-hand assistant, Nadine Petry. They brighten this business of putting pen to paper.

And you, my dear readers. Again you are in my thoughts as I write. When you choose to read this book, I want you to feel as though you have spent your time well.

Cheers and Blessings,
Mary

Prologue

Three Years Ago

On an unusually cold and wintery Monday evening, sixty-eight-year-old Virginia Wakeling was making her way slowly through the costume gallery of the Metropolitan Museum of Art. As she wandered through the exhibitions, she had no premonition that the glamorous evening would end in tragedy.

Or that she had only four hours to live.

The museum had been closed to the public because the most lucrative fundraiser of the year was about to begin, but for this hour the trustees were invited to privately study the gowns former first ladies had worn at inaugural balls.

Virginia's own gown was a copy of one Barbara Bush had worn in 1989. An Oscar de la Renta creation, it had a long-sleeved black velvet bodice and a peacock-blue long satin skirt. She knew it looked both dignified and regal, exactly the impression she wanted to give.

But she still was not sure of the makeup Dina had applied because she thought it might be too vivid. Dina had protested, "Mrs. Wakeling, trust me. It's perfect with your dark hair and beautiful skin, and it absolutely calls for a bright lip rouge."

Maybe, Virginia thought, and maybe not. But she did know the carefully applied makeup took ten years off her age. She moved from one inaugural gown to the next, fascinated by the differences in them: Nancy Reagan's one-shouldered sheath; Mamie Eisenhower's with two thousand rhinestones on pink silk; Lady Bird Johnson in a corn-yellow gown with fur trim; Laura Bush in long-sleeved silver; Michelle Obama in ruby red. All of these women—so different, but each so determined to look her very best next to her husband, the President.

Life has gone by so quickly, Virginia thought. She and Bob had begun their lives together in a small, three-room, two-family home on the then-unfashionable Lower East Side of Manhattan, but their lives had begun changing immediately. Bob had been born with a knack for real estate, and by the end of their first year of marriage he had put a borrowed down payment on the house they were living in. That was the first of many brilliant choices he was to make in the real estate world. Now, forty-five years later, her homes included a Greenwich, Connecticut, mansion, a Park Avenue duplex, an oceanfront showplace in Palm Beach, and a condominium in Aspen for skiing vacations.

A sudden heart attack had taken Bob five years ago. Virginia knew how pleased he would have been to see how carefully Anna was running the business he had built for them.

I loved him so, she thought wistfully, even though he

had a hot temper and was so domineering. That never really bothered me.

Then two years ago Ivan had come into her life. Twenty years younger, he had approached her during a cocktail party at an art exhibit in a small studio in the Village. An article about the artist had caught her eye, and she had decided to attend the show. Cheap wine was being served. She was sipping from a plastic glass and taking in the assorted mixture of people who were studying the paintings. That was when Ivan joined her.

"What do you think of them?" he asked, his voice even and pleasant.

"The people or the paintings?" she replied, and they both laughed.

The exhibition ended at seven. Ivan had suggested that if she wasn't busy, she might want to come with him to a small Italian restaurant nearby where he guaranteed the food was delicious. That was the beginning of what had become a constant in her life.

Of course, it was inevitable that, after a month or so, her family wanted to know where she was going and with whom. Predictably, their response to her answers had been one of horror. After he graduated college, Ivan had followed his passion in the sports fitness field. He was a personal trainer for now, but he had a natural talent, big dreams, and a strong work ethic, perhaps the only traits he shared with Bob.

"Mom, get some widower your own age," Anna had snapped.

"I'm not looking for anyone to marry," she told

them. "But I certainly enjoy having a fun and interesting evening." Now a glance at her watch made her realize that she had been standing still for minutes, and she knew why. Was it because despite the twenty-year age difference, she was seriously considering the possibility of marrying Ivan? The answer was yes.

Shaking the thought away, she resumed her study of the dress forms of the former first ladies. I wonder if any of them realized or even suspected that they would have a day like this in their lives, she asked herself. I certainly never dreamed of how my life would change. Maybe if Bob had lived longer and gone into politics, he might have been a mayor or a senator, even a president. But he did create a company, and a neighborhood, and a way for me to support causes I believe in, like the museum.

This gala drew A-list celebrities and the city's most generous donors. As a member of the board of trustees, Virginia would be front and center that evening, and she had Bob's money to thank for the honor.

She heard footsteps behind her. It was her thirty-six-year-old daughter, Anna, whose dress was as beautiful as the one Virginia had commissioned for herself. Anna had scoured the Internet for a gown similar to the gold lace Oscar de la Renta that Hillary Clinton had worn to the inauguration in 1997.

"Mom, the media are arriving on the red carpet and Ivan was looking for you. He seemed to think you'd want to be there."

Virginia tried not to read into her daughter's words. On the one hand, "he seemed to think you'd want" was passive-aggressive, as if Anna knew better what her mother would want. On the bright side, apparently Anna had had a cordial conversation with Ivan and had come searching for her at his request.

Oh, how I wish my family would accept whatever decision I finally make for myself, she thought, slightly annoyed. They have their own lives and everything they will ever need. Give me a break and let me live my life the way I choose.

She tried to brush away the thought as she said, "Anna, you look gorgeous. I'm so proud of you."

They walked out of the gallery together, Virginia's blue taffeta rustling next to Anna's gold lace.

Later that evening Virginia's black hair and colorful gown were spotted by a jogger as he ran through Central Park. He stopped when he realized his foot had grazed an object protruding from the snow. He was shocked to see that the woman he was looking at was not only dead, but her eyes were still open and her expression frozen in fear and horror.

Virginia Wakeling had fallen—or been thrown—from the roof of the museum.

1

Laurie Moran could not ignore the satisfied expression on her nine-year-old son's face as he watched the waiter place her breakfast on their table.

"What's the secret?" she asked with a smile.

"No secret," Timmy replied. "I was just thinking how really cool you look in that suit."

"Well thank you so much," Laurie said, pleased, even as she reflected on the fact that Timmy's use of the word *cool* was another sign that he was growing up. School was closed while teachers were at an education convention. Because of that Laurie had decided to go in late so she could take Timmy and her father to breakfast. Timmy had been to Sarabeth's restaurant for breakfast at least twenty times, but never approved of Laurie's choice of the eggs benedict with salmon.

"No one should eat fish for breakfast," Timmy pronounced with confidence. "Right, Grandpa?"

If Laurie had to handpick a rival for her son's affections, she couldn't have chosen a better role model than her father, Leo Farley. While other kids Timmy's age were starting to admire athletes, comedians, and musicians, Timmy still looked at his grandfather, retired NYPD First Deputy Police Commissioner Leo Farley, as if he were Superman.

"Hate to tell you this, kiddo," Leo said crisply, "but you can't keep eating pancakes with chocolate and powdered sugar on them for the rest of your life. Thirty years from now, you'll understand why your mom's eating fish, and I'm pretending to enjoy this turkey bacon that tastes like paper."

"So what do the two of you have planned for the rest of the day?" Laurie asked, smiling.

"We're going to watch the Knicks-Pacers game," Timmy said. "We recorded it last night. I'm going to look for Alex in his courtside seats."

Laurie suddenly put down her fork. It had been two months since she and Alex Buckley last spoke—and two months before that Alex had taken a break as the host of her television series to focus on his own law practice. Before Laurie even realized how important Alex was to her daily life, he was gone.

There was a reason she often joked that she needed a clone. She was always busy, both at work and as a mother, but now that Alex was gone, there was an unmistakable void in her life. She kept herself going, one day at a time, focusing on her home and her work, but that was no help.

Given Timmy's mention of Alex, she expected her father to jump in and ask, *How is Alex, by the way?* Or, *Does Alex want to join us for dinner this week?* But instead, Leo took another bite of his dry turkey bacon.

Laurie suspected that Timmy also wondered why they hadn't seen more of Alex recently. If she had to guess, she'd say he was picking up on his grandfather's cues not to ask about it directly. So instead, he had mentioned Alex's courtside seats.

Laurie tried to sound matter-of-fact. "You know Alex donates them to charities most of the time. His seats will be there, but there might be other people in them."

Her son's face fell. Timmy had managed to survive witnessing the murder of his own father. Heartsick, she realized that he was trying to replace him with Alex.

She took a final sip of coffee. "Okay, time to earn my keep."

Laurie was the producer of *Under Suspicion*, a series of true crime–based television "news specials" focusing on cold cases. The show's title reflected its format of working directly with the people who were unofficial suspects in the investigations. They had never been formally charged, but still were living under a constant cloud of suspicion. It was always so hard for Laurie to commit to one case for each special, but she had narrowed the newest possibilities down to two.

She dropped a kiss on Timmy's head. "I'll be home for dinner on time," she promised. "We'll have roast chicken?" She constantly felt guilty for not preparing more healthy meals for her son.

"Don't worry, Mom," Timmy said. "If you're late, we can have pizza."

Leo pushed back his chair. "I need to pop over to task force headquarters tonight. I'll go after you get home and be back for dinner by eight." A few months ago, her father had stepped back into law enforcement waters by joining the NYPD's anti-terrorism task force.

"Sounds perfect," Laurie said. She could not believe how blessed she was to have these two gentlemen—her sixty-five-year-old father and her nine-year-old son—always trying to make her life easier.

Fifteen minutes later she arrived at work and another man in her life immediately gave her a headache. "I was starting to wonder if you were coming in." It was Ryan Nichols, calling out to her from his office as she passed his door. He had been hired as the host of her television show a mere three months earlier, and she still had no idea what he was doing at the studio full-time. "I have the perfect case for us," he shouted as she pretended not to hear him.

2

Laurie deliberately ignored Ryan's call and made it to her own office before having to deal with him. Her secretary, Grace Garcia, immediately sensed that she was not happy. "So, what's wrong? I thought you were taking your handsome son out to breakfast." Sometimes Laurie thought that Grace valued the idea of Laurie taking a much-needed break more than she worried about her own time off.

"How can you tell something's wrong?" Laurie asked.

Grace looked at her as if to say, *Did you really just ask me that?* Grace had always been able to read her like a book.

Laurie dropped her bag on the desk inside her office, and a minute later Grace followed her carrying a cup of hot tea. Grace was wearing a bright yellow blouse, an impossibly narrow pencil skirt, and black sling-back pumps with five-inch heels. How she managed to carry anything without tipping over was a mystery to Laurie.

"Ryan saw me get off the elevator and made some crack about my coming in late," she said, spitting out the words.

"He's one to talk," Grace exclaimed. "Ever notice how he's never here on the mornings after he attends some high-society event covered on Page Six?"

Honestly, Laurie never noticed Ryan's absence. As far as she was concerned, he didn't need to be here at all until it was time to turn on the cameras.

"Oh, are we talking about Ryan's double standards for office hours?" The voice belonged to Laurie's assistant producer, Jerry Klein, who had stepped from the office adjacent to hers to linger near her door. As much as Laurie pretended to disapprove of the constant flow of gossip between Jerry and Grace, the truth was that the two of them provided some of her most enjoyable moments at work. "Did Grace tell you that he kept dropping by here, looking for you?"

Grace shook her head. "I was trying not to ruin her morning. She'll see that guy soon enough. Tell me, Laurie, has anyone told him you're the boss? He's like a clone of Brett running all over this place."

Technically, Grace was right. Brett Young was the head of Fisher Blake Studios. He'd had an enduring, successful television career. He was as tough as a boss could be, but he had earned the right to run his own ship, as tightly as he wanted.

Ryan Nichols, on the other hand, was an entirely different story. To be sure, before he turned up at Fisher Blake less than four months ago, he was an up-and-coming star in the legal world. Magna cum laude from Harvard Law School, followed by a Supreme Court clerkship. In just a few years as a federal prosecutor, he had already won the kinds of cases that were covered by the *New York Times* and the *Wall Street Journal*. But instead of continuing to develop his skills as a practicing lawyer, he left the U.S. Attorney's Office so he could become a part-time talking head on cable news stations, offering instantaneous analysis about legal issues and trial coverage. These days, everyone wanted to be a celebrity, Laurie thought.

The next thing she knew, Brett Young had hired Ryan as the new host of the series without consulting her. Laurie had found a perfect host in Alex and working with him had been a pleasure. He was a brilliant lawyer, but he recognized that Laurie's programming instincts were what made the series successful. The fact that he was a skilled cross-examiner made him the ideal questioner for show participants who thought they could get through production repeating the same lies they'd told during the original investigation.

Ryan had only appeared in one special so far. He had neither Alex's experience nor his natural skills, but he had not been nearly as disastrous as Laurie had feared. What bothered Laurie most about Ryan was the fact that he clearly saw his role at the studio differently than Alex had ever seen his. He was constantly finding ways to undermine Laurie's ideas. He also served as a legal consultant to other shows at the studio. There was even talk about his developing his own programming. And it was certainly no coincidence that Ryan's uncle was one of Brett's closest friends.

So to get back to what Grace had intended as a rhetorical question: *Did Ryan know Laurie was his boss?* Laurie was starting to wonder.

She took her time getting settled at her desk, and then asked Grace to call Ryan and let him know she was ready to see him.

Maybe it was petty, but if he wanted to see her, he could be the one to walk down the hall.

3

Ryan stood in her office, with his hands on his hips. Looking at him objectively, she understood why one of the raging debates among fans of her show was "Who's cuter? Alex or Ryan?" She had an obvious preference for one, of course, but Ryan was undoubtedly handsome, with sandy blond hair, bright green eyes, and a perfect smile.

"This view is amazing, Laurie. And your taste in furniture is impeccable." Laurie was on the sixteenth floor, overlooking the Rockefeller Center ice skating rink. She had decorated the office herself with modern, but welcoming, furnishings. "If this were my office, I might never leave."

She took a small amount of pleasure in the hint of jealousy she detected in his voice, but she didn't need his small talk.

"What's up?" Laurie asked.

"Brett seemed eager to get started on the next special."

"If it were up to him, we'd have two specials a week as long as the ratings held. He forgets how much work it takes to completely reinvestigate a cold case from scratch," she said.

"I get it. Anyway, I have the perfect case for our next episode."

She could not ignore the use of the word *our*. She had spent years developing the idea for this show.

As many unsolved murders as there were in this country, only so many of them met the unwritten criteria for the cases explored by *Under Suspicion*. Some cases were *too* unsolved—no suspects, the equivalent of random guesses. Some were essentially solved, and the police were simply waiting for the evidence to fall into place.

A very narrow category in between—an unsolved mystery, but with an identifiable world of viable suspects— was Laurie's specialty. She spent most of her time scouring true-crime websites, reading local news coverage all around the country, and sifting through tips that came in online. And always there was that intangible instinct that told her that this case was the one she should pursue. And now here was Ryan, certain that he had a novel idea for *them* to work on.

She was confident that she would already be familiar with any case Ryan mentioned, soup to nuts, but did her best to appear appreciative that he had a suggestion. "Let's hear it," she said.

"Virginia Wakeling."

Laurie recognized the name immediately. This wasn't a homicide from the other side of the country. It had occurred just a couple of miles from here, at the Metropolitan Museum of Art. And it wasn't especially cold, either. Virginia Wakeling was a member of the museum's board of trustees and one of its most generous donors. She had been found in the snow behind the museum on the night of the institution's most celebrated fundraiser, the Met Gala. It was one of the most star-studded, high-profile events in all of Manhattan. She had died after a fall—either a jump or a push—from the museum's roof.

Wakeling was a big enough presence in the art world that there were murmurs the museum might even suspend the annual gala the following year when there was still no explanation for her death. But the party continued on, despite the absence of a solution to the ongoing mystery.

Laurie remembered enough of the facts to offer an initial opinion. "It seemed pretty clear that her boyfriend did it."

"As in '*Under Suspicion*,'" Ryan said, wriggling his fingers in quotes.

"It looks like a closed case to me. He was considerably younger than Mrs. Wakeling. It seems as if the police are sure that he was the killer even if they can't prove it. Wasn't he a model or something?"

"No," Ryan said. "A personal trainer. His name is Ivan Gray, and he's innocent."

The knot in Laurie's stomach grew tighter. As strongly as she had ever felt about any of her cases, she had never been certain about anyone's guilt or innocence, especially at the outset. The entire purpose of her show was to explore an unsolved case with an open mind.

She was fairly certain that Ryan had not stumbled

onto this case by accident. "Do you happen to know Mr. Gray?" she asked.

"He's my trainer."

Of course, she thought. It made perfect sense. When Grace and Jerry were discussing Ryan's idiosyncratic hours, they may as well have analyzed his various workout hobbies: hitting golf balls at the Chelsea Pier driving range, spin classes at SoulCycle, circuit training at the gym around the corner, and, if Laurie had to guess, some latest workout craze with his new pal, Ivan Gray.

"Yoga?" she guessed.

Ryan's face made his opinions about yoga clear. "Boxing," he said. "He's the owner of PUNCH."

Laurie wasn't exactly a gym rat, but even she had heard of the trendy workout spot dedicated to boxing. Their flashy ads were emblazoned on subways and the sides of buses, depicting perfect-looking New Yorkers in fashionable exercise clothes and boxing gloves. The thought of punching an object named Ryan Nichols actually sounded pretty good to Laurie.

"I really appreciate the suggestion," she said coolly. "But I don't think that case is right for the show. It's only been three years. I'm sure the police are still investigating."

"Ivan's life has been basically ruined. We could help him."

"If he owns PUNCH, apparently it hasn't been ruined entirely. And if he killed that woman, I'm really not interested in helping him. He could be using us to try to get free publicity for his gym."

Laurie couldn't help but think back to the grief Ryan had given her only a few months ago. He hadn't even been officially hired yet, but he took it upon himself to tell her that the case of a woman already convicted of killing her fiancé was unsuitable for her own show because he was so certain she was guilty.

Ryan was looking at the screen of his iPhone. If it had been Timmy, Laurie would have told him to put it away.

"With all due respect, Ryan, the case isn't even cold yet," she said dismissively. Her own husband's murder went unsolved for five years. Even without any suspects, the NYPD kept assuring her the entire time that they were "actively working" the investigation. "The last thing I want is to hurt our relationship with law enforcement by interfering."

Ryan was tapping on his phone screen. When he finished, he tucked his phone in his pocket and looked up at her. "Well, let's hear him out. Ivan's in the lobby and is coming up."

4

Only one word came to mind when Laurie saw Ivan Gray walk into her office: huge. The man was enormous. He was at least six-foot-three, but his height was not what stood out about his appearance. There wasn't an ounce of spare flesh on his body. He looked trim and powerful. His hair was short and dyed brown. His eyes were hazel green.

She was almost afraid to shake his hand, expecting a grip that would crush her fingers. She was surprised when he greeted her with a normal, human handshake rather than a painful clasp.

"Thank you so much for inviting me in, Laurie." She had not, in fact, invited him, and had not asked him to call her by her first name.

"Well, Ryan speaks so highly of you," she said flatly.

"The feeling's mutual," Ivan said, giving Ryan a friendly punch in the arm. "The first time he came in for a session, I thought, This guy'll be begging to leave in twenty minutes. But he trains hard. Might even be able to defend himself against one of my better fighters if he keeps up the work—the female fighters, I mean."

It was the type of inside joke that immediately reminded the outsider—in this case, Laurie—that she wasn't part of the gang. Laurie wished that Ryan would show the same kind of dedication to learning basic rules of journalism. She mustered a smile.

She would normally study a case for hours before interviewing the primary suspect. She was at a loss for how to transition from their banter about Ryan's latest workout obsession to a woman's murder. Once she gestured for Ivan to have a seat on the sofa, she decided to jump right in. "So Ryan told me you're interested in having us reinvestigate the death of Virginia Wakeling."

"You can call it a reinvestigation if you'd like, but if you ask me, the NYPD hasn't investigated it for even the first time. All they needed to know was that a sixty-eight-year-old woman was dating a forty-seven-year-old man, and they made up their minds. They didn't seem to care about the complete lack of any evidence against me."

Laurie did the simple arithmetic in her head. Virginia had died three years earlier, making Ivan fifty years old today. He looked more like he was forty, but she suspected that he may have had some assistance in that area. His skin was tan, even though it was January, and that short hair might be hiding the onset of baldness.

The case had been in the news so recently that Laurie was able to recall most of the reported facts from memory. From what she gathered, Virginia's money was at the heart of the original police investigation. Her husband had been a real estate genius, successful enough to leave Virginia an extremely wealthy widow. Laurie could only imagine what Wakeling's family and friends thought when she began dating a personal trainer more than twenty years her junior.

But, despite what Ivan said, his age and profession were not the only reasons he became the leading suspect.

"With all due respect," Laurie said, "to call it a complete lack of evidence is not entirely fair to the investigation, is it? Motive, after all, is a type of evidence. There were financial concerns, as I recall."

After Virginia's death, police discovered that several hundred thousand dollars of her money had been spent on Ivan's various expenses. Her children were adamant that their mother had not authorized the expenditures. They speculated that their mother may have discovered that Ivan was stealing from her, and could have been planning to pursue criminal charges against him. That would give him a powerful motive to silence her.

"Nothing irregular at all," he said. "Yes, she helped me with some bills. The Porsche was her birthday gift to me. I tried not to accept it. It was far too generous, but she insisted. She told me that she loved the idea of being driven around in it with the top down in the summer. She said it was more a gift to herself than to me."

Laurie hadn't remembered that an expensive sports car was involved, but even a Porsche didn't amount to the kinds of expenditures at issue. "My recollection is that it was more than a car. Substantial funds were missing."

"They weren't." He punched his right fist into his left palm to emphasize the point. Laurie found herself flinching. It wasn't the first time that she had reminded herself she might be speaking to a killer. It was the nature of her work. She had a sudden eerie image of him lifting Virginia Wakeling and throwing her from the roof of the museum. Whoever killed her had to have been strong, and this man clearly fit the bill.

Ivan's voice was calm when he continued his explanation. "The money wasn't missing. Like I said, she covered some small bills of mine, plus the car. The rest of the money was an investment in PUNCH. That's my gym."

Laurie nodded to signal that she was aware of his business.

"It was a dream of mine, and Virginia knew that. She was a client. I'd have her do some boxing exercises—nothing heavy, mostly some rope jumping and shadow-boxing. It's a great workout, and totally different from everything else. People love it, and I knew that I had a winning idea. I never asked her to help me. I was absolutely shocked when she told me she'd give me the seed money. I found an old-school boxing gym and convinced the owner to sell it to me so I could transform it into a hot spot. He's technically a partner, but the business is all mine. Virginia believed in me. She knew I'd succeed, and I did."

Laurie could tell that he was proud of his accomplishments. Had they been built on the murder of an innocent woman? "How much money did she front you?"

"Five hundred thousand dollars."

Laurie could feel her eyes widen. People had killed for far less.

"I don't understand, Ivan. If she was investing in your

business, why didn't you have a written agreement or some other proof of her intentions? My understanding from news reports at the time was that the children were adamant that their mother would never have agreed to give you that kind of money."

"Because that's what Virginia told them. Her children are greedy. They've had everything handed to them, and it's never enough. They took one look at me and assumed I was a gold digger. To get them off her back, Virginia assured them that she wasn't giving me anything. She wouldn't even let me tell them that she'd paid for the Porsche. They had to suspect she was hiding it from them. I made a decent living as a trainer, but I would never have spent that kind of money on a car. But then after Virginia was killed, they made me out to be some kind of thief to the police."

"Spending money on luxuries like sports cars is one thing. You don't think a mother would tell her children that she was investing a substantial amount of money in a business?"

He shook his head. "I know that she didn't. Don't get me wrong: Virginia loved her children, and was very close to them. But they didn't really know their mother. Virginia was going through a tremendous change when she was killed. Bob—that was her husband—had been gone for five years. She was finally living her life beyond just being his wife and their mother. She was completely independent and finding such joy in her philanthropy. She had stepped back from some causes that were important to Bob and had chosen her own. That, of course, included a seat on the board at the Metropolitan Museum."

Laurie couldn't help but notice the gentleness in this big man's voice when he spoke about Virginia. "And how did your gym fit into that?"

"My point is that she was happy—really, truly happy—forging her own identity. But her children second-guessed everything. They wanted her in a time capsule. They didn't like the idea of her changing, and I was part of that change. We were very serious about getting married. I had already bought a ring for her. But she wasn't ready to tell the family. Virginia believed that once my boxing business was off the ground, her children might start to accept me. That's why she helped me, and that's why she didn't tell anyone about it."

"But there must have been checks that she signed, something to prove she consented to the expenditures."

"She did it all electronically. Virginia was older than me, but better online than I am. She could donate a hundred thousand dollars to a charity with a few keystrokes."

Or alternatively, Laurie thought, you knew her passwords and figured she was so wealthy and generous, she would never miss the money.

"She wired about half of that money directly to my partner for my initial buy-in," Ivan explained, "and then the other half went to pay for equipment, improvements on the space—the costs of starting up a business. But it wasn't gone. It was in a business that she believed in, which would have been part of our income after we were married."

Ryan had been quiet up until this point, but Laurie could tell from the way he was leaning forward in his seat that he was eager to interject. "It's just like I said, Laurie. Ivan was stereotyped from the very beginning, but he didn't actually have a financial motive to hurt Virginia. First of all, there wasn't a shred of evidence to prove that the money Virginia put into PUNCH was stolen. Even if Ivan had stolen money from her—"

"Which I didn't—"

Ryan held up a palm to cut Ivan off. "Of course not. But assume for the sake of argument that he had, it would have been Virginia's word against his if she had accused him of taking the money without her permission. They were in a close, romantic relationship. They weren't officially engaged yet, but had clearly discussed marriage in the future, as evidenced by the purchase of a ring from Harry Winston. She had obviously spent other amounts of money on him voluntarily, including the Porsche. I'm telling you as a former prosecutor, no lawyer could have proven a case of theft against Ivan beyond a reasonable doubt. In a worst case scenario, they would have reached some kind of settlement where he repaid her from the business, as if she were an investor."

Laurie could see the logic of Ryan's argument. If anything, the only consequence of Virginia's murder would be to ensure that Ivan never got to marry into her money. Her death had also called attention to her finances, virtually ensuring that Ivan would be the leading suspect. She had to hand it to these two. In a short meeting, they had managed to spin her perception of Ivan on its head. From this new perspective, she could see Ivan's argument that he had nothing to gain and everything to lose from murdering Virginia.

Ivan must have recognized that she was beginning to get pulled into his side of the story. "I swear to you, Laurie, I didn't do it. I loved Ginny. That's what I called her. She told me that when she was young that was her nickname, but her husband wanted her to be called Virginia after he started to become well known. We would have been married within months if she had lived, and we would have been happy."

Ryan added, "Laurie, I know you hate it when I step on your toes around here, but I'm telling you: this case will be a hit for *Under Suspicion*. It's perfect. And we'd be helping a good man."

Normally by the time she asked the most important question, she had already mastered every publicly available fact about the case. But, at the risk of jumping in too soon, she asked it now, because she had to know. "If you didn't kill Mrs. Wakeling, who did?"

When Ivan immediately looked to Ryan instead of answering the question, she believed her first instincts had been right. When the pause grew longer in silence, she began to stand from her chair. "Okay, I think I can mull things over from here—"

"No, wait," Ivan exclaimed. "It's not that I don't have my theories. Trust me, I do, and facts to back them up. But I've got a training session in fifteen minutes with an A-list movie star, and I never expected you to hear the full side of my story. I'm not sure I want to start naming names unless you really think you might use Virginia's case. I've managed to go on with my life, even though I know a lot of people think I'm a murderer. If I stir all of this up again, I want it to be for a good reason."

She didn't know what to think of Ivan's logic. On the one hand, it seemed like an innocent person would drop everything for a chance to clear his name. On the other hand, she could picture Ryan cajoling Ivan into coming up to the studio, in which case Ivan might be having second thoughts about saying too much.

"Fair enough," she said. "Let's each take a day to mull it over. We can meet again tomorrow if we both think it's worthwhile."

Ivan nodded his agreement. "Thank you so much, Laurie, for your time and for keeping an open mind," he said. "It means so much to me." This time, when he shook her hand, the grip was tight enough to burn.

5

Grace and Jerry nearly spilled through her door the second Ryan escorted Ivan out of her office.

"So *that's* why Ryan was skulking about all morning?" Jerry asked. "Ivan Gray? My guess is it's not because he thinks you need boxing training."

"I'm surprised you recognized him at first sight," Laurie said. "I don't think I would have."

"I was really hooked on the Wakeling case and I read every word about it," Jerry said.

"Then fill me in," Laurie told him.

"After she was found, the media began highlighting Ivan's role in her life—first as her trainer at an elite health club hidden near the Plaza Hotel, then as her surprising boyfriend. He was even her date the night she died. But as time passed, the news coverage faded. Ivan managed to keep his name and face out of the papers."

"You really did follow this case, Jerry."

"Think about it, Laurie. Virginia Wakeling is the only person who ever died at a black-tie gala at the Met."

"Let's go back to Ivan," Laurie said. She found herself

making a mental note that viewers might be interested in hearing from him about how he had navigated his privacy in the ensuing years.

"The minute I saw Ryan hustling Ivan Gray into your office, I just knew that Ryan would be pitching him as our next case," Jerry said.

Grace jumped in. "Ryan likes things that just fall right into his lap. And lately, all he talks about is his boxing gym. When I think about it, Ivan Gray might be good for the show. He's a totally different kind of suspect, and that could be really interesting."

"Laurie, what's your take on him?" Jerry asked. "What did you think?"

She shrugged. "It was a short meeting, but my gut says it's not right for us. It's a very recent case. I assume the police are still investigating. And maybe I'm being unfair based on the age differences and the amounts of money at stake, but Ivan struck me as dishonest. You know me—I won't label someone a killer without hard evidence, but I can see why Virginia's family was suspect about his intentions."

"So you think he's a gold digger," Grace concluded.

"You said it, not me."

"The setting would be amazing," Jerry said. "I mean— the Met!"

Recognizing that a longer discussion was about to ensue, Grace announced that she was going back to her desk, but Laurie should call her if she needed anything. Once she was gone, Jerry immediately continued his point.

"Laurie, we couldn't ask for a more glamorous, iconic setting. The annual costume exhibit is one of the most famous parties in the world. And the night when Virginia was killed, the theme was 'Fashion of First Ladies,' featuring the clothing of American first ladies throughout history. I hate to be cynical, but even if we just rehashed what we know from news reports, the film footage alone would be catnip for viewers."

"Trust me, Jerry, I know. But we can't even be sure the museum will let us film there—"

"Then let me find out. I can make some calls."

Laurie rarely cut Jerry off, but she found herself holding up a palm now. She knew that the Met Gala was the museum's biggest fundraising event of the year. She knew it drew top celebrities and the city's most generous donors. She knew that people held viewing parties at home to weigh in on the red carpet's fashion hits and misses. And as a member of the museum's board of trustees, Virginia would have been front and center on the red carpet. Laurie didn't need Jerry to tell her all the reasons the case would make for great television.

"Laurie," Jerry said persuasively, "I'm not telling you how to run your show, but normally you'd at least want to do some research before making a decision. Look, I know we just got off the high of clearing an innocent person with our last episode. But that's not always going to be the case. Sometimes the ones under suspicion are the ones who actually did it. If Ivan's guilty, then if anything our show could help prove that."

"Sure, in theory. But Ryan's obviously biased. He's got

his little bromance going with his new favorite trainer. Maybe if we still had Alex," Laurie countered.

"Well, that ship has sailed."

Laurie felt the immediate sting of those words, but didn't blame Jerry. He only meant that Alex was gone from the show. He had no way of knowing that he might be gone entirely from her life.

"Ryan has worked out better than we thought," Jerry said. The ratings for their last episode were just as strong as the most recent show featuring Alex in the role of narrator.

"Granted that's true," she conceded, "but Ryan's not objective. I fought him tooth and nail on the last special because he was so sure he was right—and he wasn't. I can already see the same thing happening again with Ivan, but this time would be worse. Ryan would be the trusted contact person with the central suspect."

Jerry nodded, showing that he got her point. It would be one more step toward turning over control of her show to someone else.

"So, okay then. No Virginia Wakeling investigation. We'll find something else."

He was about to leave her office when she stopped him. "See if you can find out if filming at the Met is even a possibility."

He looked surprised by the request, as if he'd thought the subject had been put to rest.

"I'm the one preaching about keeping an open mind, right?" Laurie asked. "Might as well start now."

6

Once she was alone, she sat at her desk and looked at the framed picture she kept there. It was a picture of Greg with Timmy and her at a friend's beach house in the Hamptons. Only three months later, a man would approach Greg while he pushed Timmy on a playground swing set and end his life with a single shot to the forehead.

After Greg died, she went through a period where she could barely make herself work, and then suffered a string of failures at the studio. She realized that she had been holding back her best idea—a show that reinvestigated cold cases through the eyes of the people affected by them—because she was afraid of being seen as the damaged widow, immersing herself in unsolved murders because she still had no idea who killed her husband.

Once she finally launched the program, it was a hit. More surprisingly, the police were finally able to identify the killer whom Timmy had described only as Blue Eyes. Since then, she saw *Under Suspicion* as more than just a job. She saw it as a way to help people.

Now looking at Greg's face in that photograph, she finally realized what was really bothering her about the Virginia Wakeling case. It wasn't entirely about Ryan's involvement. It was the way the case came to her—with an introduction to Ivan Gray. Yes, Ivan had said that he loved Virginia and wanted to marry her. But he sounded more like a man who wanted to clear his name than a man who had lost the woman he wanted to spend the rest of his life with.

She wasn't attached to the case, because she didn't yet feel a connection to anyone who was affected by Virginia Wakeling's death.

But Ivan Gray wasn't the only person in Wakeling's life.

She opened her Internet browser and Googled *Virginia Wakeling obituary*. The write-up in the *New York Times* was lengthy. She couldn't help but notice that it began, not with any accomplishments of Virginia's, but with a summary of the work done by her husband, Bob. The developer had made a fortune by transforming what was once a run-down industrial area of Long Island City into a thriving neighborhood of high-rise luxury apartments and trendy restaurants, all within minutes of Manhattan.

The obituary then went on to note Virginia's work as a philanthropist after she was widowed five years earlier. She endowed a charity that promoted childhood literacy by providing new books to inner-city children. She was recently honored by Dress for Success, a charity that provided professional attire to women working toward self-sufficiency. A long list of arts and cultural organizations and institutions followed. *Mrs. Wakeling is survived by her daughter, Anna Wakeling; son-in-law, Peter Browning; son, Carter; and grandchildren, Robert III and Vanessa.*

It was too early to know whether Ivan Gray could be trusted or not, but she believed him about one thing: Virginia had spent decades as a wife and mother, and had begun a remarkable new phase of life on her own. She had to have been loved, if not by Ivan, then by others. She had two children who lost their father, and then their mother only five years later. They, like Laurie and Timmy at one time, went to bed each night unsure about who had killed their mother, if indeed anyone had killed her, and why.

When she looked at the case from their perspective, and not Ivan's, Laurie found herself caring. She had promised to keep an open mind, and now she would.

7

Leo Farley hopped into the car waiting for him out-side the building on Randall's Island feeling as if he were twenty years younger.

He was sixty-five years old. If someone had asked him a decade earlier to look into a crystal ball and envision his retirement, he never would have predicted his cur-rent life. His wife, Eileen, died much too young. Then his daughter's husband, Greg, was murdered, under circumstances none of them could have predicted. Leo had never been the planning type, but he had always assumed he would still be on the job by the time his number came up.

But, contrary to what he had expected, he had retired six years ago, at the age of fifty-nine, to help his daughter, Laurie, raise her son, Timmy. He went from roll calls and classified briefings to oatmeal breakfasts, walks to St. David's, and chicken dinners at his daughter's apartment.

He was an apple who never thought he'd be an orange. He had gone from being the first deputy commis-sioner of the NYPD to being a retiree who was helping raise his grandson. But then, three months ago, he had been invited to join an anti-terrorism task force with the NYPD, with headquarters right across the Triborough Bridge from the Upper East Side. He would work several evenings each month, such as tonight, and could do much of his work from home, leaving plenty of time to be around for Timmy and Laurie.

By the time he got back to Manhattan, Laurie already had dinner on the table.

"If I didn't know better," he said, stepping into her apartment, "I would think my daughter had learned how to cook."

Laurie was a woman of many talents, but they weren't found in the kitchen. "I'm tempted to tell you that I found a new recipe," she said.

"I love you, sweetheart, but I'm still a cop at heart. I know when you're twisting the truth."

"It's a new carryout service called Caviar. I can't even claim credit for discovering it. Timmy placed the order."

Leo scanned the options on the table: hanger steak, mashed potatoes, cooked carrots, and a green salad.

"Sorry to use up your one red-meat night for the week, Dad," Laurie said, "but this place is supposed to be fantastic." A year ago, Leo had had a heart problem and had two stents inserted in his right ventricle at Mount Sinai. He wished Laurie had never known about the procedure, because now she was determined to transform him into a gluten-free, miserable vegan.

Leo was running the last slice of meat on his plate through a dollop of béarnaise sauce when Laurie changed the subject from a fundraising auction at Timmy's school to a case she was thinking about covering at work.

"What do you remember about Virginia Wakeling? She was the board member pushed from the roof of the Metropolitan Museum of Art on the night of the annual gala."

By then, Leo had already retired from the NYPD, but the case had been front page news for at least a couple of weeks. "It was a horrible scene, a terrible way to die. Officially, the case is still open, but the unofficial word is that her boyfriend did it. He was after her money."

"Except, according to him, she had willingly loaned him money," Laurie said. She filled in her father on everything she had learned about the case that morning from Ivan Gray. "If anything, his gravy train dried up once she was gone."

"Isn't that the kind of case you look for?" Leo asked. "You need to find multiple sides to the story."

She shrugged.

"That's not like you, Laurie. What's bugging you?"

"The case came in through Ryan."

Leo set his fork down on his plate. He had only met Ryan Nichols a couple of times, but Leo thought the man's ego got in the way of his brain. "Did he know Mrs. Wakeling?"

"No, worse. He's friends with the boyfriend, Ivan Gray. He's absolutely convinced the guy is innocent and the police unfairly stereotyped him."

"Hey, Mom?" Timmy was nibbling on three French fries at a time.

"Yes?"

"I don't want to judge you or anything, but other mothers don't talk about murder at the dinner table."

Laurie gave her son a poke on the side of his waist. "How are you going to be the number one detective in all of North America if we don't poison your mind at a young age?"

"The head of security at the Met is on this anti-terrorism task force I joined. We were just meeting about potential threats at high-occupancy targets. The head of detectives for the Central Park Precinct is part of the group, too. Do you want me to see what I can find out about the state of the pending investigation?" Leo asked.

Laurie was beaming at him as she cleared the dishes. "Is there anyone in this city you don't know, Dad?"

He made two calls—one to the head of security at the Met, and one to a homicide detective he knew. Neither was detailed, but they ended in the same conclusion.

He found Laurie in the kitchen, loading the dishwasher. "Sorry, kiddo, I'm no fan of Ryan, but this case might be right up your alley."

"How so?" she asked.

"It's chilly to the extent the police aren't working active leads, but apparently there are still plenty of angles for you to pursue. A security guard saw her go upstairs, but the cameras were off. No one has any idea who might have been up there on the roof with her. Apparently there was a lot of money at stake. Any number of people had something to gain from her death."

Laurie wrung out a sudsy sponge and propped it on the side of the dish rack. "That's interesting, but frankly I was hoping you'd tell me it wasn't my type of case."

"Nope. From what I can tell, you might be able to do some good here. They need a new lead, or the case might go ice cold."

"I don't know. I've always been the lead contact for the person who's—quote, unquote—under suspicion. If we do this case, I'll be ceding a certain amount of power to Ryan."

"Well, for what it's worth, the head of Met Security said he'd be willing to meet with you anytime you want. He was there the night Wakeling died. I know better than to tell you what to do, but don't turn a good case away just because it comes from Ryan. Even a broken clock is right twice a day."

Leo had little regard for Ryan, but he had a feeling that Laurie had her own reasons for resenting the young lawyer. It was about Alex Buckley, not Ryan. *She looks so unhappy. Of course, she misses him. How could she not? And Timmy and I miss him too,* he thought.

8

Alex Buckley looked out the oversized windows of his apartment's living room, staring at the lights reflecting off the East River. The call had ended, but he still held the phone in his hand, replaying the words he had just heard from the other end of the line.

He had known for weeks that his name was under consideration, but the entire process had seemed like practice for a dance that might not end until years down the road. But, tonight, he got the call from the senior senator of New York, who had just spoken personally with the President of the United States. It was going to happen.

"Yes!" he said to himself triumphantly, raising his free hand into a small fist pump.

He heard his butler, Ramon, clear his throat as he entered the room. "No snow yet, Ramon?" he asked.

The forecast was predicting the first snow of winter. They'd made it through New Year's without a flake. But Ramon had something else on his mind. "Is that the call you were hoping for?" he asked.

"It was indeed. I'll go to D.C. next week to fill out the

rest of the questionnaire required for Senate confirmation. I've been warned the process is grueling."

"If anyone can sail through smoothly, it will be you, Mr. Alex. I'm so glad I was here to answer the phone. I feel like I'm a small part of history."

Ramon had taken the rare week off to visit his daughter, Lydia, in Syracuse. At sixty-one years of age, he was now officially a grandfather to a baby girl named Ramona. He had only been back in the city one day, and had already shown Alex at least fifty photographs of the baby. Ramon could not get over the fact that less than thirty years after moving to the United States from the Philippines, he now had a beautiful little granddaughter, a natural-born citizen.

"Thank you, Ramon."

"I know it's late, but a celebration seems in order. Is there something small we can do to mark the moment?"

Ramon insisted on calling himself the butler, but he was also Alex's assistant, chef, friend, and honorary uncle. Alex lost his own parents more than fifteen years ago, and had been appointed legal guardian to his younger brother, Andrew. Andrew had expanded their two-man family by marrying Marcy and fathering three adorable kids, but Alex considered Ramon to be part of the Buckley clan, too.

Alex could see that Ramon shared the sentiment. His round face beamed as proudly as if a member of his own family had gotten that phone call. "A port sounds nice if you'd like to join me."

"A port sounds perfect, sir."

The senator's phone call had been to notify Alex that the President was nominating him for a judicial appointment to the United States District Court of the Southern District of New York. It was one of the most prestigious trial court positions in the country. A press release would go out first thing in the morning.

Ramon returned with a small silver tray, topped with two port glasses. "Perfect timing," he commented, looking out the window. The snow was starting to fall.

As he and Ramon held up their glasses for a toast, Alex realized that, even though he was about to be named for a dream job, part of him would have been even happier if the phone call had been from someone else.

He went to bed that night thinking not about a career on the bench, but about Laurie Moran. A little more than two months ago, he had taken a risk with their relationship, telling her that he needed to step back from her until she was truly ready to let him into her life.

He looked out the window at the snow, wishing he could watch it fall with Laurie. Was she ever going to call?

9

Laurie had a love-hate relationship with New York City. Some days, she stepped outside, looked up at the towering buildings, soaked in the anonymity of walking on a crowded sidewalk, and thought to herself how lucky she was to live in the most exciting city on earth. On other days, all she could notice was the sounds of horns and sirens and the smells of engine exhaust and garbage.

The morning began on an "I love New York" note when she walked out of her building to find pillows of clean, white snow lining the edges of a freshly plowed sidewalk. She got a hello from her favorite coffee cart operator, and stepped down to the platform for the finally completed Second Avenue subway to find her train pulling in, with plenty of seats to spare.

Then the train inexplicably came to an abrupt halt between stations. The conductor said something over the speakers, but the words were garbled and incomprehensible. The lights flickered on and off. A frightened woman started banging futilely on the glass of the exit door. The man next to her told her to knock it off.

Other passengers picked sides in the heated but pointless debate that ensued. Laurie closed her eyes and counted until they started to move again.

By the time she emerged from underground, the snow along Sixth Avenue was black from dirt, and the sidewalks were filled with gray slush. The two-mile commute had taken her nearly an hour.

So much for loving life in the city.

When she got to her office, Grace had a tall skinny latte and a miniature croissant from Bouchon Bakery ready for her on her desk.

"You're an angel," Laurie said, unwrapping a jade-green scarf from around her neck. The coffee was still hot.

"When you're not here by nine-twenty, I know something happened that warrants a little treat."

"I was trapped in subway hell."

"Well, I wish I had better news for you, but Brett came by five minutes ago asking to see you ASAP."

Of course he did, she thought to herself. It was going to be that kind of day.

Brett Young's secretary, Dana, waved Laurie into the boss's inner sanctum.

"How bad is it?" Laurie asked.

Dana waggled a hand, signaling that her boss was in one of his moods, but they had both seen worse.

When she walked in, Brett was on the phone. He held

up one finger, told the person on the other end of the line to get back to him immediately, and gestured for her to sit down as he hung up. Brett expected the world to move at five times its actual pace.

"Why aren't you covering the Virginia Wakeling case?" he asked.

"Who said I wasn't?"

"So you are doing it? Why didn't you tell me?"

"The subject was only raised yesterday, Brett. It's under consideration."

"There's nothing to consider. It's perfect. Better than anything you've featured so far."

The insult burned. "Where's this coming from, Brett? I would have thought by now that I had earned a certain amount of trust." They'd had four features in the *Under Suspicion* series, and each had been a hit in the ratings. The episodes also triggered viral social media activity on Twitter and Facebook that helped grow the kind of young, trendsetting audience that advertisers craved.

Brett waved a hand dismissively, as if to tell her to get over herself. "I'm the guy who pays the bills, which means I get to nose around when I think you're missing the boat. You're not missing the boat?"

"I'm honestly confused about what you're asking me, Brett."

"A little bird told me that you have some beef against the muscleman boyfriend. What's his name: Igor?"

"Ivan. Ivan Gray."

"Perfect name for a murderer. I love it."

"I don't have a beef, Brett. And he may or may not be

a murderer. That's why I do due diligence before jumping in."

"Three words, Laurie: It. Doesn't. Matter."

She started to protest, but he immediately cut her off. "I don't care if Ivan, Igor, Whatever, is guilty or innocent. It's a rich lady in a formal gown, thrown to her death from the roof of the Metropolitan Museum of Art during their fanciest event of the year. The black hair, pale skin, and blood against a snowy Central Park backdrop. Celebrities in dresses. It's a no-brainer."

"I never said no, Brett."

"Well, you apparently didn't say yes either."

"We don't know yet if the family will participate. We don't know if the Met will let us film there. There's work to be done."

"Then go do it. Here's the deal: unless you come back here with a darn good reason, your next case is Virginia Wakeling."

"Message received."

She was on her way to his office door when he stopped her. "Don't sue me for being politically incorrect, Laurie, but sometimes I wonder why you're so hard on Ryan. You're like two little kids chasing each other on the playground. I confess it's kind of fun to watch the two of you go at it. He's single you know—a real catch, if you ask me."

Laurie managed to keep down her half-consumed latte.

● ● ●

She had just gotten back to her office and was about to call Ryan when a *New York Times* alert popped up on her phone: "White House names celebrity defense attorney to elite federal bench."

She clicked on the alert to see a photograph of Alex. It was one of her favorites, the headshot the studio had taken when he first joined as the narrator of her show. His blue-green eyes looked straight through the camera behind black-rimmed glasses. She felt the latte stirring again.

She knew how Alex dreamed of being a federal judge. He always assumed that his work as a criminal defense lawyer might stand in the way of an appointment. Now he was finally getting his dream job.

She pictured him getting a phone call, from a senator or perhaps even the White House directly. She wondered whether he even thought to call her with the news, or if he had totally moved on without her.

Her thoughts were interrupted by a tap on her door. It was Ryan.

She didn't bother trying to hide a roll of her eyes. "Ryan, we agreed to take a day to think it over. You didn't need to go over my head to Brett."

"I'm sorry, Laurie." He did not sound at all sorry. "I saw the way you looked at Ivan yesterday. You don't believe him."

"You don't know me well enough to assume to know what I'm thinking, Ryan. For what it's worth, I did some research last night to address my concerns that the case might be too fresh." She didn't see the need to tell him that the relevant phone calls had been made by her father. "I was going to move forward with the investigation anyway. Jumping to conclusions and pulling power plays with the boss is not the way to make friends around here."

"With all due respect, Laurie, making friends isn't my priority. Ivan will be here in fifteen minutes. He's ready to tell us about the other suspects."

10

Ivan filled a good third of the long, low, white leather sofa that sat beneath her office windows. He assumed the pose she always associated with so-called "alpha" males: knees apart, feet firmly planted, taking up as much space as possible.

He was telling them about the last time he had seen Virginia Wakeling. "She looked so beautiful that night. Through my eyes, I didn't even see our age difference. The dinner had just ended, and they were preparing the stage for the musical performances. My guess is it was around nine-thirty. We were working our way through the room—they set it all up around the temple," he added, referring to the museum's giant Egyptian show-piece, the Temple of Dendur. "Ginny was very much in demand. I would just nod and say hello. But when the museum director was talking to Ginny, his wife made a point of striking up a conversation with me. I told her I was a trainer, and she had endless questions about Pilates versus yoga, free weights versus cross-training. When I finally got free, I couldn't find Ginny anywhere."

"Where were you when you found out she had died?"

"In the main hall. I had worked my way there after not finding her in the temple. I was looking for her when I heard the sounds of people in shock, then a woman screamed something about a woman in a blue gown. I knew right then in my gut that something had happened to Ginny. A guard said later that she had asked to go up to the roof for fresh air. Someone must have followed her upstairs and pushed her."

"You said you had thoughts about who that might be," Laurie said.

"You asked me that yesterday: If I didn't kill Ginny, who did?"

"It's the question I always ask when we start to work a new case."

"Well, to start with, you need to take the *if* out of the question. I'm an innocent man."

Once again, Laurie thought he was more concerned about clearing his name than identifying Ginny's killer.

"We know you are," Ryan said.

Laurie ignored Ryan's comment and spoke directly to Ivan. "You said 'to start with.' What other concerns do you have?"

"I need you to know I take no pleasure in pointing a finger at any of these people. I cared about them, whether or not they felt the same way toward me."

"Fair enough," she said.

Ivan took a deep breath, as if to steel himself for what

he was about to say. "I've spent three years asking myself your very question, and can see the only explanation for Ginny's death: it was her family.

"Her family hated me," Ivan said, spitting out the words. "They despised me. Loathed me. Take out a thesaurus and pick any word. They looked at me as if I were subhuman. I tried so hard to get their approval. Any comment I made—*that's a nice dress, it's a beautiful day*—was met with a scoff or an eye roll, at best."

"Which family members are we talking about?"

"Carter, Anna, and Peter. All three of them a united front of disdain." Laurie recognized the names from Virginia's obituary. Carter was the son, thirty-eight years old and apparently unmarried at the time of his mother's death. Anna was the daughter, two years younger than her brother. Peter was Anna's husband. She jotted down their names on the notepad in her lap.

Ivan's tone softened. "Well, at least the grandkids, Robbie and Vanessa, liked me, but they were toddlers, and all I had to do was pick them up and spin them around and I was their best buddy."

He smiled sadly at some memory he was having of the kids who might have been his step-grandchildren if things had worked out differently.

"Why did the family dislike you so much?" Laurie asked.

"If you asked them, they'd say I was too young, too poor, and only after their mother for one reason. But, honestly, I don't think their feelings had anything to do with me personally. They would have found a reason to disapprove of anyone Ginny allowed into her life."

"Her husband had passed on five years earlier. They didn't want her to find happiness with someone else?"

Laurie remembered one of her last conversations with Alex. *I know this sounds cold, Laurie, but it's been six years.* Six years since Greg was murdered, and, still, she had pushed Alex away so many times that he had tired of waiting.

"They didn't want her to change. Ginny loved her husband, don't get me wrong, but in the time I knew her, I saw her grow from under his shadow. She was sharper, funnier, more alive. And as much as I'd like to say it was because of me, it wasn't. But that's not how her kids saw it. They thought their mother was going through a phase. They wanted her to be the same exact woman as when she had been Mrs. Robert Wakeling."

"That may have been a reason not to like you," Laurie said, "but I'm afraid I don't understand why you suspect them of killing their mother."

"They were terrified that I was going to gain access to the family money. When Ginny and I were talking about our plans to get married, we discussed her plans for her fortune. She left behind a two-hundred-million-dollar estate, plus half the shares in Wakeling Development."

Laurie resisted the urge to let out a whistle. She wrote "$200M" on her notepad and underlined it three times.

"So obviously, I was going to sign a prenup, which I completely understood. But she thought her children should be self-sufficient."

"She was going to cut them off?" Ryan asked.

"Not precisely. After Bob died, Anna and Carter took

over the family business and each held a quarter of the stock. She never would have taken control of the company from them. The plan all along was for Ginny to leave them the rest of the stock when she passed. But she was coming around to the view that people are strongest when they're self-made."

"As her husband, Bob, was," Laurie noted.

"Precisely. She had no problem giving someone a head start—her kids inherited a successful company from Bob, for example, or the money she was fronting me for the gym. But she wanted them to have to work for a living, and, frankly, I think they always assumed otherwise. Bob's major project in Long Island City was over and done with. She wanted them to have an incentive to work just as hard as he did. She was planning to change her will to leave the bulk of her estate, other than the company, to charity."

Laurie had read articles about some of the nation's wealthiest billionaires announcing that they were leaving almost the entirety of their money to charity. She wondered if Virginia had been influenced by those same stories.

"Did she tell the kids she was changing her will?" The family would have no motive to kill their mother to inherit under the current will, unless they knew she had plans to amend it.

"Well, that's the hitch. I think so, but I can't prove it. Anna's husband, Peter Browning, is a commercial real estate lawyer. He was practically Ginny's third child, she trusted him so much. He was also the executor of her will. My theory is that she talked to Peter about her plans. I told the police, but I have no idea if they ever investigated it."

Laurie jotted down "Peter/executor/$$" on her notepad.

"So which of the kids do you think did it?" Laurie asked.

"I have no idea."

11

I van spent the next few minutes trying to describe each of Ginny's family members in a nutshell. According to him, Anna was the harder worker of the two children and was more deeply involved in running the company. "As much as Anna despised me, I always felt sorry for her. My impression is that Bob always assumed that Carter would be the future leader of the family empire, all because he was the boy and the firstborn. But Carter was the laziest one of the bunch. Anna at least makes an effort. Ginny, of course, knew that Anna had a real head for business, but Anna had this chip on her shoulder that she couldn't get rid of."

"Whoever killed Ginny was strong," Laurie noted, trying not to sound accusatory. "Ginny didn't look frail in the photographs I saw of her. Could her daughter really have pushed her over the roof's ledge?"

He shook his head. "Trust me, I know Ginny was strong, because I trained her. No, if Anna was involved, she had help."

"For example, her husband, Peter," Ryan noted.

Ivan nodded. "And/or her brother, Carter."

"Tell me about him," Laurie said.

He shrugged. "He's capable enough, but less serious and more spoiled than his sister. A bit of a playboy. He had a brief marriage in his early thirties, but it only lasted a couple of years. He told Ginny he didn't think he would ever marry again. She was hoping he'd change his mind, but he seemed determined to remain uncommitted."

"Can you think of any other possible suspects?" Laurie asked.

He remained silent. She could tell that he was torn about whether to speak up.

"We want our investigation to be thorough, Ivan. We don't jump to conclusions."

"You should probably talk to Penny, Ginny's assistant. Penny Rawling."

"She was at the Met that night?"

Ivan nodded. "Penny was chomping at the bit to go, but Ginny had not intended to invite her. Most socialites don't include their assistants at that kind of event. Ginny was extremely generous to Penny. Too much so, in my opinion. Penny's mother had been Bob's longtime secretary at the firm. When she passed away as Penny was graduating from high school, Bob hired Penny to work for him and then, out of loyalty, Ginny took her on as her personal assistant after Bob died."

"Why would Penny kill someone who was so generous to her?"

"I'm not saying she did. Like I said, I think it's the kids. But Penny could be resentful. She had hoped to work her way up to a more substantial job at Wakeling Development, but it was fairly clear that the family saw her only as an assistant, and not a particularly good one at that. In my opinion, she was unreliable and constantly distracted. She often left early and came in late. Ginny was willing to overlook her shortcomings out of loyalty, but I don't like to see kindness taken advantage of. I spoke to her multiple times about needing to develop a stronger work ethic."

It was Ivan's second reference to the importance of a "work ethic." If Ivan was telling the truth, he may have had more influence on Ginny's plans to change her will than he was acknowledging or even knew.

"If Penny hurt her, it's because she thought I would fire her if we got married, cutting her out of the small inheritance she expected to get one day. It wasn't much— seventy-five thousand dollars—but it was a lot to Penny."

"Was Penny strong enough to throw Ginny from that roof?"

He shook his head. "Even weaker than Anna. The girl's a twig. But the distractions I mentioned? She was constantly on the phone with some mystery boyfriend and seemed terribly concerned about her appearance at the gala, after lobbying so hard to attend. I got the impression her unknown suitor would be there. But she showed up with one of the older trustees whose husband couldn't come." Ivan's voice became more husky. "Man, I hope it wasn't Penny. I don't want to believe I indirectly played a role in Ginny's death by giving her a hard time."

"Well, it sounds like you don't really think Penny was involved."

"No, I wouldn't, except for one nagging fact. Penny,

more than anyone, saw Ginny and me together. She saw that we had something real. Despite the difference in our backgrounds, we were deeply in love. We knew each other. Truly knew each other." His gaze drifted away momentarily. It was the first time Laurie believed that this man was mourning Virginia Wakeling.

He blinked a few times before speaking again. "When the tabloids made me out to be a gold-digging monster, Penny never defended me. She threw me under the bus, saying I had asked Ginny to buy me that Porsche, which totally wasn't true. I never have found an explanation for that. It makes me think she was trying to pin the blame on me, and why would she possibly do that?"

Laurie was now jotting notes in her pad at a frantic pace. She looked up to see Ryan staring at her. His face said, *I told you so.*

He had been right: this case was perfect.

As soon as they had walked Ivan to the elevator, Ryan looked to her for confirmation. "What next?"

"I try to get the family on board. And I talk to the folks at the Met. Those pieces have to fall into place for this to work."

She expected him to invite himself along on both counts, but he simply nodded. She was the producer. He was the host. He had no official role to play until they moved into production.

As he turned toward his office, she said, "Ryan, it's a good case."

"Thanks. And you were right: going to Brett was a jerk move."

It was nice to know they agreed on something.

Two phone calls later, she had a schedule that would please even Brett Young. The head of security at the museum could meet with her after lunch. And, much to her surprise, Anna Wakeling's assistant scheduled her for an appointment the following morning.

12

That afternoon, Laurie was enjoying life in New York City again as she entered the Metropolitan Museum of Art. She remembered the first time her parents brought her here. They waited until she was in the first grade because they wanted to make sure that she would be able to appreciate it as a special place.

Her mother had held her hand and assured her that nothing bad would happen as she approached a mummy in its sarcophagus. She marveled at the suits of armor and mannequin horses in the Arms and Armor wing. She and her father had replicated the day with Timmy when he was the same age, pausing at the pool in the Temple of Dendur to toss in a coin and tell Laurie's mom they wished she were there. As far as Laurie was concerned, this building was one of the most beautiful places in the world.

She was asking a security guard at the reception desk for Sean Duncan, the head of security, when a dark-haired man in a pin-striped suit approached. "That would be me. You must be Ms. Moran, right on time."

"Call me Laurie." He greeted her with a friendly

handshake, but was otherwise formal in his mannerisms. She noticed that the uniformed security guard stood straighter in his boss's presence. She guessed Duncan might be ex-military.

He led the way through the main hall toward the medieval sculpture garden. "My wife is a huge fan of your show. She's loves everything crime-related. Am I allowed to tell her we met, or is this a top-secret visit?"

"Sure, but we haven't made a decision yet. I'm just doing research at this point."

"Got it." When they arrived at an elevator, she noticed another security guard adjust his posture. "I figured we'd start with the scene of the crime."

Laurie had only been to the Met roof when it was open for exhibits during the summer. Today, it was closed to the public. The roof was completely empty, providing a pin-quiet view over a snow-blanketed Central Park and the surrounding skyline.

"Wow, how do you not just live up here?"

"There's a reason my office is just over there," he said, gesturing through an adjacent window.

He walked to the west edge of the roof and pointed to a spot in the snow below. "She was found right there. We had snow on the ground then, too."

Beyond a waist-high railing, the roof's concrete ledge was thick, lined with low hedges. There was no way a fall could be accidental. A person would either have to jump or be thrown with a great deal of force.

"You were head of security at the time?"

"Second in charge. Got bumped up last year."

"Congratulations. Did you know Mrs. Wakeling personally?"

"Only to say, 'Hello, Mrs. Wakeling,' when she was here. She seemed like a nice lady. The director adored her."

"There was no camera footage of her fall?"

He shook his head. "We conduct our annual camera maintenance on the night of the gala. We turn them off for testing and replacement while the galleries, roof, and other non-party spaces are closed to the public for the party."

"How was Mrs. Wakeling up here if the roof was closed?"

"She was a museum trustee. They're allowed to go wherever they like, whenever they choose."

She sensed that Duncan didn't approve of the system. "Do you know what time she came up here?"

"Our VIPs each have an assigned security guard as their liaison for the party. Mrs. Wakeling's was named Marco Nelson. He said he showed her to the elevator shortly after nine-thirty, not long after the dinner ended, and before the music started." That timeline matched Ivan's. "According to Marco, Mrs. Wakeling said she needed fresh air, but didn't want to go to the front steps. It's an absolute madhouse during the gala, full of paparazzi and celebrity watchers. She asked to come up here, making a point to say she wanted to be alone."

"Did she say why?"

"No, but Marco said her lips were pursed and she kept looking back toward the party, as if something there was upsetting her. Marco had the distinct impression that she'd been in an argument or had some other reason to be unhappy."

"Did he come upstairs with her?"

He shook his head again. "According to Marco, the last time he saw Mrs. Wakeling was when she was stepping onto the elevator alone. About ten minutes later, a jogger in the park found her body. Can you believe we had guests complain that we didn't go on with the concert that night?"

Unfortunately, she could. In Laurie's work as a journalist, she had seen the best and worst of humanity.

"Is Marco working today? It would be helpful to talk to him."

"Marco left a couple of years ago to work in private security. He's probably earning three times what I make as the boss here, but then again, he doesn't get to spend most of his waking hours in the Met."

"It's one of my favorite places on earth," Laurie said.

"My wife said the best present I ever gave her was on our third date; I walked her around the museum after closing. She said she felt like Claudia Kincaid in *From the Mixed-Up Files of Mrs. Basil E. Frankweiler*."

The book, about two siblings who run away from home and live secretly at the museum, was one of Laurie's favorites as a child. She could tell how much this man loved the museum.

"You said Marco thought Mrs. Wakeling might have had an argument. Did anyone actually witness her in a dispute that night?"

"Not to my knowledge."

"Did anything else unusual happen that night?"

"We try hard to avoid any surprises, but there is one thing. Shortly before Mrs. Wakeling's body was found in the park, an alarm in the galleries was tripped. It was in the display area of the costume exhibit, after we had closed it to the partygoers. The guards who responded saw no signs of a problem. But after Mrs. Wakeling's body was found, police speculated that the killer may have set off the alarm to distract us. While we were chasing down a false alarm, someone could have slipped into a staircase and followed Mrs. Wakeling to the roof."

"How did the guests react when they heard the alarm?" Laurie asked.

"The guests didn't know," Sean explained. "It was a silent alarm triggered by a motion sensor. The only ones who would have been aware of it were the on-site security personnel."

"Were you able to determine the whereabouts of Mrs. Wakeling's various friends and family at the time she went up to the roof?"

"By friends, I suspect you mean Ivan Gray, specifically."

Laurie smiled. "I meant anyone who might be relevant. We keep an open mind at *Under Suspicion*."

"I'm not sure I'd say the same of others. Her family was pointing the finger at Mrs. Wakeling's date before the police even arrived. It was quite a scene. But if you're asking whether any one person had an ironclad alibi, I'm not the person to ask. Our priority was keeping the guests calm and managing ingress and egress. The police handled the actual investigation. The lead detective's name was Johnny Hon, if that helps."

"It does, thanks. I'll give him a call. We'll also be talking to her children, son-in-law, and assistant, since they were all there that night."

"Don't forget the nephew."

"What nephew?"

"Oh, what was his name? John? No, Tom, that was it. Tom Wakeling. And he made sure to use his last name to finagle two tickets to the ball. It happens all the time. People show up saying they're a Kennedy or a Vanderbilt. Turns out they're third cousins. Anyway, I got the impression this kid was a bit of a black sheep. Mrs. Wakeling approved him for the list, but made a point of saying that her table was full because the director and his wife were seated with her. It was obvious she wanted some distance from the nephew."

"Was he a suspect?"

"I doubt it, but, like I said, I wouldn't know. I only mentioned him because you were listing family members."

This was the first Laurie had heard of Virginia's nephew. She assumed that Ivan was either unaware of the nephew's attendance or did not consider him a suspect.

As always seemed to be the case, the number of people she needed to interview was expanding instead of dwindling. She jotted down two more names in her notebook: Detective Johnny Hon and Tom Wakeling.

13

Brasserie Ruhlmann was as quiet as Laurie had ever seen it when she arrived promptly at five-thirty that evening. Named for the French Art Deco designer Émile-Jacques Ruhlmann, the restaurant evoked a high-end Parisian brasserie, complete with soaring ceilings, red velvet chairs, and crisp white tablecloths. It was also directly downstairs from Fisher Blake Studios, making it one of Laurie's favorite spots.

As she shook off her coat and handed it to the hostess, she spotted Charlotte throwing her a small wave from a corner table next to the back bar. They exchanged quick kisses on both cheeks before Laurie took a seat across from her.

Charlotte already had a martini on the table.

"You got here early," Laurie noted.

"Practically a snow day at Ladyform. I sent out an email last night telling the entire staff to use their discretion about whether to come in. Of course, we got three inches instead of nine, and half the office stayed home anyway." Laurie's friend Charlotte ran the New

York City operations of her family's business. Under Charlotte's watch, Ladyform had grown from a manufacturer of "lady's foundational garments" to a brand renowned for its high-end athletic clothes.

Laurie had met Charlotte after featuring the disappearance of Charlotte's younger sister on an episode of *Under Suspicion*. After production ended, Charlotte invited Laurie to lunch, and the two had become fast friends.

Laurie ordered a white wine instead of joining Charlotte in a martini and then listened as her friend vented about a fabric supplier who decided to add another 5 percent of Lycra to a product without notifying her. "I've got ten thousand bolts of the stuff. I made up one sample garment to see how it worked. The pants looked like Olivia Newton-John's in the final scene of *Grease*."

Laurie pictured the iconic, skintight, shiny black leggings. "Maybe you'll start a new trend?"

"Sure, if disco makes a sudden comeback." She waved a hand, whisking the stress away. "I'll get them to replace it. Just a headache, that's all. Oh, hey, don't let me forget this."

She reached into her bag, pulled out a heavy book, and handed it to Laurie. *First Ladies of Fashion* was emblazoned in glossy letters on the front jacket.

"I forgot I had it until I got off the phone with you."

When Charlotte had called Laurie to suggest an impromptu drinks date, Laurie had been leaving the museum and mentioned that she was looking into the Virginia Wakeling case. She was surprised when Charlotte told her that she had been at the gala that night. Apparently, Ladyform purchased a table each year to support the museum's Costume Institute and to help equate the Ladyform brand with fashion as well as function.

Laurie flipped through the pages of the coffee table book published to commemorate the exhibit being celebrated the night Virginia Wakeling died. "It was printed before that night," Charlotte explained, "so it won't have any mention of the death. But I thought you might be able to use it somehow."

Sean Duncan had said it would be possible for Laurie to film at the Met, but of course they wouldn't be able to replicate the actual fashion exhibit. Jerry could work wonders, however, with still photographs. She assumed they could request high-resolution versions of any images she wanted to use. The book had hundreds to choose from. "This is great, Charlotte. Thanks."

"I wish I knew more about the actual case." Charlotte had already explained that she had been in the ladies' room when she heard murmurs from other partygoers about a woman who had fallen. Her table was nowhere near the prestigious seating enjoyed by Virginia Wakeling. In short, she had no firsthand knowledge related to the investigation. "Otherwise, I could have been the first person in history to appear on your show more than once, other than Alex of course. Speaking of Alex, I saw him two nights ago at the Bronx Academy of Letters benefit."

Charlotte had invited Laurie to take one of the seats at Ladyform's table for the event, a fundraiser for a public school in the poorest congressional district in the country. Unfortunately, the event had conflicted with taking

Timmy to Jazz at Lincoln Center. Once again, Laurie needed a clone.

"How did he seem?" Laurie asked, trying not to sound overly curious.

"He seemed fine." Laurie could tell that Charlotte was holding something back.

"Did he say something about me? Oh, strike that from the record. I sound like a twelve-year-old."

"It didn't really come up. We just said hello, and he introduced me as having met him through *Under Suspicion*." She wrinkled her nose, as if she realized she had let something slip.

"He introduced you . . . to whom?"

"Kerry Lyndon."

Laurie recognized the name. She was a news anchor for the local CBS affiliate. Long blonde hair, big blue eyes, impeccably dressed in front of the camera at all times. Laurie had a sudden image of Kerry Lyndon standing next to Alex, the two of them looking perfect together.

"They weren't together-together, though. I noticed in the program that they were both listed on the auction committee. I think they were just greeting guests."

Or, alternatively, Kerry had been Alex's plus-one for the evening. Until he had started dating Laurie, Alex had been a staple on the social pages of the newspapers, always accompanied by an accomplished woman known in her own right.

"Did you hear the news?" Laurie asked, not wanting to speak any longer about Alex's date for the benefit. "He's being named to the federal bench."

"Wow. The Honorable Judge Alex Buckley. It's got a nice ring to it. Is he totally psyched?"

Laurie shook her head. "I have no idea. I read it in a *New York Times* alert this morning."

Charlotte reached across the table and placed a hand on Laurie's. "Sweetie, I'm so sorry. I just assumed you'd hear about the appointment from him. I know you two are on a break, but I figured something as big as that . . ." Her voice trailed off. Thanksgiving, Christmas, and New Year's had passed without a word between them other than an exchange of mailed holiday cards and the delivery of a new video game as a Christmas gift for Timmy. Why would he have reached out to tell her that he was finally getting his dream job?

Charlotte was looking at her with an expression that approached pity. "I never should have mentioned seeing him at the benefit."

Laurie feigned a smile. "I promise, Charlotte, you have nothing to apologize for. Alex is free to share his company with other women. We're not together."

Charlotte paused, sensing that Laurie was putting on a brave face, but then changed the subject to an upcoming fashion segment she had planned for the *Today* show the following week.

The moment had passed without further emotion, but, inside, Laurie's heart was sinking.

14

The following morning, Laurie arrived to find Grace already at her desk, even though it was well before nine. Grace's makeup was flawless, as usual, but today, she wore her long, shiny black hair in a tight bun at the nape of her neck. Instead of one of her standard clingy dresses, she had on a bright green silk blouse tucked into wide-legged black pants.

"You look like you're going on a job interview. You're not quitting on me, are you?" Laurie asked. She couldn't imagine losing Grace.

"I'm toning down my look for a change. My sister said people would take me more seriously. We'll see."

Laurie felt a pang of guilt. It had never dawned on her that Grace, one of the most confident people she knew, worried about how she was perceived by others.

Before she could say anything, Jerry arrived for their scheduled status conference to discuss the next edition of the series. "Are we ready?" he asked.

"Let's do it," Laurie said.

Jerry began by running down the items they could

already check off their to-do list. He was working with the museum's legal department so they could film on-site. "You'd think we were filming at the Vatican with all these hoops, but it's manageable. I'm more worried about getting the Wakeling family on board. What do they have to gain?"

"I have the same concerns," Laurie said. "It's only been a few years, and it's clear that Ivan's still the number one suspect. If they realize Ivan has a personal connection to Ryan, they'll never trust us." Laurie was reminded once again how much she wished Alex had never left. "But Brett made it clear that this is our next case, as long as we get at least one member of the family to participate. I can't stand the idea of telling him that I struck out."

"So then we won't let that happen," Jerry said confidently. His phone buzzed against the coffee table and he checked the screen. "Perfect timing. The car is here."

Their appointment with Ginny's daughter, Anna Wakeling, was in twenty minutes. Laurie noticed a shadow fall across Grace's face as she headed back to her desk. She thought about what Ivan Gray had said about Ginny's assistant, Penny. She was loyal, but felt unappreciated.

Laurie realized that Jerry had ascended from an intern fetching coffee to being a valued part of the production team. Grace, however, remained in the same position.

"Can you join us, Grace?" Laurie asked. "You always have a good read on people."

Grace's smile was infectious. "Absolutely."

15

The offices of Wakeling Development occupied two
floors of a converted warehouse in Long Island City overlooking the East River. As they waited in the reception
area, Laurie realized that she could see Alex's apartment
across the water. She wondered whether he was home
or at his office, or maybe in court or in a meeting. She
remembered when they used to talk on the phone every
single night about nothing in particular if they didn't see
each other in person.

The appearance of a young woman through a set of
double doors pulled her from her memories. "They're
waiting in the conference room for you." She offered
neither a name nor a handshake, and began leading them
down a long hallway.

"You're not Penny Rawling, are you?" Laurie didn't
know yet where Virginia's personal assistant had landed
after Virginia's death. Jerry, the resident social media
researcher, had located a Facebook profile for a Penny
Rawling in Astoria, but her page had the highest privacy
settings available. No access to photos, posts, or back-

ground information unless you were a Facebook friend of hers.

The woman who greeted them appeared confused by the question and explained that no, her name was Kate. She walked them into a luxurious conference room with a marble table and white leather chairs. A row of three people flanked one side of the table, the lone woman stationed in the center.

Laurie recognized her from media reports as Virginia's daughter, Anna. She had shoulder-length, honey-blonde hair and wore a perfectly tailored navy blue sheath dress and four-inch nude heels. On one side of her was her husband, Peter Browning, whom the media described as a brilliant but quiet lawyer who quickly became a trusted member of the Wakeling family once he married the beloved daughter, Anna. On her other side stood her older brother, Carter. He was now forty-one years old based on Laurie's count, but his appearance was boyish. His sandy-blond hair was tousled, he had remnants of a tan even though it was January, and, according to the social pages, he was still very much a busy bachelor.

"I'm Anna Wakeling." She still used her maiden name, Laurie noticed, and she barely bothered to introduce the men at the table with her. "I appreciate your coming out to Long Island City to meet. So many Manhattanites refuse to cross a bridge or tunnel."

Laurie made a point to admire the view from the corner windows. "I remember when this area was primarily industrial. I can see why your father was so proud of the mark he made."

"Which is exactly why our company is still located here. Daddy would never have wanted us to leave."

Laurie already knew from her phone conversation with Anna that she was familiar with *Under Suspicion*. Laurie had also explained that their show was interested in reinvestigating the circumstances leading to Anna's mother's death.

Once they were all seated, Laurie steered the conversation to the subject of the family's primary suspect. "Our understanding is that your family was of a single mind when it came to Ivan Gray."

Anna answered immediately. "That man murdered our mother. End of story."

"Yet the police have made no arrest," Laurie said. "Didn't he have more to gain from marrying your mother than harming her?"

Anna waved a dismissive hand. "Please, she said they'd get married 'when the time was right,' but my mother was never going to marry him. He was a phase, a distraction." Laurie couldn't help but notice that both Carter and Peter were deferring to Anna. "I hate to say this, but we were embarrassed for her, running around town with this boy toy on her arm. She was old enough to be his mother."

"Our understanding is that their engagement was imminent. There was even a ring."

"Which my mother paid for, I'm sure," Anna said. "And which she did not wear, at least not in public. I'm sure she enjoyed being seen with him, but it was a dalliance, and Ivan knew it. That's why he stole that money to start his ridiculous gym. When I think about how my father would have reacted. I even told her, 'Daddy's the one who worked for this money. He would be destroyed if he could see the way you are spending it.'" She shook her head at the memory. "That was the day before she died."

Her husband, Peter, reached over and touched Anna's hand to comfort her.

"Mr. Browning," Laurie began—

"Call me Peter."

"Okay, and I'm Laurie. My understanding is that your mother-in-law trusted you when it came to her personal finances. Did she speak to you about her plans when it came to Ivan?"

"Well, as a family member, I can tell you that she assured all of us that she was not supporting him financially. She said Ivan had his own 'working man's' income that she only supplemented in 'modest ways,' and that she would never allow another man to get his hands on the money earned by Anna and Carter's father. So of course it came as a complete shock when we learned about all that money going into his business."

Laurie noticed that Anna's brother, Carter, was nodding in agreement, but did not seem to be following the conversation closely.

"Peter, you made a point to note that you were speaking as a family member. Weren't you also the executor of her estate? Surely she must have talked to you about her plans in the event she got married. Was she going to change her will?" According to Ivan, Virginia was planning to make drastic reductions to her family's inheritance.

"Now I need to replace my family member hat with my lawyer hat. That question is clearly covered by attorney-client privilege, which survives Virginia's death."

Laurie noticed that Peter used the more formal name that Virginia's husband, Bob, had preferred. "But Anna and Carter, you're not covered by an attorney's privilege."

They both shrugged, but seemed to share a knowing glance.

"I'm telling you, Ms. Moran," Anna said, "Ivan Gray embezzled hundreds of thousands of dollars from our mother and then killed her when he realized that she was onto him. The security guard who led her up to the roof said she was upset. She'd clearly had an argument. It's only a matter of time before Ivan slips and says the wrong thing to the wrong person, and then the police will swoop in for an arrest."

"Did you see your mother arguing with Ivan, or anyone else, that night?"

Once again, both men looked to Anna for guidance. Laurie wished she had been able to question them separately, but unlike a police officer, she could not control the circumstances under which she met her witnesses.

Anna shook her head. "We're too honest to fabricate evidence, but there's no doubt in my mind it was Ivan. Every time I see an ad for his stupid boxing gym, I want to punch something myself."

"What about Penny Rawling?" Laurie asked. "As your

mother's assistant, she was certainly in a position to see her and Ivan interact regularly."

An awkward silence fell over the table, and this time, Carter was the one to answer first.

"We created a job for her as a billing clerk after Mom passed, but it didn't work out. I heard she was starting business classes at Hunter College, but she hasn't stayed in touch with the family."

"And what about your cousin, Tom?" Laurie asked. "We're told that he was also at the gala that night and was a bit of the black sheep in the family."

Carter let out a knowing laugh. "Boy, was he. For a while, he made me look like a Rhodes Scholar by comparison."

"That's all in the past now," Anna said abruptly. "Tom has matured tremendously. He works here at the company with us now, handling office leases."

Despite his sister's serious tone, Carter was still chuckling to himself. "Remember how annoyed Mom was that Tom used the Wakeling name to land tickets that night? She said, 'Thank God I was able to tell him in all honesty that our table was already full.'"

Even Peter and Anna were smiling at Carter's impersonation of their mother's precise diction.

"And Tiffany, his embarrassing date," Anna added.

Carter burst out laughing. "The two of them stuck out like sore thumbs. Everyone could hear Tiffany talking at the top of her lungs about her wacky grandmother, the retired cabaret dancer. She swore a series of U.S. presidents fell in love with her grandmother. But John Kennedy was her favorite. At least she showed good taste there."

The laughter grew and then subsided as Anna shifted back to business mode, but with a slightly less stilted tone now. "Anyway, cousin Tom is a changed man. He's a trusted family member and colleague." She looked directly at Carter as she spoke.

She's sending her brother a message, Laurie thought. Cousin Tom is a trusted family member. But then why wasn't he invited to this meeting?

Suddenly, Anna was standing, her attention already drifting to the cell phone in her hand. "I appreciate you're coming out here, Laurie, but I'm afraid we have another meeting scheduled."

Laurie was caught off guard. "I was hoping to talk to you about participating in *Under Suspicion*."

"I'm sure, but we'd prefer to wait for the police to complete their investigation before a television show begins poking around."

Laurie had come here thinking that she only needed to get one family member on board to be able to move forward with production, but it was clear that Anna was running the show for all of them, and had made up her mind before the meeting ever began.

"Whether you participate or not, we'll still be—quote, unquote—'poking around.'" She did not relish the idea of going forward without them, but had a feeling that Brett Young would give her no choice.

Grace surprised Laurie by suddenly handing a file from her giant purse to Peter before he could stop her. "Let us just leave the paperwork with you so you can mull it over. In the interests of full disclosure, you should know that Ivan Gray's got some strong opinions about your family, and I've gotta say: the three of you were a lot nicer in person than he made you sound."

Jerry looked as if he wanted to pull Grace from the room, but Grace wasn't finished.

"I'm just a secretary, but if it were me, I wouldn't want a man like that talking about me on national television without getting in my side of the story."

When the assistant named Kate arrived to escort them back to the lobby, Anna Wakeling's face was white as a sheet.

16

They broke into an analysis of the final minutes of the meeting the second they stepped into the elevator.

Jerry said, "Grace, I think you shook Anna to her core. I wondered if the woman was going to faint. Her skin went as pale as her mother's."

Grace was fanning her face with her hands as if she were on fire. "I'm so sorry. I was just acting on impulse. It seemed like we were about to lose them."

Laurie placed a reassuring hand on Grace's forearm. "What you said was absolutely correct. It is in their interest to present their side of the story."

"But, no offense, Laurie," Jerry said. "It can sound intimidating when it comes from the boss. Grace, I loved it when you said, 'Gee, I'm just a secretary.'" He pressed one finger into his cheek to mimic a child's dimple. "Then, boom! You lowered the hammer: 'You really don't want this man talking about you on national television.' You rattled them for sure."

The elevator came to a halt and they stepped out into the lobby.

"Fingers crossed," Grace said, crossing two dark red fingernails. Her smooth, heart-shaped face was shining with pride.

Laurie noticed two men in the lobby halt their conversation to check out Grace. One, carrying a take-out bag from Chipotle, rushed to catch the elevator doors before they closed.

His friend waved. "Talk to you later, Tom."

Laurie reached behind her with one hand, holding the doors open for the man named Tom. "Are you Tom Wakeling, by any chance?"

"Yeah," he said, squinting at her, trying to figure out if he should recognize her.

With dark, wavy hair and short facial stubble, he bore no obvious resemblance to his fairer cousins, but he shared Anna's high cheekbones and Carter's long nose.

Without losing eye contact with Tom, Laurie said quietly to Grace, "If you have an extra participation agreement, let me have it."

Grace quickly slipped the papers out of her tote bag and into Laurie's hand.

The elevator began to buzz, and Laurie hopped into the car on impulse.

"I'll meet you guys out front," she said, leaving Jerry and Grace behind in the lobby. "Tom, I'm Laurie Moran."

17

Laurie was grateful that the other Wakelings were in whatever meeting they had either scheduled or fabricated to have an excuse to cut short their conversation with her. Now they were nowhere in sight.

She followed Tom to a small office cluttered with files and notebooks. It had a window view, but she imagined the other family members in much more luxurious work spaces based on her fleeting glimpse of the conference room.

It didn't take long for Laurie to explain why she was there. Now that *Under Suspicion* was a hit show, she didn't even need to lay out the nature of her work. She stretched the truth a bit by saying she had just met with his cousins Carter and Anna "to work out the details of their participation in the next special."

"I assume you'll be willing to sit down with us, too?"

He shrugged. "Yeah, no problem."

Trying to appear nonchalant, she handed him a copy of their standard participation agreement.

While he skimmed the document's contents, she asked how long he had been working at the company.

"Two years as of last Halloween," he said, dashing off his signature and returning the completed form to her.

That would have been less than a year after Virginia Wakeling's death.

Laurie had read in Robert Wakeling's *New York Times* obituary that he had started the business with his brother, Kenneth, but had assumed sole responsibility over operations by the time Long Island City parking lots were being replaced by high-end luxury loft apartments. She asked Tom about the family history.

"God bless both Dad and Uncle Bob"—he made the sign of the cross—"but if there's a lesson to be learned from that chapter in the Wakeling Saga, it's 'family first.' They let the business get between them." He sounded melancholy as he described how the two brothers shared a dream as young men to develop a pocket of land just beyond Manhattan into a thriving, modern neighborhood. But when their dream hadn't yet come to fruition after five years of work, Tom's father, Ken, grew impatient. Bob's forte was construction. Ken was the architect in the family. "My father really was an artist at heart, while Bob was a natural businessman. Dad's artistic side wanted—no, needed—to work on other projects. So Uncle Bob bought Dad out of the business, basically paying him the land's purchase price. Dad was grateful for the return of his investment so he could move on to more reliable jobs as an architect, and his brother kept plugging away at their dream. For a while, everything was fine. Then all of the pieces of their Long Island City plan finally began to fall into place like dominos."

It was a plan that would lead to a two-hundred-million-dollar fortune for Robert Wakeling. "Your uncle didn't find a way of splitting some of it with your father?" Laurie asked.

"Nope. He said Dad made his decision. He quit, and Uncle Bob didn't. Like I said, he was all business."

"That couldn't have been easy for your father to accept," Laurie said.

He shook his head. "My senior year of high school, he sold our apartment in an Upper East Side high-rise and moved us to the west side because he couldn't stand the sight of Long Island City on the other side of the river."

"And yet here you are working at Wakeling Development."

"My father died a year before Uncle Bob, also of a heart attack. I swear, I think they'd both still be alive if they had made peace with each other. Personally, I could always see both of their sides in the feud. Dad thought Uncle Bob cut him out of a fortune while Uncle Bob thought Dad bailed on their dream, and shouldn't be rewarded for it."

"But you weren't some neutral third party," Laurie said. "One of these men was your father. Not to mention, you had to watch while your aunt, uncle, and cousins became extremely wealthy people. Carter and Anna stepped right into the family business, straight out of college. You only landed here a couple of years ago."

"Honestly, I didn't resent them for it one bit. At that point I had jobs bartending at nightclubs, and life was a party. I told myself I was having fun."

"And now things are different?" Laurie asked.

"Clearly," he said, gesturing at the stacks of documents around his office. "If I had to pinpoint the moment it all crystallized for me, I think it was that night of the Met Gala, to tell you the truth."

"Because of your aunt's death?"

"No, although obviously that was horrible. I was at the museum, surrounded by the rich and famous. I saw the way my aunt and cousins were treated there, almost like royalty. Meanwhile, I knew I only got in because of my name. They were hobnobbing with celebrities and members of the board of trustees, and I was sneaking around the portraits gallery like a kid playing hide-and-seek with some ridiculous woman. We were complete fish out of water."

"Your cousins mentioned you had a rather colorful guest with you that night."

"Ah, Tiffany Simon," he said smiling. "Absolutely gorgeous, and a ton of fun, but a complete wacko. That was our second date, as I recall. I saw her a few more times after that, but then I finally realized she loved drama. Every moment of life was like a scene in a play that she was writing as she went along. Get this: she would introduce herself to a stranger as a princess from some fictional island, just to entertain herself. It was exhausting. Anyway, running around the gala with her that night while she was drinking too much and telling insane stories about Granny the lover, I felt ashamed of myself in comparison to the rest of my family. I decided right then and there I was going to talk to my aunt and cousins to see if they had any advice for me to put my life on a different track."

"And then your aunt died."

"Talk about surreal. It was a wake-up call. I realized life is short. Suddenly, we were the next generation of Wakelings. I waited several months before approaching Anna and Carter for a job, but when I did, they welcomed me with open arms."

"Do you mind if I ask where your mother is in all this?"

"Florida. After Dad died, it was going to be hard for her to keep up with expenses in New York. She sold the apartment and got a condo in Naples. She visits at least twice a year. I think she's happy that the cousins and I were able to pull the family back together, even if it was too late for Dad and Bob to see."

It was a happy ending to the Wakeling family story, but something about it didn't ring true to Laurie. Tom had to have resented his cousins for hoarding the largess of Wakeling Development for themselves, even after their father had passed away. Carter and Anna hadn't built that company any more than Tom had, and yet they were "treated like royalty," as he described it, while he was a "fish out of water." He might have indeed decided "right then and there" at the museum to turn his life around. He may not have even waited for the gala to be over. She pictured Tom pulling his aunt aside for advice. Virginia would have been distracted, focusing on the party and her mingling with other benefactors of the museum. She could have told him it wasn't the proper time or place, or maybe she rebuffed him outright.

Laurie could almost hear Virginia Wakeling speaking from the grave, as if she were standing in the room with them. *You're even less dedicated than your father, with none of his talent. Too little, too late.* Tom might have continued to make his case. Or maybe he said something worse. *You never worked a day in your life, Aunt Virginia, and now you're squandering your money on a gold digger.*

Virginia would have been upset. She would have gone to her security guard, Marco, asking to go up to the roof for fresh air.

Laurie imagined Tom watching his aunt step into the elevator. She could see him tripping the alarm in the exhibit and then slipping into a staircase when the guards weren't watching. Knock it off, she told herself. You were ready to decide that Ivan was the killer before you met him. Now you're about to prejudge Tom because he sounds too good to be true. Don't get ahead of yourself.

"Well, thank you very much for your time, Tom," she said, forcing a warm smile. "I'll be in touch when we start planning our production schedule."

"I'm happy to go along with whatever my family wants me to do."

Jerry and Grace were waiting in the back of the black SUV that would return them to Manhattan.

"We have good news," Jerry said, looking excitedly toward Grace as Laurie climbed into the car. "You tell her! You're the one who did it."

Grace was smiling from ear to ear. "Anna's assistant

called Jerry five minutes ago. Apparently Anna, Peter, and Carter all agree to participate in the show."

Jerry said, "She specifically mentioned they didn't want a liar like Ivan Gray to present his side of the story on national television without a counterpoint, pretty much quoting Grace word for word."

"Nice work, Grace," Laurie said, offering her a quick high five. "We can add Tom's agreement to the collection."

She handed Grace the document Tom had signed.

"So how did things go?" Jerry asked. "Get any dirt?"

"Maybe. He says it's all love and happiness between him and the cousins, but I'm not so sure."

The only thing of which Laurie was certain was that their list of alternative suspects had just grown by one.

18

When they returned to the office, Laurie invited Grace to join her and Jerry in her office for lunch, wanting to reward her for the work she'd done that morning at Wakeling Development. Grace offered to stay if she was needed, but said that otherwise she had taken Ivan Gray up on his offer for a free training session at PUNCH.

Laurie wasn't sure how to feel about Grace spending time outside of work with Ivan. On the one hand, the entire reason they had this case was because of Ryan's personal connection to Ivan, so Laurie felt like a hypocrite for telling Grace she couldn't go. On the other hand, she was protective of Grace, and Ivan was still the most likely suspect in the murder of Ginny Wakeling.

Laurie was still trying to figure out what to say when Jerry blurted out a response. "Are you crazy, Grace? That man's probably a murderer."

"Laurie thinks the nephew, Tom, did it."

"I think no such thing, Grace."

"I know," she said. "I'm just so impatient. Whenever we start a new special, all I want is to know who did it. Dealing day by day with this long list of people, not knowing who's dangerous—" She shuddered. "It gives me the creeps."

She was tucking a water bottle into the gym bag that had been stashed beneath her desk. "Rest assured, I won't be working out with Ivan. I told him that to avoid any appearance of a conflict of interest, I needed to train with someone other than him. A nice woman named Tanya is meeting me in ten minutes. I'm told she knocked out a two-hundred-and-fifty-pound man cold last year when he tried to grab her purse on the F train. I think we'll be fast friends."

As they watched Grace walk away, Laurie said to Jerry, "If Grace becomes best friends with her boxing instructor, I bet she'll find out what Tanya thinks of Mr. Ivan Gray."

Now the take-out containers from their lunch had been cleared—an egg salad sandwich for Laurie and grilled salmon and asparagus for Jerry, who was torturing himself with a thirty-day "cleanse" consisting of nothing but vegetables and lean protein. They were at her office conference table, poring over the book that Charlotte had given Laurie from the "Fashion of First Ladies" exhibit. They had already marked at least fifty photographs with Post-it notes, making a point to draw equally from Democratic and Republican first ladies.

"I'm worried we won't be able to re-create the excitement of the Met Gala from still photographs," Laurie said. "But obviously it's impossible to go back and replicate the exhibit."

The museum had agreed to let them film on the rooftop, in the main hall, and in the temple room where the banquet tables had been set up, but they did not have free rein of the building, let alone access to all of the pieces that had been lent to the museum by the various presidential estates and libraries to create the exhibit.

"Are you kidding?" Jerry exploded. "These photos are stunning, and I'm sure the publisher still has high-res versions. We can also license video footage from the red carpet. I already cut two great clips of Mrs. Wakeling hugging Barbra Streisand and exchanging cheek kisses with Beyoncé. She looked so happy, and then she was dead a few hours later. I know we try not to let emotion affect us, but this one really gets under my skin. I look at Virginia and I think of my own mom, the way she finally got to focus on herself after the kids all flew the coop. It's like she spent her whole life as a moth and then became a butterfly."

Jerry had a point. They had dealt with cases involving much younger victims than Virginia Wakeling, but hers was also a life cut way too short. She had just started her life over again.

Laurie heard a tap on her open office door and turned to see Brett Young.

"Brett, I barely recognized you out of your natural habitat." Brett was the type who beckoned others to his turf. He did not roam the hallways.

He shot a glance at a band on his right wrist. "Julie has

me wired up to this contraption. If I don't make my goal of ten thousand steps a day, I'll never hear the end of it."

If anyone stood a chance of altering Brett Young's behavior, it was his wife, Julie.

"Where do things stand on your next special?"

For once, Laurie had an answer that would please even her difficult boss. "We're all set. The entire Wakeling family's on board. Jerry's working out details about filming at the museum, but we'll be fine on that front. I'm meeting with the detective in charge of the homicide investigation once I finish up here with Jerry. And Ivan's coming in this afternoon to sign his participation agreement."

Brett rubbed his palms together. "Now, that's what I'm talking about. I hate to say it, Laurie, but I think your little rivalry with Ryan has put a perk in your step. I should have hired someone to get on your nerves years ago."

"There's *absolutely* no need to hire anyone else for that, Brett," she said.

"Okay, Ms. Moran, I get it. Start putting together a schedule."

Once Brett was out of earshot, Jerry impersonated Brett's impenetrable scowl. "Can't you tell how happy I am, Laurie? Hope you can stick to your schedule this time."

"Be careful. I wouldn't be surprised if he has hidden cameras in every room. We'll see how long we can keep him happy. Notice I didn't mention Penny Rawling." They still hadn't found contact information for Virginia's former personal assistant. "I only gave him the good news."

"Well, Carter mentioned she may have registered for classes at Hunter College. I have a call in to a friend who works in their computer department."

"It's illegal for him to disclose information from academic records."

"Well, forget I said anything, then," Jerry said innocently, flipping to another page of the fashion book. "Isn't this picture amazing? There will probably never be a first lady as graceful as Jacqueline Kennedy."

On display for the exhibit was a crisp white cotton dress with cap sleeves and a full, pleated skirt. The dress was draped on a mannequin, paired with a single strand of pearls, a silver charm bracelet, and nude ballet flats.

"The dress is awfully simple for an art exhibit," Laurie noted. "I could find something like it in a department store today."

"That's the point: classic. Plus, look at her in it. She was so beautiful." Behind the mannequin was a wall-sized, black-and-white photograph of President and Mrs. Kennedy on a front porch, a young Caroline on the President's lap, holding a small stuffed giraffe. According to the book's text, the photograph was taken the summer of 1960 at the Kennedy compound in Hyannis Port, Massachusetts, just after the couple had announced Jacqueline's pregnancy with John Junior. "What an iconic photograph. Can we please use this one for production? My grandmother used to have pictures of JFK and Jackie in her den, and said how different the course of history could have been. It would be like a little tribute to her."

"Of course, Jerry. That's a wonderful idea."

Smiling, he marked with a star the Post-it note that had already been tacked to the page. "You know what else would be a good idea?"

"Hmm?"

"If you left for your meeting with Detective Hon. You and your father are supposed to be in Harlem in thirty minutes."

19

Leo checked his watch from the back of the cab. It was 2:32. He was supposed to meet Laurie at the Manhattan North Homicide Squad at three o'clock. There was a time when he could have used flashing lights on his unmarked car to make it there from the Upper West Side with time to spare. But even with his part-time position with the anti-terrorism task force, he was still a regular civilian when it came to navigating New York City transportation, which meant that he'd left his apartment half an hour earlier.

He had eagerly accepted when Laurie asked him yesterday if he was willing to meet with the lead detective on the Virginia Wakeling homicide investigation. Leo didn't know Johnny Hon personally, but the detective Leo had called when Laurie first mentioned the case to him spoke extremely highly of him. Leo was always happy when Laurie's work allowed him to dip a toe back into investigatory waters. Initially, he thought she would be worried that people would think she was relying too much on her "daddy." But having a cop on your side comes in handy when talking to other cops, and Laurie was too much of a pro to let petty misperceptions keep her from getting the job done.

Leo checked his email on his phone. He had spent the first half of his career using a typewriter for police reports. He never thought there'd come a day when everyone would walk around with a powerful computer in their pocket.

He had a new message from Alex Buckley. The subject line referenced the message Leo had sent to Alex the previous night: "re: Cheers to Your Honor!"

After Leo first met Alex through Laurie's show, the two men had socialized regularly, both with Laurie and without, primarily to talk sports. Leo could see early on that Alex's interest in Laurie wasn't solely professional, and he had watched as Alex had come to care deeply about not only Laurie, but her son, Timmy. He had also seen Laurie's feelings change. As much as she had tried to avoid the blurring of Alex's role on her show, she could not ignore the natural connection the two of them shared.

When they filmed a special at the famous Grand Victoria Hotel in Palm Beach, Leo had caught a glimpse from his terrace of Laurie and Alex having a nightcap, sitting side by side on chaise lounges next to the pool area, no other hotel guests in the vicinity. Laurie's intermittent laugh broke over the sounds of ocean waves. Leo hadn't seen his daughter so happy since Greg was alive. When Alex resigned as the show's host once they ended production, he said it was to focus on his law practice, but Leo was certain that Alex was clearing the path to have a serious relationship with Laurie without the complications of working together at the studio.

And then the name of one of Alex's former clients had come up while Laurie was investigating her next special. Leo still didn't know all of the details about who said what to whom, but by the time the special was being filmed, Laurie had accused Alex of keeping her in the dark about his client, and Alex had come to believe that Laurie lacked faith in him. In theory, it was a dispute between a lawyer and a journalist, but it had grown into something much larger. When Leo found Laurie crying one night after Timmy went to sleep, all she said was that Alex was gone.

Out of respect for Laurie, Leo had decided to keep his distance from Alex for the time being, but yesterday, when he saw the news about Alex's nomination to the federal bench, he started to pick up the phone. Alex was his friend, too. He could not let an accomplishment like this go unacknowledged. But then he imagined how the call would play out. Leo would say congratulations. Alex would say thank you. And then what? Leo would inevitably pivot to the topic of Laurie. He didn't want his daughter to accuse him of meddling.

So, instead of calling, he had sent a short note from this little gadget. *Dear Alex, or should I call you Judge Buckley now? Congratulations on the much deserved recognition. I never thought I'd root for a defense attorney to take the bench, but you're one of the finest men I've ever known. Justice will be well served. Proudly, Leo Farley.* Short and sweet.

Alex's response was similarly polite. *Leo, It's great to hear from you. Thanks for the kind words. Your support means the world to me. Now if only the U.S. Senate agrees! Best to the whole family, Alex.*

Leo read the final line of the email, picturing Alex composing it, always so precise with his words. Laurie was convinced that Alex had moved on without her, but Leo believed that Alex was still waiting, fingers crossed that Laurie would come around.

20

By the time Laurie got to the corner of 133rd Street and Broadway, her father was already standing outside the nondescript, unnamed building that housed the Manhattan North Homicide Squad, talking to a well-dressed Asian-American man with slicked back hair and wire-rim glasses. Leo waved as he saw her approach, and his new acquaintance offered a hand for a quick shake. They both had their coat collars flipped up against the cold.

"You must be Laurie. I'm Detective Johnny Hon."

"Thank you again for taking the time to speak with me, Detective. I'm sorry I kept you in the cold waiting."

"Not at all. I came down to sneak a smoke before you arrived. Don't tell my wife. I'm supposed to be quitting." She noticed a binder, about four inches thick, tucked beneath his left arm. "I hope you don't mind, but I figured I'd bring the work down to you. Commissioner Farley deserves better treatment than a dusty conference room in need of fresh paint."

Her father raised his eyebrows, knowing the description was accurate. "I told you to call me Leo, and you're calling the shots, Johnny. Where you go, we follow."

"A perk of being in Harlem's the food, and I still haven't had lunch thanks to a court hearing that went long. I'm starving. There's a spot called Chinelos around the corner. Killer tacos, only three bucks a pop. Okay by you?"

Laurie flashed him a thumbs-up. She was happy to have a second lunch if Detective Hon could help her figure out who killed Virginia Wakeling.

Hon's chosen lunch spot was a hole in the wall with fluorescent lights and tile floors, more like a deli than a restaurant, with a counter for ordering and a few tables in the back. But, at least at this time in the afternoon, it was private, pin quiet, and, as Hon promised, served delicious Mexican food.

Hon was adding a generous amount of extra hot sauce to his tacos when he asked about Laurie's meeting that morning with the Wakeling family. "I'm surprised they even agreed to speak with you."

"Not only that. They're going to appear on our show."

He let out a whistle. "Wouldn't have guessed that one. I've watched your show with Alex Buckley putting suspects in the hot seat and asking hard questions. Man, I'd like to see him make the Wakeling family squirm."

"We have a new host now," Laurie said, trying not to show the emotion in her voice, "but, yes, we like to think that we're thorough with our interviews."

Leo leaned forward toward Hon. "You make it sound as if they've been less than forthcoming with you, Johnny."

He shook his head. "Not in a suspicious way, nothing like that. But all three of them—the son, the daughter, the son-in-law—are hell-bent on seeing Ivan Gray behind bars. If you ask them any question other than 'Just how guilty do you think your mom's boyfriend is?' they get impatient, like you're nosing around in their business."

Laurie remembered the certainty in Anna's voice when she repeatedly accused Ivan of her mother's murder.

"Ivan thinks one or more of them killed Mrs. Wakeling because she was planning to change her will. According to Ivan, she was leaning toward leaving almost everything to charity. The kids would still have the business but they'd need to accumulate their own wealth."

Johnny Hon was nodding, clearly already familiar with the theory. "Problem is, until we develop a way to speak to the dead, we have no way of knowing her intentions. What we have is the will that was put into probate when she died. Ivan says she was talking about changing it, but no one backed him up on that. I called the lawyer who wrote the will. He said he hadn't spoken to Mrs. Wakeling for at least a year."

"Anna's husband, Peter, was the executor of the estate and, by all accounts, a trusted advisor," Laurie said. "When I asked him whether Virginia mentioned changing her will, he—"

"Claimed attorney-client privilege." The two of them finished the sentence in unison.

"I can understand why Virginia Wakeling would find it awkward to talk to her attorney about changing her will," Leo observed. "Her executor was her son-in-law. In essence she would have been telling him that instead of the money going to his family, the Wakeling fortune would be left to charity."

"Maybe that's why she never got around to making the change," Hon added.

"Or maybe she was prevented from going through with it," Laurie opined.

Laurie broke the brief silence that followed. "You seem pretty confident that the only thing I'm doing is duplicating work you finished three years ago."

"I've got no big ego about these things, Laurie. I want answers, whether they come from me or from a television program like yours," Hon said. "It's a little funny to hear about you walking through the same exact steps I took." He looked at Leo. "You've been in police work most of your life. You know how some cases are."

"My nine-year-old son can't wait to join the police force." Laurie smiled. "He told us he was planning to get the records of unsolved cases and solve them one by one."

"The Farley name goes on," Hon said. "Anyway, the son-in-law, Peter, remained poker-faced when I asked him about impending changes to the will."

"That didn't seem suspicious to you?"

Hon shrugged. "I figure, someone willing to kill their mom—or mother-in-law—for money would just as soon lie and tell me, absolutely not, she'd never change her will. I think Anna and Peter are all about protecting the

Wakeling name. If Mrs. Wakeling was going to change the will, they may not want the public to know about it. Their fortune would seem like ill-gotten gains, so to speak. So, if they don't think it's relevant to her murder, they find a way not to talk about it. This is what I meant when I said it would be interesting to see them getting cross-examined on TV."

"But you didn't consider them suspects?" Leo asked.

"Technically, everyone's conceivably a suspect until the case is solved," Hon said matter-of-factly.

"They don't have alibis, right?" Laurie asked.

"No. Multiple witnesses placed them all in the main hall when rumors began to spread about a death, but anyone could have made it from the roof back down to the crowd very quickly. Anna said she had gone to the ladies' room, and Peter and Carter were both working their way around the crowd, saying hello to various guests. It was impossible to pin down anyone's location to the very second. Did someone explain to you that the video cameras were down that night for servicing?"

Laurie nodded. "I met with the head of museum security yesterday, a guy named Sean Duncan."

"He's a good man. Runs a tight ship there," Hon said emphatically. "Unfortunately, he didn't have much first-hand interaction with the Wakelings on the night of the gala. The guard assigned as Virginia Wakeling's contact no longer works there. His name is Marco Nelson."

"I assume you must have interviewed him?" Laurie asked.

"Oh sure. He was the last one to see Mrs. Wakeling

alive, other than her killer, of course. I was surprised when the Met let him go."

"He was fired?" Laurie exclaimed. "Sean made it sound like Nelson had moved on to private security where he could make more money."

"Oh, I don't doubt it, but he was encouraged to look elsewhere. Bob Grundel—that was Sean's predecessor as the head of security—told me Marco was suspected of stealing high-end merchandise from the museum's retail store. Apparently, he was dating one of the assistant managers and had a tendency to sign up for purse-checking duty on nights when she was working. The theory is she was sneaking items out under his watch. A straight arrow like Sean would probably set up a sting operation and build a case. The former boss played his hunch by giving both of them a warning they might want to look for work elsewhere. Or at least that's what I'm told." Hon shrugged, knowing he was repeating gossip he'd learned on the job.

"You said before that Marco was the last to see Mrs. Wakeling, except for her killer," Leo said. "Is there a reason you used the singular of that word? Is it possible more than one person was involved?"

"I should have said 'killer *or* killers.' Correction duly noted." Hon looked at Laurie. "You have a theory?"

"As you said, everyone's a suspect. But I saw the roof. It's highly unlikely a woman would have had the strength to push Mrs. Wakeling over that wide ledge. 'Push' may not even be the right word to describe what happened. That railing is three and a half feet high and there is shrubbery on the other side of it. Whoever did this pushed her over the railing and then shoved her off the shrubbery. Or she was lifted up and thrown over in one motion. But I suppose if either Anna or Virginia's assistant, Penny, were involved, they could have had a male accomplice."

"You're casting a wide net. The personal assistant?" Hon asked.

"Ivan thinks Penny may have been worried about getting fired if Virginia and Ivan had gotten married. He apparently had strong thoughts about her work ethic, or lack thereof. And my understanding is that she did inherit under the will. He didn't understand why Penny didn't defend him to the police. According to him, she was in a position to know they were a happy couple, and that he wasn't using Ginny for money. And by the way, Ivan called Mrs. Wakeling 'Ginny,'" Laurie said, her tone reflective.

"Well, he's right about one thing: that is definitely *not* the impression that Penny gave us. She was right in step with the rest of the family. She said that Ivan was in a rush to get married, and she thought it obvious that his motives were financial. Even if he had signed a prenuptial agreement, he would have been far more comfortable as Mr. Virginia Wakeling than as a personal trainer," Hon replied.

"Maybe she was just backing up the Wakeling family because she wanted to stay in their employ," Leo suggested.

"Or here's a simpler theory: maybe all of them were telling the truth about Ivan. He was using that woman for her money, and when she found out he was stealing from her, she was going to expose him," Hon suggested.

Laurie was all the more certain that they needed to find Mrs. Wakeling's former assistant before they started filming. "We haven't been able to locate Penny. Can you help with that, by any chance?"

"Last time I spoke to her, she was working at Wakeling Development."

"Not anymore."

"Afraid I can't help you, then."

Detective Hon was already doing her father a favor by even meeting with her. She couldn't expect him to turn over private location information about a citizen for her. "What about the nephew, Tom Wakeling? Did you look into him?" she asked.

Hon wiped his hands on paper napkins as he finished his last bite of food before answering. "Oh, I went there all right. No matter how hard he tried to hide it, it was real clear to me that he resented the rich half of that family. He said he went to the gala that night to impress his date, but I wouldn't be surprised if he sort of enjoyed making his fancy aunt and cousins uncomfortable by bringing a date who clearly didn't fit in. I take it the feeling was mutual. As I recall, he only inherited fifty thousand dollars from his aunt. Not exactly nothing, but more like pocket change given the fortune at stake."

"He told me this morning that they're all one big happy family now," Laurie said.

Hon rolled his eyes. "Look at it this way. Your uncle makes a fortune off an idea that also belonged to your father, and you don't get a piece of the action? Whether he shows it or not, no way that didn't get under his skin."

"And yet I never heard one word about him until I started digging into this case. Why was Ivan a suspect, and not Tom?" Laurie asked.

"Because Tom was the one member of that family who had an actual alibi. Unlike his cousins, he wasn't mingling around in a crowd. He was with his date the entire time."

"This is Tiffany Simon?" Leo inquired.

Hon nodded. "That's the one. She provided a detailed alibi at the time of the murder. Apparently, the party was a bit stuffy for her tastes, so they snuck up to the second floor to poke around in the empty galleries. It was actually pretty cute: she said they were checking out all those stodgy old formal portraits on the second floor, mimicking their stilted poses and forced facial expressions. I confess, the next time I went to the museum with my teenagers, we gave it a try. Pretty entertaining if you're not a big art aficionado."

"Couldn't Tom have asked her to lie to keep him out of trouble?" Leo asked, frowning in concentration.

"Except their versions of the story lined up perfectly," Hon pointed out. "Some old general looked like Brad Pitt, an Italian heiress looked like Cher. Highly unlikely they cooked that up out of thin air. Besides, it was only their second date. Hard to imagine she'd lie to homicide detectives when they weren't even in a serious relationship. Good luck with your show, Laurie, but I'll make a bet with you. Come back here when it's all said and done, and you're going to agree with me about who killed Virginia Wakeling."

"Ivan Gray?"

"He's the guy. Tacos on me if you prove me wrong."

Laurie noticed Hon glance at his watch and could sense that he was ready to wrap things up.

"I'll kick myself later if I don't ask you about that notebook, Detective. Any chance it's about the Wakeling case?"

"Better than a chance." He slid the binder across the table. "I had to redact a few names and numbers under privacy laws, but otherwise, that's everything I've got. My investigation is your investigation."

She began flipping through the pages. Virginia Wakeling's will. Crime scene photos. Police reports. "I don't know how to thank you."

"*De nada.* There's not a cop on the job who doesn't look up to your father, Laurie. And maybe you and your TV show can shake something loose after all this time. It'd be nice to see Ivan Gray behind bars at last."

"*If* he's guilty."

"Oh, he's guilty all right. It takes a certain kind of cruelty to kill a woman who loves you. There's not a question in my mind that he'd hurt a complete stranger like you if he thinks you're breaking new ground. Be careful, Laurie."

21

Thirty-year-old Penny Rawling completed one last walk-through of the apartment. The property listing described a chicly renovated, turnkey-ready, three-bedroom, two-bathroom condo in the heart of the West Village featuring a spectacular sunset view over the Hudson River. In reality, the third "bedroom" was a cubbyhole at best, used by the current owner as a tiny home office. The "chic renovations" used the kind of inexpensive but trendy finishings that inexperienced buyers easily mistook for high-end. And the "view" was from a single living room window, and only if one leaned a bit to the side to glance around a neighboring building.

Given what she had to work with, however, Penny thought the place was ready to show. Just as she knew what kinds of words to use in a listing to please her employer, she had mastered the finishing touches of staging an apartment for potential buyers. With the seller's permission, she had placed all clutter and personal mementos in clear, plastic boxes that could be stored neatly beneath the bed in the master suite. Fresh flowers—a mix of lilies and roses were the best assortment at the corner delicatessen—had been arranged in a crystal vase on the dining room table. Every room looked like a page out of a modern furniture catalogue.

She removed the stack of flyers she had printed out with details about the apartment and placed them neatly next to the vase of flowers.

She stopped and looked at the lower right-hand corner of the printout, trying not to feel resentful. The woman pictured there was Hannah Perkins, a member of the firm's elite "Titanium Club" for agents who had sold at least a hundred million dollars of real estate in the preceding year.

All on the backs of minions like me, Penny thought bitterly.

Penny was more than halfway done with the seventy-five hours of training she needed to sit for the exam to get a New York State Realtor's license. In the meantime, she made twenty bucks an hour as an assistant, answering Hannah's calls, printing out contract documents, preparing flyers, scheduling appointments, arranging appraisals, organizing co-op packages, and, yes, cleaning a lazy seller's cluttered home—basically all the work except negotiating a selling price and cashing that big commission check at closing.

"Someday, I'll be the star of the agency," she promised herself, glancing in the mirror. She smiled as she took in her newly styled black hair. She had recently taken a friend's advice to try a chin-length, layered bob and knew it accentuated her bright blue eyes. The new, expensive, but on-sale, Escada slacks and jacket were a perfect fit now that she had managed to take off ten pounds. I look like a Titanium Realtor, she thought proudly as she locked the apartment door behind her.

She was stepping into the building's lobby when her cell phone chirped in her purse. Under Hannah's orders, she no longer used the cheery, pop-song ringtones she had previously favored. "No offense, Penny, but no one takes a woman seriously when her phone sounds like it belongs to a teenybopper."

Penny looked at the screen, expecting to see Hannah's name there, micromanaging her as usual. Her heart nearly stopped when she saw the number. Nearly three years later, and she still recognized it.

Her finger lingered over the screen, knowing that she should decline the call. Nothing good could come of this. But just as her memory still knew that number, the person on the other end of the line still, apparently, had some amount of control over her.

"Hello?"

"You didn't change your number."

"No. I changed everything else, but not that."

"Are you okay?"

"I'm a real estate agent now," she said, before realizing how silly it was to lie. He, of all people, would be able to check, if he were inclined to do so. "Well, almost. I'm about to take the exam." That was just an embellishment on the actual timing, and not nearly so easy to disprove.

"Congratulations. I'm proud of you."

She swallowed, hard, not wanting him to know how

much she still cared about his opinion of her. If I had been a member of the Titanium Club, would I have been good enough for you and your precious family? she wondered. Probably not.

"Why are you calling?" she asked. Her voice sounded chilly, even though her skin felt on fire.

"Have you been contacted by a television show called *Under Suspicion*? The producer is a woman named Laurie Moran."

"I know the show, but no, they haven't contacted me. Why would they—Oh," she said, connecting the dots.

"Yeah, I guess it was only a matter of time before the media circus came back around. They'll probably contact you at some point."

"Why? I was only the assistant."

"You were more than that. Always. And you were there that night. Plus you knew Ivan, arguably better than any of us."

Ivan. How many times had she been tempted to walk in when she passed his gym? But he had moved on, just as she had. Maybe she would see him again after she had her license, so he'd know that she had found that "work ethic" he was always lecturing her about.

"So that's the only reason you're calling?" she asked. "Fine. Thanks for the heads-up."

"What are you going to tell them?"

"What do you mean?"

"If the show contacts you. I mean, you don't even have to talk to them. You know that, right? You could just ignore them."

"And how's that going to look?"

"Like you want to keep your privacy. Whatever excuse you can come up with for not doing it."

Once again, he was only thinking about himself. He never cared about her, not then, and not now.

"Thanks again for the call." She hung up without waiting for him to say good-bye.

As she walked to the West 4th Street subway station, she found herself wondering how long it would take for a television program like *Under Suspicion* to get on the air. If the timing worked out, she might be a full-fledged agent by then. Having her name emblazoned across the bottom of television screens across the country wouldn't be a bad way to launch a career in New York City real estate and it would be a chance to show off to the Wakelings.

"Titanium Club, here I come!"

22

When Laurie returned to the office, she was surprised to see Ivan Gray standing at Grace's desk. Gray had been scheduled to sign the participation agreement at the end of the day. I hope he didn't change his mind, she thought, alarmed. She hurried down the corridor to catch him before he left, but when she got closer, she saw that he was handing papers to Grace. When he asked, "Do you need anything else from me?," she breathed a sigh of relief.

"I can answer that," Laurie said as she approached him. "That's all we need for now. We'll be in touch with you as we get closer to production."

"Any idea when that will be?" Ivan added quickly. "I confess I'm getting excited to put out my side of the story."

"I wish we were in a position to be more precise," Laurie told him, "but we're always juggling a million moving pieces. Rest assured, we're eager to get to the truth, but want to make sure we're thorough and fair to all sides. But I do have another question. We want to talk to Mrs. Wakeling's assistant, Penny Rawling."

Jerry chimed in. "The Wakeling family said they had heard rumors Penny was taking business classes at Hunter since leaving the family's employ, but apparently that lead was a dead end. I checked, but unfortunately, my friend at Hunter College says there's no student there by that name."

"We haven't kept in touch," Ivan explained. "When I tried to make suggestions about her work, about how to be better organized, she thought I was criticizing her. That's the only explanation I can think of for her refusal to defend me to the police."

"And her relationship with Mrs. Wakeling's family?"

He shrugged. "They thought of Penny as a secretary and not much more."

Laurie noticed Grace clear her throat.

"I'm sorry," Ivan said. "That's not what I meant. They didn't seem to have any connection to her beyond her being their mother's employee. I thought Penny and I were closer than that. Both her parents died when she was so young. I was trying to mentor her."

Laurie noticed Ivan's gaze shift, and then he was waving at someone behind her. She turned to see Ryan Nichols, raising his fists into a mock one-two-three punch.

Oh, joy, she thought.

"Laurie was just asking me about Ginny's assistant, Penny," Ivan explained. Laurie realized she was tiring of being spoken about in the third person between these two. "She and I were never friends," Ivan continued, "but we had a connection, and then she turned on me when

Ginny died. I get the impression from Laurie's expression that she was given a different version."

"If you don't mind, *Laurie* is right here," Laurie said, pointing at herself. "And, from what I understand, Penny thought you were in a terrible rush to get married."

He shook his head adamantly. "Absolutely not. The exact opposite. I know to a certainty that Penny heard me say that I would wait until we were a hundred years old if necessary. Ginny laughed and said, 'And what use would I have for such an old man?' Then she added, 'Besides, I'll have turned to dust by then.'" Ivan was smiling wistfully at the memory.

Ryan was looking down at his wing-tip shoes, appearing incredulous.

"What?" Ivan asked.

"Look, I'm going to have to ask you this at some point on camera, so I may as well pose the question now, Ivan: You said you'd sign a prenup. You had picked out a ring. And yet she refused to accept your proposal. She lied to her own children about her intentions. Why didn't you leave her in the face of such rejection? Most men would have walked away."

Laurie had been dubious about Ryan's contributions to the show, but he was finally posing a tough question to his newfound friend. She was also curious about Ivan's answer.

"I never even saw it as a rejection. She was a widow. She was deeply in love with her husband. She needed time to figure out what her life would look like, not just without him, but with another man in the picture. I was something entirely new, a major change in her life. When I offered her the ring, she said it was too soon to accept it. She needed time, and I was willing to wait, no matter how long it took. Forget the age difference. I was in love with Ginny. Why is that so hard to believe?"

23

Alex Buckley walked out of the Delta Shuttle terminal at LaGuardia and into the black car where Ramon was waiting behind the wheel.

"Everything went smoothly, Mister Alex?"

"Some rain in D.C., and protestors outside the capital, but here I am, only ten minutes delayed."

"Were you able to see Andrew and the kids?" Ramon asked.

Ramon knew how close Alex was to his younger brother, Andrew, who was a corporate lawyer in D.C. "I checked into the Ritz yesterday," Alex said, "but ended up staying the night at his house. Johnny is a bit confused and thinks Uncle Alex is about to become president, but I will say they were happy to see me."

Andrew's son, Johnny, was in the first grade and was just aware enough of government positions to confuse a lower-court judicial appointment with being elected President. His twin sisters were only three, and still thought of Uncle Alex as the man who taught them how to sing "The Itsy Bitsy Spider." To this day, they placed their fingertips together to act out the song the second they laid eyes on him.

"Johnny may have a crystal ball," Ramon said. "It wouldn't surprise me at all if you ended up President someday."

As they made their way up the Brooklyn-Queens Expressway and across the Triborough Bridge, Alex reviewed the paperwork he had been given by the Senate Judiciary Committee to complete for his confirmation hearings. The day had been a whirlwind of activity he never could have dreamed of, ending with a meeting in the Oval Office with the President himself and the other judicial nominees. Alex only wished his parents had lived to see it happen. The President had welcomed them all collectively with a joke: "You may come to regret this honor once you see the hoops you'll be jumping through."

He hadn't been kidding. The questions in these documents would take him days to answer, touching on everything from his roommates in college to his thoughts on the most influential Supreme Court decisions in United States history.

He had read all the questions twice when he flipped back to the second page in the packet. The information requested here was relatively straightforward biographical information, but one section gave Alex pause. At the top of the page, he was asked to list contact information for anyone with whom he currently lived. After that, he was asked to identify spouses, ex-spouses, children, parents, and siblings.

None of this would be difficult for Alex. He was a

bachelor who lost his parents at a young age. He had one live-in employee, Ramon, and an adult brother with his own family.

But the third question on the page was a catch-all: "Please provide biographical information for any individuals who serve a role similar or comparable to those listed in parts (a) and (b), above, regardless of legal affiliation or formal definitions of family (such as intimate partners, part-time roommates, financial dependents [whether or not adopted], etc.)."

I can only wish that I could write, "Wife: Laurie Moran Buckley, Stepson: Timothy Moran." Even thinking it was painful. Once again he asked himself if he lost Laurie by pressing her for a firm commitment before she was ready.

This is my fault, he thought. I told Laurie I would wait as long as necessary, and then I pushed her away, forcing her to experience a "freedom" from me that she never asked for.

He tucked the papers back into his briefcase, praying that something would change before he had to submit his answers.

24

It had been a long day. Anna Wakeling took a deep breath as she opened the door to her Park Avenue apartment.

From inside she could hear the voices of her two children, seven-year-old Robbie and five-year-old Vanessa, coming from the living room. The aroma of a baking chicken made her realize she had skipped lunch in the office. Thank God for Kara, she thought. She's a marvelous cook.

In the living room Vanessa and Robbie were playing word games with their longtime nanny, Marie. Both jumped up when they saw her and enveloped her in hugs.

One boy, two years older than the one girl, just like Carter and me, she thought. But her children's lives had been nothing like her own childhood. In the beginning Carter and I attended public schools in Queens, she thought. I could count on one hand the number of times our mother had relied on a babysitter. Robbie and Vanessa, in contrast, had a nanny, and next year Vanessa would be joining Robbie at one of the most elite private day schools on the Upper East Side.

In the beginning Dad treated us differently, Anna thought, taking Carter to building sites, showing him architectural drawings of new projects. But I was smarter. I wanted to learn everything Dad was talking about. I begged him to let me tag along. It wasn't long before he realized I had it all over Carter.

Unlike her parents, Anna tried so hard to treat her children equally, not like "the boy" and "the girl," the way she and Carter had been so frequently stereotyped. She never wanted Robbie to feel entitled because he was a boy, and she never wanted Vanessa to feel limited because she was a girl.

25

From the doorway Kara announced, "Dinner will be ready in fifteen minutes, Mrs. Browning."

Anna kissed the top of the heads of her children. "Okay, guys, let me get into some comfortable clothes. I'll be right back," she promised. She made it upstairs to her dressing room to change into jeans and a sweater and pulled her long hair into a loose ponytail at the nape of her neck.

Peter had spent the late afternoon in his home office. She stopped there to tell him she was home. He stood up and gave her a quick kiss. "I like you in jeans," he said approvingly.

"It feels good to be in them, but Peter, I'm worried. Do you think we made the right decision today? I mean, to get involved with that program?"

"I don't think we had any choice," Peter said, his voice troubled. "If we don't give our side of the story, Ivan could make up anything he wanted, and we'd be left having to respond after the show aired. At least this way, we'll have a chance to shoot down what he says during the actual production."

Anna nodded. They'd run through the same calculation this morning after their meeting with the producer and her assistants. "What if my mother really was planning to cut us out of the will?"

"As her executor, wouldn't she have told me that?" Peter asked. "After all, she went over the terms of her will with me after your father died."

Peter had refused to discuss his mother-in-law's plans for her will with the police, citing client confidentiality. He had taken the same approach with the television producers this morning. But he and Anna had no secrets from each other. "If Virginia had been planning to change her will, she hadn't even mentioned it to me. On the other hand," he said, "she did assure me that if she ever decided to marry Ivan, she would have him sign a prenuptial agreement."

"But did she ever say anything about leaving money to charity?"

Peter took her hands in his. "Why are you so worried about this, sweetheart?"

"Suppose she talked to her friends about leaving everything to her favorite causes? How will it look if word gets around that we inherited all this money that was supposed to go to charity? It makes us look, I don't know . . ." Her voice trailed off.

"Annie," Peter said soothingly. "You work hard. You've earned this."

She shook her head. "I haven't done anything that comes close to what Dad accomplished. We live off his work, not ours."

"We live on the business he built. You're the one who has been maintaining it and making it grow," Peter said vehemently. "You don't have to be embarrassed just because your father left you a wonderful legacy."

Anna nodded, but her expression must have betrayed her true feelings. Peter hesitated, then his voice softened, "This is about Carter, isn't it?"

"Remember that the day before Mother died, Carter told us that he was worried that she was going to change the will. He asked us point-blank if we knew anything about that. We both thought that he was being paranoid about Mother's financial plans, especially given the situation with Ivan."

Anna's voice was trembling. "After the murder, when the police started asking questions about Mother's will, no one could have sounded more distraught than Carter. Neither one of us spoke about that conversation to the police. But if my mother was going to cut us off and Carter found out—" Anna couldn't bring herself to finish the thought.

"That didn't happen, Annie. You're talking about your own brother."

"Who, to this day, pays more attention to chasing women and having fun than working for a living. Maybe he was drunk or something—"

"We saw him that night, right after we realized it was your mother who'd fallen. He wasn't drunk. He was in shock."

"Well, maybe it was an accident. Maybe they got into an argument on the roof and she stepped backwards—"

Peter put his arms around her to calm her down. "That is *not* what happened," he said firmly. "Ivan Gray killed your mother. And this show might be able finally to prove it."

"I want to believe it happened that way. But Carter did ask about Mom's will the day before the murder."

"We are the only ones who know that, and we're not going to tell it to anyone, ever. Now, let's go to dinner."

26

The apartment was pin quiet by the time Laurie went to bed that night. Timmy had gone to sleep an hour earlier. It was that rare New York City moment of complete silence: not even a car honk or a siren in the distance.

She clicked the television on, turning the volume low. She flipped channels until she found a repeat episode of *Law & Order*. She liked the background noise, the familiarity, the flicker of the dim light in the darkness.

She reached into her nightstand and pulled out the small velvet box tucked neatly into the front corner. She removed her platinum wedding band and placed it on her left ring finger, as she often did when she was missing Greg and couldn't fall asleep.

She thought about Ivan Gray's words in the office that afternoon. Ryan had asked him why he stayed with Virginia, even as she refused to formally accept his proposal. "She needed time, and I was willing to wait, no matter how long it took. I was in love. Why is that so hard to believe?"

Laurie remembered when she believed that Alex

felt the same way about her. But then she had tested the strength of his commitment by accusing him of misleading her when one of his old cases collided with her last investigation. In retrospect, she could see that Alex was only protecting his client, as he was required to do by law. But now the damage was done. Like Ivan, Alex had been willing to wait when he thought all Laurie needed was time to be ready for a new relationship. But after that argument, he became convinced that her uncertainties were about him. You're wrong, she thought. The only person who has ever made me want to move on was you, Alex.

Last night, she had tried so hard to appear nonchalant when Charlotte mentioned seeing Alex with another woman. Her heart still hurt at the thought of it. But was it fair for me to ask him to keep waiting when I still fall asleep every night thinking about Greg, and wondering what our life would be like today if only he had lived?

She twirled her wedding ring on her finger. When she wore this ring, she felt as though Greg was here with her again. She thought she might see him in her dreams and feel—just for a few minutes in her sleep—as if she never lost him. "I never thought I'd have to grow old without you, my love," she said aloud.

With her wedding ring still on, she cried herself to sleep that night.

27

Three days later, on Monday morning, Laurie stepped out of the elevator at Fisher Blake Studios, ready to look at the Virginia Wakeling case with fresh eyes. Everything had been moving so quickly since Ryan Nichols first suggested—or practically ordered—that Laurie reinvestigate the murder. She knew that she should probably be grateful. After all the worry she'd had about Ryan being a bad fit for her show, he had actually identified a good case. And, so far, the pieces of the production had fallen together perfectly.

Laurie remembered how Greg used to complain about hospital administrators who "couldn't get out of their own way." Instead of accepting a simple solution, they would overplan and overanalyze to the point of inaction. Was she doing that now?

She found Grace standing in the doorway of Jerry's office. Laurie always enjoyed their Monday morning catch-up sessions. She spent her weekends keeping up with Timmy but got to live vicariously through Grace and Jerry's carefree adventures. As she approached, she could tell that Grace was recounting yet another horrible first date.

"Oh, perfect timing," Grace said as she looked up. "I was just getting to the best part." She stepped into Jerry's office, and Laurie followed.

She couldn't help but notice that Grace was dressed nothing like herself this morning. She was wearing a pleated skirt that fell four inches beneath her knees and a white crewneck sweater. It looked more like a private school uniform than one of her usual ensembles.

Jerry, in contrast, was looking extremely dapper in a tweed vest with a checkered shirt and perfectly coordinated striped bowtie. "I don't know how this story could be any better," he said. "We're not even to the dinner course yet, and whoever this guy is, he's told Grace that she looks like the most beautiful woman he knows—which is, by the way, his mother. He's asked her to wear flats next time, so she won't be taller than him, because of course he overstated his height by three inches in his online profile. And he made sure before she ordered the steak that they'd be going Dutch on the check."

Laurie shook her head and laughed. "I don't know how you do it, Grace. Dating these days sounds like urban warfare."

"Gotta kiss some toads is how I see it," Grace answered. "Plus, I always get the best stories out of it. So, when he leaves the table to make a phone call, I tell the waiter to give us the check as soon as dinner's over. No coffee or dessert for us."

"Smart woman," Laurie said.

"We split the check, of course. And then I assume he's as anxious as I am to get out of there, but as we're leaving he says it's still so early that the shops are still open at the Time Warner Center. He wants to know if I'll go to Hugo Boss with him to help him pick out an outfit."

"That doesn't sound so strange," Jerry said.

"An outfit for his *date* the next night. He said, *She looks a lot like you, so you probably have the same taste.*"

When their laughter died down, Grace's tone suddenly became serious. "Sorry, we're rambling on too long. It's time to get to work, I know. What do you need, Laurie?"

First, the change to Grace's wardrobe. Now an apology for gossiping a little past nine in the morning.

Laurie decided she would bring up the wardrobe question later.

"To talk about the case with the two of you in my office in twenty minutes," she said.

"Sounds good," Grace said. "But do you want me to call Ryan?"

Laurie paused. On the one hand, Ryan was the one who brought in Ivan. On the other hand, she could already picture him rushing the investigation. Her gut was still warning her that they were moving too quickly. No, she did not need to "get out of her own way." Ryan and Brett had her second-guessing herself, but she had gotten this far by listening to her own instincts.

She was missing something, and she was going to keep working on it with Jerry and Grace until she found it.

28

Once they were all seated in her office, Laurie started by making a list of the participants they had already secured, placing a check mark next to their names if they were considered a potential suspect.

Ivan Gray. Carter Wakeling. Anna Wakeling. Anna's husband, Peter Browning. The cousin, Tom Wakeling.

Laurie placed check marks next to all five names.

"I thought you said the police cleared the cousin," Jerry said.

"So far they have. Tom and his date, Tiffany Simon, both said they were together in the American Wing, looking at portraits on the second floor. The story rang true to the police, I guess. And they assumed this woman wouldn't lie to protect Tom since they were only on a second date."

Grace shook her head. "But the second date was to one of the most sought-after events in the city with a man whose last name was Wakeling. To some women, that might be a relationship worth protecting," she pointed out.

"I agree," Laurie said. "That's why I still have Tom

on our list of suspects. I want to talk to his date myself."
By all accounts, Tom and Tiffany had lost touch nearly
three years ago. There'd be no reason for her to cover for
Tom now. She wrote down the woman's name—Tiffany
Simon—in a separate column: Her to-do list. "Hopefully
she'll be easier to find than Mrs. Wakeling's assistant,
Penny Rawling. Have we had any luck with that?"

Jerry shook his head. "Ivan doesn't have her cell phone
number anymore, assuming it's the same as it was then."

Sometimes Laurie longed for the old days, when you
could look up a number in the white pages or, in a real
pinch, call 411.

She added Penny Rawling's name beneath Tiffany's,
and then added a check mark. Penny wasn't the most
likely suspect, but she hadn't been eliminated from suspicion either.

She tapped her pen against her notepad. "I wish we
had a better handle on Virginia Wakeling's children. It
was hard to get a sense of them in such a short meeting."

"If you ask me," Grace said, "Anna seemed like the
boss of the bunch."

"Followed by her husband in the pecking order," Jerry
said. "Then a big step down before the brother, Carter."

Grace, always willing to jump to conclusions, de-
clared that if the children had anything to do with it,
"Anna would have been the one to call the shots. I bet
she tripped the alarm in the costume exhibit to create a
diversion, and then her husband followed Mrs. Wakeling.
How many men haven't had a thought or two about pushing their mother-in-law off the roof?"

"It is so hard to imagine anyone coming up with a plan to murder his or her own parent," Laurie said. "Maybe I'm being sexist, but it seems especially shocking for a daughter to kill her mother."

"On the other hand," Jerry said, "I could imagine Carter acting alone. We all agree he seems to live in his younger sister's shadow. That could make him resentful. If Ivan's telling the truth, then Virginia was thinking about changing her will so her children would need to support themselves through their own work for the company. Anna's clearly the one running the show at Wakeling Development, so Carter might have been afraid that she'd find a way to force him out."

"Or they all acted together," Laurie said. "Or it was Ivan, or Penny, or Tom. In that case Anna and Carter are innocent people who lost their mother." Once again, she felt as if they were grasping at straws. She realized how much she wished she could talk about the case—about everything, really—with Alex. "Whatever dynamics we noticed in the family, it's obvious that the three of them are close-knit. They're protective of each other. We need an outsider—someone other than Ivan—to give us a better idea of their relationship to their mother. That makes it all the more important that we find Penny Rawling."

"I'll keep trying," Jerry said.

"I know," Laurie said, not wanting Jerry to feel as if she were blaming him.

"What about the nephew, Tom?" Jerry asked. "He's just a cousin. Maybe he'd be willing to give us the dirt?"

"I don't think so. First of all, until I talk to Tiffany

Simon, we have to consider him a suspect, too. More important, I talked to him in person. He may have been the black sheep in the family three years ago, but today he very much wants to stay close to the pack. He won't say anything to jeopardize his position with the family."

She looked down at her list. What was she missing?

"If we go to production now, we pretty much only have Ivan's word against the family's," Jerry said.

Laurie shrugged. "That was my problem with the case from the beginning. I can't imagine we'll learn anything new."

"Well, Brett can't say you didn't warn him," Grace said consolingly.

"And I can at least make the episode gorgeous," Jerry said, his voice lifting. "I hate to say it, but viewers will tune in just to see the dresses. Are you ready for a preview?"

Grace and Laurie sat back and Jerry pinned a series of photographs to the large corkboard in Laurie's office. Grace added oohs and aahs in response to her favorites. Laurie made a point to give a little clap when he pinned the photograph of Jacqueline Kennedy in her white cotton dress. That was the one Jerry was including as a tribute to his grandmother.

"Now, these are just the still photos," he explained, "but once it's all produced, we'll cut it together with video footage of the gala. It will be snappy with lots of movement. And then we'll contrast those images with photographs from the crime scene—nothing gory, of course, but yellow tape across the roof space, maybe a few spatters of blood on the snow. I haven't selected those images yet. Obviously, this work was more pleasant to complete," he added with a smile.

"It all looks great," Laurie said. She had come to television with a background in journalism, but Jerry had majored in media arts and had started at Fisher Blake as an intern. His strength was in creating strong visuals specifically for television.

"I just wish we had access to a few of the actual dresses," Jerry said. "If we could even use three, with one tiny corner of exhibit space at the museum, I know I could work wonders."

"I'm sorry, Jerry, but the Met said it would be impossible," Laurie said. "The dresses weren't in their permanent collection. Most came from presidential libraries, the Smithsonian, and other museums."

"I know. I just wish I could snap my fingers and make it so."

"Well, if you had that magic power, I'd prefer you use it to find these two women, and pronto," Laurie told him. She held up her notepad. "Tiffany Simon and Penny Rawling might be able to give us a new angle on all of them." She still had that feeling in her gut that they didn't have all of the pieces of the puzzle yet. "I just know Brett will be pushing us to start production any day now."

"No magic powers needed," Grace announced. She was looking at the screen of her iPhone. "Penny Rawling might be keeping a low profile, but I think I found Tiffany Simon."

She handed Laurie and Jerry her phone. It was open to the website of a business called the Marriage Mobile.

Their motto was "When You're Ready to Say 'I Do,'" and they promised to show up anywhere in the tristate area with everything a bride and groom needed for a wedding. The owner and "minister" was named Tiffany Simon.

Laurie studied the picture of Tiffany, taking in the fake eyelashes, heavy makeup, and plunging neckline. Not the kind of appearance that would go over well at the exclusive Met Gala, she thought. No wonder Tom's cousins were scornful of his date.

Why wait? she asked herself, as she picked up her phone and dialed the number on the website. The call was answered by a fluttery voice saying, "Marriage Mobile, Tiffany speaking."

Her voice matches her picture, Laurie thought, as she introduced herself and explained why she was calling.

The response she received was everything she could have hoped for. "I love your reality show," Tiffany squealed. "I can't wait to be on it. Boy, can I tell you something about the Wakelings. What a snooty bunch they are."

She may be a fount of information, Laurie thought, as she offered Tiffany a chance to meet anytime tomorrow.

"Oh, I would love to," Tiffany told her, "but I have meetings with new clients in the morning and early afternoon, and I have to get everything together for a wedding I'm doing at five o'clock. The ceremony is at the pier alongside the *Intrepid*. The groom used to be in the navy and he wants the battleship in the background of his wedding pictures. Do you want to meet afterwards, say six o'clock?"

"I can do six," Laurie said.

"Great. Landmark Tavern is on Eleventh Avenue at Forty-Sixth. It's in a neat old building and would be super convenient for me. The menu is English pub fare if that's okay with you."

I'm not going for the food, Laurie thought to herself. "Fine. I'll see you tomorrow."

Laurie hung up the phone and looked at the expectant faces of Jerry and Grace. "My date is set with Tiffany Simon, and she appears anxious to dish on the Wakeling family."

29

The following evening, Laurie arrived at the Land-mark Tavern first. She took a table where she could easily see the front door. A few minutes later Tiffany came in. Laurie immediately recognized her from her picture on the Marriage Mobile website. When she stood up and waved, Tiffany slithered over to her table. Her cheeks were still pink from the cold, and she shivered as she slipped off her parka but kept it pulled over her shoulders.

"Boy it was cold out there," she said with a deep sigh. "I should have charged them more."

"It is cold today," Laurie agreed, and then added, "Thank you again for meeting me."

"No problem," Tiffany said simply. "Like I told you on the phone, I'm glad to have a chance to dump on the Wakelings."

When the waitress came over, Laurie ordered a glass of Chardonnay.

"I need something a little stronger than that," Tiffany announced. "I'll have a double Chivas Regal."

"I don't blame you," Laurie said, smiling as she sipped

her wine. "Before we start talking about the Wakelings, I have a question for you. I'm curious. How did you get into the marriage business?"

Tiffany giggled. "A lucky accident. Sort of like betting on the right horse. Two years ago, I jumped through all the hoops to marry two of my close friends who were getting hitched. It was a tiny ceremony, and they wanted every part of it to be special. You'd have thought Prince William was marrying Kate what's-her-name. So I said I'd figure out a way to officiate. Turns out, the city will let you register as long as you're a minister, and I found a church online that was willing to make me one. Hard to believe, huh? Anyway, once it was over, I realized I'd had more fun planning their wedding than any job I ever had, so I figured, what the heck? Let's give it a try. A lot of people just want to get married; they don't need a whole fancy thing. I show up with some silk flowers, a half-decent photographer, and the paperwork."

"No muss, no fuss," Laurie said.

"Yep. In fact, I used that as my motto when I first started my website. And now my job is to help people celebrate the happiest day of their lives with the person they love. Or the second or third time they find true love," she grinned.

"Good for you," Laurie said heartily. "And now let's get to the reason why we're here. I appreciate the opportunity to talk to you about Virginia Wakeling's murder."

"And I guess my name came up because that night at the Met Gala I was her nephew's date?" Tiffany asked as she signaled for another Scotch.

"Exactly," Laurie confirmed. "Any information you have about where her various friends and family members were at the time of her death would be helpful."

"Well, I can only tell you about one, which is Tom. We weren't even halfway done with dinner when I started getting bored. His family was sitting together at a nearby table. They kept giving me nasty looks, like I was dirt or something. Tom and I were at some overflow table of people who had only bought one or two tickets, so a bunch of strangers, basically. And dull ones, at that. There was a couple from somewhere in the Middle East. Their accents were really heavy, and I had trouble understanding what they were saying. Another couple was in their mid-nineties and both of them were half-asleep. I tried to liven things up by telling them stories about my grandmother, but even though I was shouting, I don't think they heard a word."

Laurie noticed tears glistening in Tiffany's eyes. "Is your grandmother still with us?"

"She had a stroke a year ago and has lived in a nursing home since then. She's very forgetful and her only memories are all the men who were chasing her when she was a dancer." Tiffany took a gulp of her Scotch. "Anyhow, Tom and I decided to get up and move around instead. When I spotted two of the security guards watching the bottom of the staircase get distracted, I grabbed Tom's hand and ran up the stairs."

"Was this when the alarm went off in the costume exhibit?"

Tiffany looked confused by the question. "What alarm?"

"I'm sorry. Never mind." For a moment Laurie had forgotten Detective Hon's explanation that it had been a silent alarm. "What distracted the guards?"

"One of them was showing the other one his phone. It looked to me like maybe he was posting pictures from the event or something. You ask me, people spend too much time on social media. No matter where you go, somebody's face is stuck on his cell phone. Right?"

"Right," Laurie agreed. She found herself liking this eccentric woman more and more by the minute.

"So, anyway, we slipped up to the second floor. No one was around. It was awesome. We roamed all over. And I still remember—because it was honestly the only fun I had that night—we were looking at the old formal portraits, making faces like the ones in the pictures. Not one of them smiling. Then I remembered I heard that the reason they all looked so grim is because they all had bad teeth. I told Tom that and he burst out laughing."

Laurie nodded. "I've read that George Washington never smiled because he was ashamed of his wooden teeth."

Laurie could see why Detective Hon's gut had told him that Tiffany was telling the truth. She told the story as if she were still seeing it in her mind today. She was remembering something that actually happened.

"But when did you realize his aunt had been killed?"

"We were hiding behind a post at the top of the stairs. After about fifteen minutes we headed back downstairs. We were waiting for the security guards to get back on their cell phones so we could slip down. But when I sneaked a peek, you would have thought a bomb had exploded in the main hall. Cops and security guards bumping into each other everywhere. Everyone was standing, and they were trying to figure out what the cops were up to. I'm sure no one even noticed us when we joined the crowd. I asked some man what was going on, and he said a woman had died. We had no idea who it was until I saw Anna next to a guy who looked like a cop. She was crying hysterically while her husband held her. It was awful to watch. I knew it had to be about Mrs. Wakeling; I'm instinctive that way. Anyhow, Tom ran over to check on her and heard Anna telling the police that if her mother was murdered, it was by Ivan Gray. What a terrible way it was for him to find out his aunt's dead." Tiffany shook her head. "I mean, I know Tom was only their cousin and it was their mother who died, but they didn't even talk to him that night. I felt really bad for him. He was crying, too. It was like a man without a family."

For a second, Laurie's mind flashed to Alex. He had told her once that he felt like a man without a family once his only relative, his brother, had moved to Washington, D.C. "Tiffany, was Tom with you the whole time you were on the second floor?" she asked, trying to focus on the task at hand. "He didn't leave for the men's room or anything like that?"

"The police asked me the same thing that night when it was still fresh in my mind. We were definitely together every minute. Are you going to need me for your show? I really want to be on it."

"I don't think so, but I'm not sure," Laurie said. "It's

late. How about having dinner? The shepherd's pie would be perfect for this weather."

Tiffany shook her head regretfully. "Nope, I've got a Pomeranian at home who's probably a few minutes away from peeing on my rug."

Laurie signaled for the check and told Tiffany she didn't need to wait if she was in a hurry.

"I'm not letting the puppy keep me from finishing this great Scotch. It makes me feel nice and warm."

Laurie took another sip of her wine. She did not think that Tiffany had anything else to tell her, but she wanted to establish a friendship with her just in case she decided to put her on the show.

Tiffany made it easy for her by saying, "I'd really love to be on your show, even if for only a couple minutes. If you can possibly mention that I'm a wedding planner, that would be really great. And I can't leave without asking how Tom is doing."

"He seems fine, from what I could tell in one meeting. He's working for the real estate development company that his father and uncle started together. From what I was told, he's much more career-focused now than he was three years ago. He's still single, in case you're interested."

"I'm not. Sure, I know plenty of women who'd be thrilled at the chance to date someone in that family, but he was definitely not for me. No spark. No pizzazz. And there's no fun in that family. Honestly, part of me wanted to warn Ivan to run away. He was the most interesting person there, if you ask me. I don't think for one second that he killed Mrs. Wakeling. The way I see it is that he was teaching her how to enjoy life."

"You gathered all of that from meeting them that one night?"

"I have a sense for these things."

She said it as if it needed no further explanation. "So who do you think killed Virginia Wakeling?" Laurie asked.

Tiffany didn't even pause before answering. "I bet she jumped."

"No one said anything about her being depressed or despondent."

"That's not the way it goes. My guess is that she realized when she was with an interesting guy like Ivan that she just didn't have it in her to keep fighting her kids about him. They drove her to it."

"You really believe that?"

"Oh, definitely. I met these people for, like, ten minutes. Trust me, if I were stuck with that pain-in-the-butt bunch, I might jump off a roof, too."

30

Looking across the cafe table at Tiffany Simon, Laurie was certain that she was not lying to cover for Tom Wakeling. She was obviously unimpressed by the family, and certainly was not trying to curry favor with them.

After paying the check, she thanked Tiffany once again for her time. As they were walking out, Tiffany paused and held up a finger as if she had just thought of something. "Did you talk to the assistant?"

"Do you mean Virginia's assistant, Penny?"

"Right, that was her name. So sweet and old-fashioned. The name, I mean." Laurie could tell from the last comment that Tiffany did not think highly of Penny Rawling. "When I said some women would have been thrilled to date a Wakeling? Penny certainly fit the bill."

"Meaning?"

"It's been so long, I can't remember her exact words to me. Something like, 'Tom's only the cousin, but still . . . lucky you.' It was tacky, like I had hit the jackpot by landing a date with Tom. But here's the thing. Then Penny said something like, 'I've got my eye on the prince.' Or maybe she said the 'golden boy.'"

"You think she was interested in Virginia's son, Carter? He was the only son in the family."

"Funny. At the time, I was thinking of the daughter's husband. He was a lawyer, maybe? But looking back, that's probably because, to me, he was the more interesting one. But, yeah, I suppose the son makes more sense. Regardless, I got the impression she had something going with one of them."

Laurie remembered Ivan's description of Penny, always on the phone with a mystery boyfriend. And according to Ivan, Penny had been fussing about her appearance for the gala, leaving him with the impression that her unknown suitor would be there.

Tiffany reached into her jacket pocket. "I can see you're not wearing a wedding ring. But you're close to making a decision. I have feelings about these things . . ." Her voice trailed off.

Laurie realized Tiffany was staring at her with her eyes half-closed. What's wrong with her? she asked herself.

Then Tiffany's eyes opened wide and she smiled. "I didn't tell you that I'm a psychic. I tell people something about themselves, and bingo, it happens. You're not wearing a wedding ring. That's because you're about to make a big decision."

She pulled her card from her pocket and shoved it over to Laurie. "If you make the one I think you should make, give me a call. I'll put together an amazing, fabulous wedding for you."

Once Laurie was in the cab, she removed her note-pad from her purse. She crossed off Tiffany's name from her to-do list and scratched out the check mark that had been next to Tom's name. And then she drew a big circle around the name Penny Rawling.

The taxi was only six blocks from Laurie's apartment when her cell phone rang. The screen identified the caller as Alexis Smith, an entertainment reporter with the *New York Post*. Laurie was tempted to let it go to voice mail, but never wanted to miss an opportunity to plug her show.

"Hi, Alexis."

"Hey there, Laurie. Long time, no see. I saw your old host last week at the premiere of a documentary about wrongful convictions, and then remembered that you got someone new. Alex was great, but Ryan's a real up-and-comer on television."

"Thanks," Laurie said, not sure what else she should say. She wished everyone would stop reminding her that Alex was apparently everywhere in New York City other than with Laurie. "Were you calling about Ryan?"

"No, but I am calling about *Under Suspicion*. Can you confirm that your next special will feature Virginia Wakeling's unsolved murder?"

How did word get out already? Laurie still didn't trust Ryan, plus Alexis had just mentioned him. But she knew Alexis would never reveal her source, and Laurie couldn't ask without confirming the report. Instead, Laurie gave her standard response. "We're always pursuing fresh angles on cases that have run cold, and look forward to announcing our next special once we have an airdate."

As Laurie stepped out of the cab, she felt as if a timer had just been set on a clock ticking over her head. Brett was already rushing her, and now they'd have the additional pressure of a newspaper article highlighting their investigation. And, still, Laurie could not shake the nagging feeling that they were moving too quickly. She was missing something important. She needed to find Penny Rawling.

31

Penny Rawling snagged the last empty table at the Starbucks on Cooper Square. She was happy to find a copy of today's *Post* left behind. As she sipped her skinny venti mocha, she flipped through the pages, skimming the headlines.

Most of her attention was elsewhere, though. Ever since she'd gotten that phone call from her ex-boyfriend about that television show, she couldn't stop thinking about him. *I'd hoped I was totally over him,* she thought to herself. *He moved on, and so did I, or at least, that's what I wanted to believe. But here I am, daydreaming about him again.*

He had tried to sound nonchalant about *Under Suspicion* when he called, but she still knew him better than everyone, after all these years. She could tell from his voice that he did not want her involved with the production. But who was he to tell her what to do? After Virginia died, he had dumped her like a piece of trash.

When he first called, she had thought a reality show would be a good way to launch her real estate career, but after she thought about it further, she realized an additional benefit to participating on the show. She might be able to see him again. She imagined them both showing up at the studio. He would see her and realize she had been the right one for him all along.

Or if he knew that she was going to be interviewed about Virginia's murder, he might call again. Maybe he'd want to meet her in person to find out what she planned to say. When he saw how far she had come, certainly he would be interested in her again, right?

The only problem was that the program's producers hadn't contacted her yet. And if she took the initiative to reach out to them, they'd ask her how she knew about the production. It was a catch-22, and so she had to wait. It will happen, she told herself. Just have faith.

She flipped to another page in the *Post*, even though she hadn't paid attention to anything so far. She nearly dropped her cup when she saw a photograph of Virginia Wakeling entering the Met with Ivan Gray at her side. She immediately recognized the gown, with a black velvet bodice and flowing blue skirt. Penny had helped her decide the final finishing touches with the designer. It was absolutely perfect.

Virginia would die a few hours after this photograph was taken.

Penny set down her mocha and focused on the text accompanying the picture. It was a snippet from Page Six:

Another 'Punch' for Wakeling Murder?

A hit reality TV show may soon rock the highest levels of the art, real estate, and fitness worlds.

Page Six has learned exclusively that Under Suspicion, *which reinvestigates cold cases with the participation of actual suspects, might be featuring the murder of Virginia "Ginny" Wakeling in its next special. True crime aficionados will recall that Virginia Wakeling was the wealthy widow of real estate magnate Robert Wakeling. She was killed after a fall from the roof of the Metropolitan Museum of Art during its annual Costume Institute Gala. The prime suspect was her boyfriend and personal trainer, Ivan Gray, more than twenty years her junior.*

Now, three years later, apparently it's Ivan Gray himself who is leading the charge to clear his name. A reporter for the Post *overheard Ivan bragging to a client at his sought-after boxing gym,* PUNCH, *that* Under Suspicion *is "on the case." Meanwhile, the show's producers would neither confirm nor deny Ivan's version. Laurie Moran, Executive Producer, said, "We're always pursuing fresh angles on cases that have run cold, and look forward to announcing our next special once we have an airdate."*

So is Ivan Gray in the know or making up tall

tales for his clientele? We at Page Six hope there's truth to his report. Under Suspicion has been on a winning streak. Will they find justice again? Stay tuned. . . .

Penny homed in on the name of Laurie Moran. That was the name her ex-boyfriend had used when he called to see whether a producer from the show had called her yet about Virginia's murder.

She took out her phone and searched Google for Laurie Moran. A minute later, she was jotting down the phone number for Fisher Blake Studios. She had now found an excuse to call.

32

The morning after Laurie met with Tiffany Simon, she had the *New York Post* open on her conference table to the Page Six column, which, ironically, was now on page twelve of the paper.

At least it wasn't Ryan who had leaked their current case to the *Post*. According to the write-up, Ivan was overheard talking about it during a training session.

Now, she and Ryan were in her office, trying to decide what to do about it.

"I honestly don't see the problem," Ryan said. He was actually smiling smugly, as if proud of the development. "It's free publicity for the show. Ratings are the currency of our business."

He was sounding more like Brett every day. Laurie wondered if he knew about the image that was making the email rounds throughout the studio's staff. It was a picture of Brett holding the hand of a smaller version of himself, on which someone had pasted the image of Ryan's face. The thought bubble above Brett's head read, "I love my mini-me." Laurie strongly suspected that Jerry was the culprit behind the Photoshop job, but she certainly wasn't going to point an accusatory finger.

"We're not the only team that can delve into this case, Ryan. Now that word's out that we're working on it, other media outlets could beat us to the punch. Ivan breached his participation agreement by telling a client about our project."

"So what do you want to do about it now, Laurie? Pull the episode after all this work?" He gestured to the documents and photographs covering Laurie's office. "Hold back Ivan's participation fee? Trust me, he doesn't need it. Look, I'll talk to him about the article. He was chatting with a client. He didn't mean for it to wind up in the press. I'll tell him to be more discreet."

She realized that, under the circumstances, there was nothing else to do about it. They had gone too far to pull the plug now. "Fine. When you talk to him, can you ask him if he knows anything about Penny Rawling dating someone in the family?" She brought him up to speed on her interview of Tiffany Simon, including Tiffany's suspicions that Penny had a romantic interest in someone in the family. "She thought Penny had a secret boyfriend in the picture who might have been at the gala that night. If it was a member of Virginia Wakeling's family, that might change everything."

"It would have to be Carter, right?"

"Unless it was Anna's husband, Peter. Marriage doesn't stop some people."

"Scandalous," Ryan whispered conspiratorially. "I'll ask Ivan what he knows."

• • •

Two hours later, Jerry was giving Laurie a preview of a preliminary slide show he had put together for their episode. As he suggested, it was a contrast between glamorous photos of one of the most selective parties in the city and darker images that hinted at the violence that had unfolded on the roof above. A gurney covered by a sheet. Blood in the snow. Crime scene tape at the roof's entrance.

"This is just a slide show. Once we jazz it up, it will be much more dynamic, like moving images."

Laurie was flipping through the notebook that Detective Hon had compiled for her, making sure that they didn't miss any critical information or images. "I can't shake this feeling about the alarm that went off that night." The alarm was tripped by someone crossing a sensor around an exhibit of six mannequins. Laurie was looking at photographs of the portion of the exhibit that was entered. The exhibit appeared undisturbed. "It was just minutes before Virginia went over the railing. I don't buy that as coincidence."

"I don't think the police thought it was a fluke, either. The alarm distracted Security, which allowed her killer to slip into a staircase to the roof."

"And yet Ivan was their leading suspect."

As usual, Jerry was following her train of thought with ease. "If he acted alone, he'd have had to trip the alarm, run upstairs, kill her, and come back down."

"Certainly possible," she said. "But previously when

we talked about the connection between the alarm and the murder, we were assuming that one person set off the distraction, while the killer or killers ran upstairs."

"So if it's Ivan, did he have someone helping him?"

Laurie thought about Tiffany's account of Penny gloating over a relationship with someone in the family. According to Tiffany, Penny said that she had her eyes "on the prince," or perhaps the "golden boy." Ivan was positioned to be the future Mr. Virginia Wakeling. Was it possible Penny's mystery man was Ivan? Ivan had been the one to mention Penny as a potential suspect, but he also insisted he had no way of helping them find her.

It was a stretch, but it was possible. Laurie was about to lay out her theory to Jerry when Grace tapped on her door and then poked her head in.

"Sorry to interrupt, but I thought you'd want me to. I've got Penny Rawling on the phone. She saw the Page Six piece and wants to speak to you."

33

Now that Penny had Laurie Moran on the phone, she wasn't entirely sure what to say to her. She didn't want to sound too eager to be involved in the production. "Ms. Moran, I'm calling because I read in the *Post* that you're working on a special about the murder of Virginia Wakeling."

"I'm afraid I can't confirm that."

Penny had already heard from one of the participants on the show that it was happening, but she couldn't show her cards. On the other hand, she could imagine the producer being wary of disclosing details over the phone. For all Laurie Moran knew, Penny wasn't actually Penny. She could be a reporter seeking out information. She decided to press forward.

"Well, in the event the story is true, I wanted you to know how to reach me. Virginia Wakeling was my employer, as was her husband, Bob, before he passed. My mother was Bob's secretary for more than fifteen years. I was very fond of both of them."

Penny smiled to herself, confident that she had struck

the right tone. Caring, but not personally invested. And the detail about her mother's work for Bob might help convince the producer that she was not an imposter.

"Do you still work for the Wakeling company?" Laurie asked.

The question struck Penny as odd. Surely the producers would have asked that question of the Wakeling family by now. She realized that the woman was testing her, still unsure about her identity.

"No. I'm still in the real estate business, but not with the Wakelings. I found more challenging opportunities elsewhere after Virginia passed." All of the time Penny had put in working for women of a certain class, she liked to think that some of their airs had rubbed off on her. She sounded so mature and dignified.

"Were you with Mrs. Wakeling the night she died?"

The question was obviously another test. "Not on the roof with her, of course," Penny said, "but, yes, I attended the gala."

Laurie must have been satisfied that Penny wasn't some crackpot calling in with false claims, because she said, "Well, we're always looking for fresh angles on cold cases, and the Wakeling murder is certainly a compelling mystery. Any chance you'd be willing to meet with me to talk about what you remember of that night?"

"I suppose I could make the time, if it might be helpful. Anything for dear Virginia."

"I can come to you at your home or at work if that's convenient," Laurie offered.

The only space Penny had at work was a tiny cubicle

next to the coffee machine, and the last thing she wanted was for a television producer to see her shabby studio apartment in Flatbush. Before she even realized what she was doing, she was rattling off a different address, this one of a luxury apartment in Tribeca. "Or, you know what, I don't want to trouble you to come all the way downtown," Penny offered. "I'll go to your office."

"It's no trouble," Laurie said. "You're doing me a favor, Penny. The least I can do is save you a trip. What would be a good time for you? It's short notice, but I'm free this afternoon and this evening."

Penny held the phone away from her ear and used her thumb to flip quickly through her calendar, and then returned to the conversation.

"Sorry, but I'm all booked up today. I can meet you at my apartment tomorrow at one-thirty. How does that sound?"

"One-thirty tomorrow. Perfect," Laurie said.

They exchanged cell phone numbers in case either of them was running late. As Penny hung up, she prayed that Laurie ran right on schedule. The apartment's owner would be gone tomorrow afternoon from one until five, and Penny had already arranged for the buyer to arrive at three o'clock with her contractor to take measurements needed for a planned remodel. They'd have to speak quickly.

34

Laurie had just hung up the phone when she noticed Ryan lingering in her doorway. She waved him in.

"What's up?"

"I just got back from PUNCH, where I spoke to Ivan in person. Consider him properly chastised. He won't be talking about the show to his clients, or anyone else for that matter."

"Thanks. Did he say anything more about who Penny's mystery boyfriend might have been?"

He shook his head. "He said he never noticed any kind of flirtation between Penny and either Carter or Peter. His initial reaction was to remind me that Tiffany came across like a crackpot with a wild imagination."

"She was eccentric," Laurie said, "but she had a distinct memory of Penny saying something about her maybe being involved with someone in the family. I see no reason for Tiffany to lie about that."

"Fair enough. I did press Ivan on it, and he certainly conceded the possibility. He said Carter was the more likely of the two, since he was always dating around. He said he'd never heard a word about Peter being unfaithful to Anna, but he also said it wouldn't surprise him if Peter got tired of being—quote—'bossed around by Queen Anna.'"

"Another thought dawned on me after you left," Laurie said. "What if Tiffany was talking about Ivan?"

"That doesn't make any sense. The entire reason Ivan named her as a suspect was because Penny didn't take his side after Virginia was killed."

"Maybe she didn't take his side because she didn't want the family to know she was seeing Ivan behind her boss's back." Laurie was thinking out loud now, the way she used to with Alex. "Or she could have suspected Ivan after the fact and tried to keep her distance."

"Then why did Ivan point us toward Penny?"

When she had these brainstorming sessions with Alex, each of them would build on the other's observations, getting closer and closer to the truth. But, with Ryan, every statement felt like an argument, as if his immediate instinct was to shut down her ideas.

"He didn't point us to Penny," Laurie said. "Not really. He gave her to us as an alternative suspect, but didn't tell us where to find her."

"Speaking of which, I heard you call whoever was on the phone by the name Penny. You found her?"

"She contacted me, actually. She saw the write-up in Page Six."

"So Ivan helped us after all."

"Accidentally, yes."

"You're meeting her tomorrow at one-thirty?"

Laurie made a mental note to start closing her door during phone calls. "Yes, at her apartment down in Tribeca."

"Great. I'm free. I'll swing by here at one. We can take my car."

35

That afternoon, Laurie sat alone at her conference table, studying the binder she had received from Detective Johnny Hon. Specifically, she was looking at photographs taken of the exhibit space that night, after Virginia Wakeling's body had been discovered in the snow behind the museum. Technically, the costume exhibit being celebrated at that night's gala wasn't an actual crime scene. Whatever caused Virginia to fall to her death had happened on the museum's roof.

But by all accounts, an alarm had gone off inside the "Fashion of First Ladies" exhibit just minutes before Virginia was found. Was it a coincidence? Possibly. But it was also possible that someone had triggered the alarm to divert Security to one area of the museum while Virginia's killer—or killers—followed her upstairs.

What was bothering Laurie was the location of the alarm that was triggered. According to the investigation that night, the museum's Security Department told police that the alarm was set off in "Gallery C" of the exhibit. Looking at photographs, Laurie saw that Gallery C was a large, open room with two rows of mannequins positioned on either side, with a wide aisle in between for visitors to roam. The alarm that was triggered was set off when someone—or something—crossed a light beam protecting the display on the east side of the room.

Without seeing the actual physical space, Laurie was having a hard time visualizing the layout of the exhibit. However, according to its preface, the official book attempted to capture the exhibit as its curator intended, presenting the exhibit's contents in the same order they would have been encountered if the reader had walked through the galleries in person. Based on what Laurie inferred from the book, she believed that Gallery C was located roughly in the center of the exhibit. If she was correct, that would mean that it was not immediately adjacent to either the entrance to or exit from the exhibit.

If you were trying to set off an alarm as a diversion, Laurie wondered, would you wander all the way to the middle of the gallery space? The decision struck her as strange.

Her thoughts were interrupted by a light tap against her open door. She looked up to see Grace.

"Hey there," Laurie said.

"Do you have a second to talk?" Grace asked.

"Of course. Come on in."

36

Grace, always so confident, appeared tentative as she walked over to her usual spot on the white leather sofa. She carried a spiral notebook in one hand, a pen in the other. Laurie joined her by the windows, sitting in the adjacent chair and looking to Grace expectantly. Grace cleared her throat, as if steeling her nerves.

Laurie smiled, hoping to calm her. "I've actually been meaning to speak to you, Grace. I think I know what this might be about."

"You do?"

She nodded. "I just hope I'm not too late. You aren't giving me your notice, are you?"

Grace's eyes widened. "Of course not. Are you kidding? I love my job here."

"Oh, thank goodness," Laurie said, letting out a sigh of relief.

"How could you even think I'd leave?"

Laurie shook her head. "You just seemed so serious when you walked in. And I've noticed recently that you've been dressing differently—more staid and reserved. I was only half-joking when I said I was worried you might be going out on job interviews."

"No, the thought never even crossed my mind."

"I can't tell you how happy I am to hear that. I really don't know what I'd do without you, Grace. So what did you want to talk to me about?"

"Remember how yesterday morning, Jerry said he wished we had access to some of the dresses from the first ladies exhibit at the museum?"

"Yes."

"Well, I couldn't stop thinking about how excited he was about the idea, so I started looking up information about where the dresses came from."

"According to the head of security at the Metropolitan Museum, the dresses weren't a part of their permanent collection. Most came from presidential libraries and other museums."

"I know, but that's not all of them. A few came from private collectors, so I started researching what I could find out about those people. One of them is a guy named Gerard Bennington."

The name did not ring a bell to Laurie. "And who is Gerard Bennington?"

"Quite the character from what I can tell. He's a renowned fashion photographer. He is a regular in the front row at Fashion Week and is friends with all the snazzy tastemakers. He also fancies himself a talented vocalist. He even auditioned two years ago for *Find a Star*."

Find a Star was a talent show produced by Fisher Blake Studios. After launching the careers of three

Grammy Award–winning pop artists, the show's popularity had waned in the last few years. Laurie's understanding from Blake was that the show was still a money-earner for the studio because of all of the product placements.

"I wonder if he still owns the dresses."

"That's why I wanted to talk to you. I hope you don't mind, but I took the initiative. I got his number from one of the production assistants on *Find a Star* and called him. He has two dresses that he lent to the museum for the exhibit—one was Jacqueline Kennedy's; the other belonged to Betty Ford."

"Is there any chance he'd allow us to use them for our production? Jerry would be thrilled!"

"I already asked him. And I'm really sorry, Laurie, but he had seen the Page Six piece. When I told him I was calling from our show, he immediately realized that I was calling about the Virginia Wakeling case. He says we can use the dresses as long as he gets his name in the credits and at least one minute of airtime. He attended the party that night so he could either talk about the dresses themselves or the atmosphere at the museum after Virginia's body was found."

"That should be doable. A few words from an objective guest who was there that night would add some color, actually."

Grace held up her pen to indicate they weren't quite finished yet. "He had one more condition," she added sheepishly.

"Should I be scared?"

Grace let out a chuckle. "No, but the producers of

Find a Star might be. Gerard would like a second shot at stardom."

"Another audition?"

Grace nodded.

Laurie was friendly with the show's executive producer and was confident she could gain his cooperation. "I'll make a call right now and let you know when we can make it official."

"Do you want to be the one to contact Gerard?"

Laurie noticed that this was the second time Grace had used the man's first name. She had a way with people, that much was certain. "Eventually, when it's time to begin interviews. But why don't you remain his contact person for all the details? You're obviously doing a great job so far."

Grace's smile lit up her heart-shaped face. "Thank you, Laurie."

"No, thank you, Grace. Those dresses will elevate the production quality of the show."

Grace was about to stand but Laurie wanted to say one more thing. "You know how much we value you here, don't you, Grace?"

"I think so."

"You said something last week about your sister suggesting you'd be perceived differently if you changed your wardrobe. Is that why you've been dressing differently? You don't think you're taken seriously?"

Grace shrugged, and Laurie felt a pang of guilt for making Grace uncomfortable.

"Well, for what it's worth," Laurie said, "you could

wear a pink tutu and bunny slippers, for all I care. You are all kinds of serious, and anyone paying attention can see that."

Grace walked out of her office with an extra bounce in her step. Laurie made a mental note to look at her budget to make room for a much-deserved pay raise.

37

❦

As predicted, Jerry was elated when he learned that he'd have access to two of the first ladies' dresses for production, after all. Once Laurie had confirmed that the producers of *Find of Star* would allow Gerard Bennington to audition a second time, she had let Grace work out the details with Mr. Bennington and secure his signature on the necessary documents.

She had also left it to Grace to deliver the news to Jerry that afternoon in Laurie's office. Jerry told Grace that she was a lifesaver and pulled her into a tight hug.

He immediately reached for the heavy book of photographs from the exhibit, searching for the two dresses on loan to the museum from private collector Gerard Bennington. The Betty Ford dress was a floor-length silk teal sheath with flowing organza sleeves. The photograph that accompanied the display at the exhibit was of Mrs. Ford dancing with a famous comedian during a state dinner held in honor of the president of Liberia.

Jerry let out a gasp when he saw the second acknowledgment of Mr. Bennington in the book. It was for the crisp white cotton dress that Jerry had already shown to Laurie. He had been planning to include the iconic photograph of the Kennedys on their porch in Hyannis Port as a dedication to his grandmother, who had admired the Kennedys. Now he'd be able to feature the actual dress in the production.

"I'll need to call the Facilities Department at the museum right away. If I can get even one corner of gallery space, we could create the illusion of being in a much larger exhibit and could ask some of the participants to walk through as though they were viewing the costume exhibit that night at the gala."

"Sounds like a plan," Laurie said, her own attention focused once again on the large binder she had received from Detective Johnny Hon. She was still wondering about the placement of the alarm that had been triggered the night of the murder. If it was set off by the actual killer, the person would have wanted to be able to slip away quickly and follow Virginia to the roof, taking maximum advantage of the time during which Security was distracted. Even if an accomplice had been the one to set off the alarm, Laurie believed the natural instinct would have been to select a location near the exhibit's entrance or exit, so the accomplice could escape more quickly and easily.

She looked again at the photographs of the east side of Gallery C, the area that was apparently trespassed. One of the dresses on display there was the white cotton dress that Gerard Bennington had lent to the museum. Laurie found herself smiling with pride. Grace had worked a miracle getting access to two historic dresses, and Jerry was at his planning board, both looking as excited as Laurie had ever seen them. They were as invested in the show as she was.

As her eyes moved from Jerry's planning board back to her own binder, she noticed a discrepancy between two images.

"Jerry, remind me again where you got all those photos you're using for planning."

"They're almost all copied from that book Charlotte gave you." He walked over to the conference table, pulled the book from beneath a legal pad, and tapped the cover. "It's practically my bible these days."

"Including the photo of Mrs. Kennedy's white dress?" she asked. "That's from the same book?"

"Uh-huh."

"And you said that the exhibition book would have been prepared before Virginia's murder, right?"

"Definitely. They like to have the books available in the gift shop once the exhibit opens. Why? What's up?"

She rotated the binder in front of her to face him and placed her finger on the photograph depicting the east side of Gallery C. "Take a look."

Jerry's eyes moved between the photograph in the binder, taken by the NYPD, and the photograph of the white dress for the official exhibit book. "The dress looks exactly the same."

"The *dress* does, yes," Laurie said in agreement, "but look right here." With her fingertip, she drew an imaginary circle around the wrist of the mannequin. "No bracelet."

In the official exhibit photo, the dress was paired with a strand of pearls and a silver charm bracelet. By the time the police photographed Gallery C after Virginia Wakeling was killed, the bracelet was gone.

Grace was looking eagerly over Jerry's shoulder. "So when did it go missing?" she asked.

Jerry shrugged. "Conceivably, it could have been anytime between the production of this book and the night of the murder."

"True," Laurie noted, "but we know for a fact that the alarm that night was set off when someone crossed the sensor protecting these six displays. If someone specifically wanted that bracelet, it would explain why the alarm was set off in the middle of the exhibition, assuming I'm correct about the layout."

"So how do we find out for sure?" Jerry asked.

Laurie knew that calling Sean Duncan, the current head of security at the museum, would be useless. According to the Security Department's incident reports from that night, "nothing was out of place" when security guards responded to the alarm.

"I know where we could start," she said. "Grace, can you call your new friend, Mr. Bennington, and see if he has time to speak with us?"

"Will do," she said.

A few minutes later, she returned to Laurie's office. "He's driving back from his country house in Kent tonight, but said he'd be happy to meet with you in the morning. He's coming here at ten."

That would have to be soon enough. In the meantime, she knew at least one other person who had attended the gala that night who might be available.

Laurie used her cell phone to send a text message to Charlotte. *Dad's taking Timmy to a Knicks game tonight. Takeout at my place? Warning: I plan to pick your brain a bit.*

She smiled as she watched dots at the bottom of the screen, indicating that Charlotte was typing a reply. *Sounds perfect, but, these days, I can't promise anything useful will come out :-). 7 pm? I'll bring the wine.*

Laurie typed a final message. *See you soon!*

38

Laurie passed the container of sliced chicken and mushrooms toward Charlotte, who politely declined. "I can't manage another bite. Is it possible to get a high from too much MSG? I can't believe how much food you ordered!"

"I wanted you to have choices," Laurie explained. They were at her dining room table, surrounded by barely touched take-out containers. "Timmy and I are going to be eating leftovers for days."

She watched as Charlotte refilled her wine glass with sauvignon blanc.

"Speaking of Timmy, he must be thrilled to be at the Knicks game with his grandfather," Charlotte commented.

"He loves it. I think he got a little spoiled last year with Alex's season tickets. Tonight's tickets are courtesy of one of Dad's cop friends. Not courtside like Alex's, but it beats the television."

Charlotte took a sip of her wine and then asked quietly, "So have you spoken to Alex at all since I saw you at Brasserie Ruhlmann?"

Laurie shook her head.

"I thought maybe he would have called you after the judicial nomination, or vice versa."

"No, he didn't call me, and I don't think I should call him until I'm ready to give him some kind of grand gesture."

"A grand gesture?" Charlotte asked with an arched brow. "What? You're going to show up at his office with a radio, ready to serenade the future judge?"

"Nothing so dramatic," Laurie said. "But, yes, something . . . determined, let's say. Anyway, it's complicated."

The table fell silent for the first time since Charlotte had arrived. "So, you said you wanted to pick my brain about something," Charlotte said, changing the subject.

"Yes, let's do that now, before I get too far into this glass of wine." Laurie got up from the table and returned with both the official exhibit book Charlotte had lent her and the binder of documents she had gotten from Detective Johnny Hon. "How well do you remember the 'Fashion of First Ladies' exhibit?"

Charlotte let out a sigh. "I can barely remember what I had for breakfast these days. That was three years ago, and I just did a quick walk-through before the gala. What do you need to know?"

Laurie pushed aside enough take-out containers to make room to open her two books. She showed Charlotte the two photographs of the mannequin in Jacqueline Kennedy's white cotton dress.

"I would wear that today," Charlotte said. "Maybe I should do a knockoff for Ladyform's new weekend lounging collection."

"I'll buy it," Laurie said, "but, for now, this is what I'm more interested in." She explained the absence of the silver charm bracelet by the time Virginia Wakeling was killed. "I don't suppose you remember whether the bracelet was there when you walked through the exhibit, do you?"

"Oh, gosh no. I wouldn't have even noticed something like that."

"What about the layout?" Laurie spelled out her theory that Gallery C, where the alarm was triggered, was in the middle of the exhibition. "Here are pictures of the room," she said, shifting Hon's binder in Charlotte's direction.

Charlotte studied the photographs and then leaned back and closed her eyes, as if trying to re-create a memory in her head. "I do remember that room. It was the only one that was long and narrow. Most of the other rooms were big squares with items on all four sides. I was comparing the two because Ladyform was in the process of planning a few pop-up stores, and I was contrasting the two approaches. You're right. That room was basically in the middle."

"So to get back to the rest of the gala, you'd have to go through a few other rooms?"

"Right."

Laurie was getting more convinced that the alarm that night was connected to the missing bracelet. What she couldn't figure out was how either one of them was connected to Virginia Wakeling's murder.

She was thinking aloud to Charlotte as they carried

the take-out containers into the kitchen. "There is one troubling fact I can't ignore," she said. "The NYPD homicide detective told me that he heard a rumor that the security guard assigned to Virginia that night—Marco Nelson—was fired because of suspicions that he was stealing high-end merchandise from the gift shop."

"So you think Sticky Fingers may have stolen that bracelet while everyone else was working on the gala?"

"Maybe."

"But as a security guard, wouldn't he have been able to turn off the sensor? Or step over it, or sneak under it, or something?"

"I'm not sure about that. I'd have to ask the Met how much individual security guards know about the placement of sensors."

"And how would that connect to Virginia's murder?" Charlotte asked.

Laurie shook her head. Charlotte did not have the same kind of analytical skills as Alex, but she could feel the rhythm of this conversation beginning to pull disparate threads of thought together in her mind. Charlotte's questions were pressing Laurie to contemplate the possible connections among a number of seemingly unrelated facts.

"If Virginia wanted to be alone, she might have wandered into the exhibit. If she found Marco stealing pieces from the exhibit, he could have killed her before she could report him. But then how did he get her to go up to the roof?"

"Maybe that's why she was upset. Maybe she caught

him and wanted to go up to the roof so she could decide what to do about it."

The theory didn't sound right to Laurie. She couldn't imagine a member of the board of trustees having the slightest hesitation to report a security guard caught stealing something from an exhibit. "He could have given her a story to buy himself time," Laurie said. "Maybe he told her the director of security was up there or something. What I do know is that Marco Nelson was the only witness who told police that Virginia was upset that night, as if she had argued with someone. He was the one who said Virginia wanted to be alone."

"And if he's not telling the truth—"

"That might change everything. I just know that when I call him, he'll have an excuse not to talk to me. Even if he's a hundred percent innocent of anything related to Virginia's murder, he's not going to want his current employer to know that there are rumors that he was stealing from the Met."

"Who's his current employer?"

"A private security company called the Armstrong Firm." Laurie had looked up Marco's LinkedIn profile after she first spoke to Sean Duncan at the museum.

"So I'll talk to him instead. Ladyform may need to hire private security for our next fashion show. He comes in to interview with me, and you can be waiting there with some questions."

"I don't know, Charlotte. The last time you tried to help me at work, I almost got you killed."

Just a few months ago, both of them had been held

at gunpoint after Charlotte got too close to the truth in one of Laurie's cases. "First of all, *you* didn't do anything except come to my rescue. And second, a meeting in my office sounds like a fairly safe way to help you out."

Laurie considered the offer and realized it was the easiest way to get a face-to-face meeting with Marco Nelson. "Great. Let's do it."

"I'll set it up in the morning and text you the details."

39

Leo watched from the stands at Madison Square Garden as the Knicks left the court and the cheerleaders rushed onto the floor. He placed a protective hand on his grandson's shoulder as Timmy waved enthusiastically to the players jogging to the locker room for the pep talk coming after a bruising second quarter.

Even though the team was having a rough season, tickets were getting tougher to come by with tourism raging in New York City. Attending tonight's game was an unexpected surprise. The deputy police commissioner had called Leo two days earlier to say that he needed to fly to Washington, D.C., for a multi-jurisdictional meeting with the Department of Justice, and he offered his two tickets to Leo. Leo never thought that his nine-year-old grandson's calendar would be busier than his, but once he confirmed that Timmy was available, the two of them happily accepted the invitation.

The seats were decent, but not nearly as good as Alex Buckley's tickets near the court. Timmy had wanted to snag Alex's attention as soon as they arrived, but Leo had made him promise to wait until the second quarter ended. Now that the buzzer had sounded, Timmy was on his tiptoes waving toward Alex. They were at least forty rows behind him. When Timmy stopped waving, Leo feared that his grandson was going to be upset that Alex hadn't seen him. Instead, he asked Leo for his cell phone. Leo couldn't believe how quickly Timmy's fingers flew across the screen. The next thing he knew, Alex was turning his head, scanning their section. His eyes brightened when he spotted them.

Leo watched as Alex excused himself from his guests, an older couple and a woman who was probably around Laurie's age. Alex took the steps two at a time, a smile spread across his face.

Timmy nearly ran into Alex's arms to give him a big hug.

"Are you using all of your seats tonight?" Timmy asked with a grin.

"I'm afraid so, Timmy. My other friends might be a bit miffed if I ask them to change seats."

He turned to see Leo's gaze lingering on his guests. "I brought along a fellow criminal defense lawyer and his wife, and their daughter who's visiting from California while her husband's here on business."

Leo was certain that Alex wanted to make clear that he was not on a date.

"We miss seeing you, Alex." Timmy peered up at Alex with wide brown eyes. "How come you haven't been over lately?"

Leo placed an arm around Timmy. "You may have

been on a school break, but the grown-ups get busy this time of year. Not to mention, Alex was nominated by the President of the United States to be a federal judge. It's one of the biggest honors a lawyer can have. His calendar is crowded."

"That's awesome!"

"Thanks," Alex said with a chuckle. "I think that's a good word to describe it."

"The only bummer is that I guess now you won't be going back to Mom's show. She *hates* Ryan Nichols."

"We don't use the word 'hate,' Timmy," Leo scolded.

"Sorry. When you're a judge, can I come see the courtroom and bang the hammer like on TV?"

"Sure thing, buddy."

"And maybe you can come to my trumpet recital next week! I'm doing the solo from 'C Jam Blues' by Duke Ellington."

Alex looked to Leo for guidance. Leo could tell that he desperately wanted to accept the invitation, but knew how Laurie would feel if he orchestrated a meeting between them.

"Let's talk about that later, Timmy. Jerry, Grace, and Charlotte all said they wanted to come, and I'm not sure how many people we're allowed to bring."

As Alex made his way back to his guests, his eyes nearly welled at how quickly Timmy was growing up. He'd give up his basketball tickets for the rest of the season for a chance to watch this boy take on a song like "C Jam

Blues." He wished he could spend the rest of the game with Leo and Timmy. What he really wished was that Laurie were here with them, just so he could see her again. When he pictured himself with the three of them, he pictured a family. But Laurie was probably fine without him. She had a family already, with Timmy and Leo. She had a successful career, and she had friends who were excited to see her son play the trumpet. Her life was complete without him. He had made a terrible mistake. He had pushed her too hard, and now he had lost her.

40

Laurie was curled up on the sofa with a blanket on her lap, reading the latest Karin Slaughter novel. She jumped at the sound of keys in the door, then turned to see Leo and Timmy walk in. Timmy was wearing what appeared to be a new Knicks hat.

She forced herself to mark her page, consoling herself that she could savor the ending before she fell asleep.

"I'm going to need to find a bigger apartment if you bring home something new every time your grandpa takes you to a game."

"Don't blame me," Leo said. "He bought it with his Christmas money."

Timmy went straight to the refrigerator in the kitchen and returned with a piece of string cheese and an apple. She had no doubt that he had eaten pounds of food at the stadium, but her son was a fast-growing boy, constantly hungry. He plopped down on the sofa next to her.

"Mom, we won! A three pointer in the final seconds. And we saw Alex!"

"You did?" She tried to sound carefree.

"Yeah. We couldn't sit with him because he had other people with him. But, we at least got to talk to him at half-time."

"Who was with him?" She was embarrassed at how quickly she had asked.

"A lawyer, his wife, and daughter." Timmy had a knack for remembering every detail of a conversation.

"The daughter was visiting from California," Leo added. "Her husband has business here."

She nodded. Message received.

"Can we invite Alex to my recital next week?" Timmy asked eagerly.

"I told him we already had five people coming," her father quickly said. He was offering her an out. "I wasn't sure we could bring a sixth."

Laurie knew how much Alex would enjoy seeing the progress Timmy had made with his trumpet in the past two months. It would be such a convenient reason to call him. The night would be about Timmy, not the two of them. But she didn't want to go back to that familiar cycle where they saw each other regularly, without ever defining what exactly they meant to each other. She could still remember Alex's response when she told him she wanted things to go back to the way they were before they got into that awful argument about her last case: "And how exactly was that? Where were we, Laurie? And what are we now that I'm no longer your host? I'm your dad's sports buddy, your son's pal. But what am I to *you*?"

No, if she called him, it could not be to invite him to be part of Timmy's recital audience. If she reached out to him, she needed to mean it. She needed to be ready to open her heart to him. It wasn't a decision she was going to make tonight.

"You can bring an entourage to your performances once you're a famous musician," Laurie said. "For now, I think we have a big enough crowd."

She finished her novel that night in bed. When she was done she placed the book on her nightstand and then reached into the drawer almost out of habit, slipping on her wedding ring before pulling the covers up to her neck.

She closed her eyes to try to sleep, but when she did, she pictured Alex in his living room that last night they spoke. *Admit it, Laurie: you'll never admire me, not like Greg. So you can keep telling yourself you're trying to move on. But you won't. Not until you find the right person, and then it will just happen. It will be effortless. But this? This has been nothing but effort.*

If she could go back in time, she would have stopped him at that moment and told him how wrong he was. She knew that in Alex she had again found the right person. But he was wrong. It wasn't always true that real love "just happens," although that had been the case with her and Greg. And maybe Alex's love for her had simply "happened." But *I believe finding my soul mate the second time was harder,* Laurie thought. *It took time, and now I may have lost him, too.*

She'd been heartsick longer than she'd allowed herself

to admit. But more than anything else, she had Timmy to think of. He barely remembered the father he'd lost. Now, Laurie thought, I can't allow him to become attached to another man unless he's going to be around for the long run. But Timmy already thought about Alex that way.

So, Alex, you were wrong when you said this should be effortless, she thought defensively. It was no gift to say that you were setting me free. It's not effortless, not for me. It's taking work, work that I continue to do even though you insisted on "setting me free."

She sat up again and slipped off her ring, forcing herself to tuck it away again inside its box in the nightstand drawer.

Greg, I loved you so dearly, she thought. I'm so happy that I have your son, and that with him, you and I will always have a part of each other. But Greg, I am so lonely. I have been so alone since that terrible day.

Laurie closed her eyes, reliving with an unexpected surge of joy sitting next to Alex in his apartment, his arm slung around her as they watched a Giants game with Timmy and her father.

The three people I now love best in the world, she thought. Pray God, it's not too late.

41

The following morning Gerard Bennington arrived at Fisher Blake Studios at 10 A.M. sharp, precisely as scheduled. In photographs Laurie had found of him on the Internet, he tended to favor eccentric, attention-grabbing clothing. In one shot, featured in *New York* magazine, he wore a kimono paired with red plaid pants. This morning, he had selected a relatively staid tweed suit and a paisley tie. The only flashes of his signature flare were a bright blue-and-canary-yellow pocket square and oversized blue-rimmed glasses to match. According to the Internet, he was fifty-one years old but had the energy of a teenager.

Her guest was not the only person who had made a surprising wardrobe choice that morning. As Grace escorted Mr. Bennington into Laurie's office, Laurie noticed that she had paired her black turtleneck dress with red ankle-high boots with six-inch heels. The old Grace was back.

As Grace left, Bennington's eyes scanned the room with disapproval. "Where are the cameras?"

"I'm sorry if there was a misunderstanding, Mr. Bennington. This morning is just an informational session. The more we prepare, the more efficient we can be when we bring you back for production."

"Oh, your darling girl, Grace was very clear about that. But I thought this was a reality show. Aren't there cameras rolling at all times? I mean, what if I say something amazing that you want to use on-screen?"

Laurie realized now that Gerard had already prepared by having his own makeup applied for filming. "You've got an excellent point, Mr. Bennington. Why don't we meet in one of our small studios? I can hit record, and that way we'll have the option of using today's footage if we need to."

"Excellent." Striking a pose, he said, "Any opportunity to use a camera, I say, take it!"

Once the single camera in the interview room was rolling, Laurie started by thanking Bennington for lending them his two dresses from the first ladies exhibit.

"By all means. I was so happy to share them. People ask me why I bother spending all that money on my own private collection, to say nothing of the cost of storing them properly. I feel it is a small price to pay to own a little piece of history. A dress is a bargain compared to Civil War memorabilia and other collectibles, and so much more appealing to the eye. So much more cheerful, too."

"Well, we'll take very good care of them during production," Laurie assured him.

"I'm sure, but I must tell you that my lawyers have checked to see that your studio is very well insured."

He doesn't miss a trick, Laurie thought, and began, "We certainly appreciate the dresses, but I do need to ask you about these pictures." She had brought copies of the relevant photographs from her office. She showed him the photograph of the dress belonging to Jackie Kennedy that Jerry had found in the official exhibit book and then the one taken after Virginia Wakeling's murder.

"Mr. Bennington, would you mind comparing these two?"

He studied the photographs, then shook his head. "They're the same. Aren't they?"

He did not notice the difference until she pointed out the missing bracelet.

"Oh dear," he said with concern. "That is a mystery, isn't it?"

"Did you lend the museum the bracelet as well? As you can see, the picture in the official exhibit book shows a bracelet that was missing after Mrs. Wakeling's body was found."

"When the dress was put on display, I had nothing to do with where the accessories came from. But I do remember it is the kind of trinket Jackie favored. Very youthful, don't you think, but simple and timeless."

The conversation was going nowhere. Laurie tried another tack. "Do you remember where you were when you heard about Mrs. Wakeling's death?"

"Oh, absolutely. I was in the main entry hall, gushing to Iman about her gown."

Laurie recognized the reference to a famous super-model who spent most of her career using only one name.

"Versace made her this amazing piece based on Martha Washington," Bennington explained. "So avant-garde. The thing was the size of a refrigerator. The poor girl couldn't even sit at the dinner table in it—not that she eats, of course, but still."

Laurie was beginning to appreciate the fact that she was recording this interview. If nothing else, Grace and Jerry would eat up every last word when they watched it. She could also imagine Gerard Bennington's more colorful lines providing some much-needed comedic relief in the actual production. "How did you hear about Mrs. Wakeling's death?" she asked him.

"How could I *not* hear about it? Some man on the edge of hysteria came running through the hall yelling, *A woman fell from the roof!* It was very dramatic. Of course, half the people there were trying to rush out of the museum, as if we were under some kind of terrorist attack or something. But the police made everyone stay until they had the lay of the land, cordoned off the crime scene, that kind of thing."

"But they didn't question everyone, did they?"

"Oh, heavens no. That would have been impossible. They didn't speak to me, for example, because I didn't know anything. It wasn't until I was walking out that my friend Sarah Jessica told me that poor Virginia was the one who fell."

"So you knew Mrs. Wakeling personally?"

"Not really. I met her at the previous year's gala, and

of course she had a high enough profile that I knew who she was. But we weren't meeting for tea or anything."

"Were you aware of an alarm being triggered that night in the gallery, shortly before she died?"

A look of concern crossed his face. "No, this is the first I heard of it. Do you think it's related to that missing bracelet?"

"For now, it's just a theory."

"It sounds like a delicious one to me," he said eagerly. "I wonder if it could be related to what happened to Virginia." He rubbed his palms together. "I can't wait to hear what you come up with. Of course, I assume you're looking closely at Ivan. That would be inevitable."

"Do you know him personally?"

"Never met him."

Laurie realized that Bennington was the type of person who used first names for everyone, even strangers.

"What a terrific story though, right? *Older widow meets hunky personal trainer.* Talk about scandal. Everyone I know says he did it. I mean, who else would want to hurt such a gracious and generous woman? The only thing is, and not to be crass about it, but shouldn't he have waited until they were married? I'm not too sure how bright of a bulb that one has, if you know what I mean."

Laurie watched as he shook his head vigorously and gasped, "Oh, that was *awful.* Please don't use any of what I just said in your show. Promise! I wouldn't want anyone to think I'm anything but horrified by what happened to Virginia. Sometimes I'm catty just for the sake of entertainment."

"I understand," Laurie assured him.

"When something like this happens, you realize that even the rich and famous are just people. Everyone has secrets. No one's perfect. Am I right?"

"I've certainly learned that in my line of work, Mr. Bennington."

"Call me Gerard. Anyhow, I mean, look at that perfect Wakeling family—smart, successful, each one of them prettier than the next. But even they had that little tiff that night."

Laurie felt herself sit up straighter at the mention of a tiff. Marco Nelson, the security guard who saw Virginia go upstairs to the roof, reported that she appeared upset, as if she'd been arguing with someone at the gala. But no other witnesses had seen her in a dispute that night.

"Virginia was arguing with her family?" Laurie asked.

"No, not her. It was the sons. Or, I guess one is the son. The other's the son-in-law. I saw them in the temple room shortly before everyone was seated for dinner. They were off to the side of the room a bit. I couldn't hear what they were saying, but even from my vantage point, I could tell the conversation was intense. And then I saw the daughter, Anna, spot them as she was heading toward their table. She clearly saw the same dynamic I had sensed and began moving their way. Ever curious—sorry, I admit it, I'm nosy—I steered myself in that direction to see if something interesting would happen."

He paused, clearly for dramatic effect.

"And?"

"It was a big letdown. She told them they had already argued enough for the day, and that they shouldn't be talking about something so morbid in public."

"This is the first I've heard about it."

"I was probably the only one who noticed. Most of the guests spend their time gawking over the biggest celebrities. I like to watch people who don't think they're being watched. So much more interesting."

"And did you mention any of this to the police?"

"Oh, heavens, no. If someone had called the police every time I bickered with my six siblings, the entire NYPD would have been millionaires from the overtime pay."

Laurie hadn't learned anything new about the bracelet that was missing from the exhibit, but her time with Gerard Bennington had been worthwhile. The night Virginia Wakeling was murdered, her son, Carter, and his brother-in-law, Peter Browning, had been arguing. Mr. Bennington had overheard Anna refer to the conversation between her husband and her brother as "morbid"—something perhaps as dark as their concerns about the family matriarch changing her will.

It was all the more important that she reach the security guard who was Virginia's contact person during the party. Once Bennington left, she sent a quick text to Charlotte to follow up on her suggestion from the night before: *Any luck reaching Marco Nelson?*

Her phone pinged a few minutes after she returned to her office. *We must have a psychic connection. I just got off the phone. He'll be here tomorrow at 9 AM. Hope that works for you!*

She had just confirmed with Charlotte when Ryan Nichols knocked on her open door. "Are you free to leave now?"

She looked at her watch. It was only eleven-thirty. They were supposed to leave at one to meet with Virginia's former personal assistant, Penny Rawling.

"Our appointment's not for two hours."

"I know, but her apartment's only two blocks from Locanda Verde. I made a lunch reservation. Care to join?"

Laurie's first instinct was to decline, sparing herself from even having to share a car ride with Ryan. But she did love the food there, and a reservation at the Robert De Niro–owned spot was almost as hard to come by as *Hamilton* tickets.

"Sure, that sounds great," she said, reaching for her coat.

Whether she liked it or not, she had to make the best of this situation with Ryan. No matter what happened between her and Alex in the future, it was clear that he would never be returning to her show.

42

When Laurie and Ryan arrived at the address Penny Rawling had given them, they were surprised to find one of the new, modern condo buildings that were popping up along the narrow cobblestone streets in Tribeca. Penny was only thirty years old. She had certainly come a long way since working as Virginia Wakeling's personal assistant only three years earlier.

"This view is amazing," Laurie said once they were done with introductions. Penny's apartment was large, with high ceilings and a wall of windows overlooking the Hudson River. Snow still lined the river's edge on the New Jersey side of the water.

"Summer sunsets on the terrace are the best part," Penny said. "Please, have a seat. Ryan, I didn't realize you'd be here, too. I've seen you on television. This is very exciting."

Laurie was accustomed to people misunderstanding the roles that various people played on her show. Everyone assumed that the face they saw on the screen was the one doing all the heavy lifting. She had used that perception to her advantage on more than one occasion. People had a way of underestimating her friendly smile and un-assuming demeanor.

Laurie had not seen any photographs of Penny, so this was her first chance to take in her appearance. She had dark hair, almost black, with crystal-blue eyes and pale skin. She was a natural beauty. Laurie found herself wondering again about the mystery boyfriend Ivan suspected she'd had at the time of the murder.

Ryan thanked Penny for taking time off in the middle of the day to meet with them. "What did you say you do again?" he asked.

Laurie assumed that Ryan was wondering the same thing she was: how could Penny afford this apartment?

"I'm working in real estate," Penny said vaguely.

"Well, it must be treating you well," Ryan said. "We don't want to waste your time, so I figured we'd get straight to the point. We've spoken at length with Ivan Gray, and a couple of things aren't lining up for us. The police got the impression that you were suspicious of Ivan's motivations for dating Mrs. Wakeling, but Ivan swears to us that you saw the two of them together and knew they were truly in love. Which is the right story?"

"Both of them, actually. Do I think Ivan would have given a woman twenty years his senior the time of day if she'd been strictly middle class? No, I don't. I suspect he had certain parameters for a romantic partner, and that probably involved financial security. But I also think they loved each other."

"You make love sound very . . . transactional," Ryan observed.

"I mean, think of it this way: I have plenty of friends who are only willing to date men with good jobs and stable incomes. Is this really any different? If Virginia was the man, and Ivan was the woman, no one would think twice about their relationship."

"But that's not the way the Wakeling family saw things," Laurie said.

Penny shook her head. "Her children all thought she was behaving like a fool. I'll never forget the time that Anna told her mother, 'Daddy's the one who worked for this money. He would be destroyed if he could see the way you are spending it.'"

Penny sighed. "I was tempted to step in and remind Anna that she'd had everything handed to her by birth, but Virginia didn't need my help defending herself. She said, 'Anna, you witnessed firsthand how angry your father could be. For once, I'm finally having fun. This is my second chance at life.' I thought Anna was going to stomp out of the room. It turned into a huge argument about whether Anna had a right to judge her mother's choices. It was as if they both forgot I was there."

So far, Penny hadn't said anything to directly contradict what she said to the police, but she seemed to be painting a more nuanced picture of the Wakeling family dynamics than she did at the time, Laurie thought. "Did you mention that particular argument to the police?" she asked.

Penny looked up at the ceiling as if searching her memory. "I don't recall. Probably not. I mean, Virginia had just died. There was no reason to air her family's dirty laundry."

"Unless it related to her murder," Ryan suggested.

"But I'm sure it didn't. The Wakelings argued like any family—maybe more, since there was the business to consider—but they were loyal to each other to a fault. The very thought of Anna or Carter hurting their mother is unimaginable to me."

"Yet you can picture *Ivan* hurting her?" Laurie asked.

"No, not really. But statistically, aren't husbands and boyfriends the usual suspects? And he did take all that money for his gym."

"According to Ivan, Virginia gave it to him as an investment," Ryan said. "Isn't that something you'd know about?"

"No. I didn't get involved in the finances unless you count doing her shopping and picking up the dry cleaning."

"What about her plans to marry?" Laurie asked. "Her kids seem to think she never would have gone through with it."

Penny answered immediately. "Oh, I think she was going to marry him. My guess is she was just waiting awhile, hoping that Anna and Carter would come around to accepting him and wishing them well."

Laurie could see Penny thinking, as if she was pondering whether to say more.

"It would be understandable if there were things you didn't mention three years ago out of loyalty to your boss," Laurie said. "But now that her murder remains unsolved, it's important that we know everything."

"Well, I do know that she may have been considering changing her will," Penny said haltingly.

This was the first time anyone other than Ivan had mentioned the possibility.

"And what makes you think that?" Ryan jumped in with the question.

"I would find these little pieces of paper balled up in her office trash. There would be names of people and various charities with numbers next to them. Almost everyone had a dollar amount listed next to their name— fifty thousand here, two hundred thousand there. But Ivan was usually listed first, with a portion noted instead of a dollar amount—a half, or a third, a quarter. That's what made me think she was assuming they'd be married."

"You didn't by any chance save these notes from the trash, did you?" Laurie asked.

"No, I didn't," Penny replied.

"What about Virginia's family?" Ryan asked.

Penny frowned. "It seemed as if they were almost getting cut out. I remember one version had two hundred thousand, but another one only had fifty thousand. That's a lot of money to most people—and I assume she would have still left the company to them—but it's a drop in the bucket to people like Anna and Carter. It seemed as if she was planning to leave most of her wealth aside from the real estate business to charity. The kids would have had to keep the company going on their own."

This was consistent with what Ivan claimed she'd been planning. "Why didn't you tell anyone about this earlier?" Laurie asked.

For the first time, Penny looked away from them, glancing at her watch while she answered. "I didn't think it mattered. It was just little notes balled up in her garbage—the way I scribble down notes about vacations I'll probably never take. If she had made up her mind, she would have called a lawyer to make it official. And I didn't want it to cause problems for the family—if, you know, Ivan tried to challenge the will or something. I wanted them to get what was theirs."

Laurie suspected that Penny didn't want anyone to know that she snooped into her boss's private notes, but Ryan was pursuing another possibility.

"And you to get what was yours?" he asked. "You inherited also, didn't you?"

Laurie wished Ryan hadn't moved to hostile territory so quickly. Until now, Penny had been extremely cooperative.

"Seventy-five thousand dollars," she confirmed. "I was very grateful. That's what I made in two years as her assistant."

"And those little notes you found: was she planning to cut your part of the inheritance as well?" he asked, pressing the point.

"I—I don't remember."

"And yet you remember an awful lot about what Ivan and her children might have been inheriting," he challenged her.

Laurie interrupted, sensing that Penny was a few questions away from asking them to leave. Looking at Penny, she could see that she wasn't strong enough to have pushed Virginia from that roof on her own. If she was involved in the murder—which was a big *if* right now—she had to have had an accomplice.

"Do you remember Tiffany Simon from the gala?" Laurie asked. "She was Tom Wakeling's date—Virginia's nephew."

"Oh yeah," she said, as if the memory was coming back to her. "Virginia said she seemed like a perfect match for someone on that half of the family. She took Bob's side regarding the split with his brother, Kenneth, so there was no love lost, even for Kenneth's son. She said that her nephew was just like his father—he wanted all of the rewards without doing any of the work."

"That nephew works at Wakeling Development now. He's doing quite well from what I'm told," Laurie said.

A flash of resentment crossed Penny's face. "Nepotism, I'm sure. He probably wore his cousins down once Bob and Virginia were both gone."

"Well, his date from that night seemed to think that you were seeing someone at the time—maybe someone who was at the gala?"

Penny shook her head, and once again, her gaze drifted to her watch.

"Maybe even someone close to Virginia?" Laurie nudged.

"That's ridiculous. Virginia's friends were three times my age."

"Her son, Carter, wasn't," Ryan said. "Neither was her son-in-law, Peter Browning."

"Now you're suggesting I had an affair with Anna's

husband? I'm so glad I decided to try to help you," she said sarcastically.

"We're just trying to be thorough," Laurie explained. "Ivan also mentioned that he'd heard you on the phone with a boyfriend. If we knew who that person was, we could be certain it wasn't related at all to Virginia's murder. We want to turn over every stone."

Penny was on her feet now, heading toward the door. "I'm on a tight timeline, so I'm afraid I need to get back to work."

Laurie tried one last time. "I'm sorry we offended you. I just need to know: did you tell Anna, Carter, or Peter—or anyone—about those notes you found? If they knew Mrs. Wakeling was going to change her will—"

A look of panic crossed Penny's face, and she suddenly seemed even more rushed to end the conversation. "I've told you everything I know. Good luck with your production. I won't be speaking to you anymore."

43

Laurie and Ryan rehashed their interview of Penny in his car on the way back to the office.

"Did you see how many times she checked her watch? She was expecting someone she didn't want us to meet."

Laurie had had the same thought.

"And how did she pay for that apartment?" Ryan asked. "Her seventy-five-thousand-dollar inheritance from Virginia wouldn't touch the down payment. Even if she's renting, that place has to be at least six grand a month. And when I asked about her job? She barely gave an answer. Real estate? That's like us saying 'media.' Totally vague."

Laurie tried not to be irked that he clumped their jobs together. "Maybe she moved in with a boyfriend," she suggested. "I didn't see a wedding ring." She began to look up Penny's address on her phone to see what she could find out about the cost of the apartment or the owner.

"Well, I solved one part of the mystery," Laurie announced, holding up her phone. "The apartment? It's listed online as 'in contract.' The asking price was an even four million."

Ryan let out a whistle. "So Penny came into money well beyond Virginia's will."

"Nope. I'm looking at the original real estate listing here. The agent's name is Hannah Perkins. She has her office phone, cell, and email address listed. And if all else fails, she also has a number for her assistant. Want to guess the assistant's name?"

Ryan's eyes widened. "Penny?"

"You got it. No last name, but the phone number's a match."

"So it's not even her apartment? It's a client's? Why would she fake that?"

Laurie thought it over, trying to place herself in another person's shoes. "Because she's ambitious. She didn't want us to know that her current position's no better than the one she had three years ago."

"I noticed how annoyed she seemed when you told her the nephew, Tom, has a good job at Wakeling now."

"Exactly."

"So if she found out Virginia was going to cut her out of the will instead of giving her the kind of job she felt entitled to, maybe she got mad enough to do something about it."

Laurie shook her head. "No, I can't picture it. Seventy-five thousand dollars is a lot, but it's not life-changing. And Virginia's death meant she wouldn't have any job at all. It would also mean she lost entree to a world she desperately wanted to be part of. I doubt her current boss lets her tag along to the Met Gala, for example. If she's lying—"

"Oh, she's definitely lying," Ryan said.

Laurie found herself agreeing with him again. "Ivan believed Penny was hiding a boyfriend. And then, completely separately, Tiffany Simon got the feeling Penny had her eye on someone in the family. It lines up. If Penny were secretly seeing either Carter or Peter, she could have mentioned those notes about the will, not realizing the damage that might be done. She looked scared when I mentioned the possibility. I think it honestly never dawned on her that the family might be involved."

"If they were, it's possible Penny's the one who got Virginia killed, all because she snooped in her garbage. If only we knew for sure what was scribbled on those notes."

"We do know what Virginia wrote in her own will," Laurie said, thinking aloud.

"Right. I saw a copy of it in that big notebook you got from the NYPD."

Irritated, Laurie wanted to tell Ryan she had been trying to make a point. "What I'm trying to say is that the will was hers, written solely for her purposes, shortly after her husband passed away." Laurie's eyes clouded, remembering how she had rewritten her own will more than a year after Greg was killed. It was another reminder that he was really gone. Her father had said he felt the same way after getting nagged by his lawyer to redo his will after her mother passed away.

Ryan was following her train of thought. "The original will written when Robert Wakeling was alive would have reflected what the two of them jointly decided, in the event something happened to both of them at the same time."

"We should compare that to Virginia's will. It's a long shot, but maybe it will give us some indication of if and how she revised it."

"That's a good idea."

"I don't think I want to contact the Wakelings to ask for a copy," Laurie said.

"Not a problem. I'll get in touch with the Surrogate's Court as soon as we get to the office. It's public record once the estate's in probate."

"You're willing to do that?" She would have thought that Ryan would see such a menial task as beneath him.

"Consider it done. Teamwork, right?"

When they returned to the studio, they nearly bumped into Brett Young as they stepped out of the elevator. He was carrying a mini-bag to transport what looked like three golf clubs. Laurie knew that Brett, in addition to annual winter trips to Scottsdale and the Bahamas to work on his golf game, kept his swing in check with regular lessons indoors at Chelsea Piers.

"Looks like a short game session today," Ryan said, holding out a palm to stall the elevator doors while he chatted with the boss.

Laurie had no idea how Ryan could tell that from what she was seeing, but she guessed it was related to the fact that none of Brett's clubs had cute, fluffy covers on them.

"Just sand, fringe, and greens," Brett said.

He may as well have been speaking Farsi from Laurie's perspective, but she knew that Ryan—as the nephew of one of Brett's closest friends—was a frequent golf partner. "My handicap would be several strokes lower if I didn't regress over the winter," Ryan said.

"Let's go, then," Brett said, waving Ryan back into the elevator.

Ryan started to follow and then paused. "I need to get a document for our show," he said.

"Laurie can do it. Can't you, Champ?" The elevator was starting to buzz from being held, but Brett was planted firmly between the doors.

She watched, speechless, as Ryan stepped from her side to Brett's.

"By the way," Brett added, "we had to pull our Valentine's Day special because Brandon and Lani are announcing their divorce tomorrow in *People*. Oops."

Laurie recognized the name of the C-list reality-star couple that got married a mere two years ago after meeting on one of the studio's multiple matchmaking series. "I swapped in your next special for the time slot. *When love proves deadly*—thought it might be a good tagline," he called out as the doors finally closed.

When Laurie got back to her office, she started to look up the process for ordering a copy of a will that had gone into probate, and then decided that this 'champ' was absolutely not going to do it. She picked up her phone and left a message for Ryan, reminding him that he was tasked with the assignment. Reviewing the Wakelings' joint will from more than seven years ago was a shot in the dark. She wasn't going to slow herself down by doing an errand that belonged to Ryan, especially now that his buddy, Brett, had set an arbitrary deadline.

She had real work to do.

44

Margaret Lawson, the woman who was buying the Tribeca apartment Penny had tried to pass off as her own, arrived earlier than scheduled, less than five minutes after Laurie and Ryan left.

Thanking her lucky stars that she hadn't been caught in an outright lie, Penny patiently waited while Lawson went over revisions she intended to make on the layout when she met with her contractor.

"Take your time," Penny assured her. "Like my mother used to say, measure twice, cut once."

"Given what this guy's charging, I want to be sure he gets all this straight," Lawson said grimly.

Penny tried to push away a pang of envy. Margaret Lawson was only five years older than she was, but was already a successful banker. She could afford not only to buy this apartment, but to remodel its perfectly nice bathrooms to her precise specifications. Someday, Penny vowed to herself, I'll have a home as nice as this one, plus a beach house in East Hampton, right on the ocean.

When she had called the *Under Suspicion* producer,

she really didn't think she had anything relevant to say. She just liked the idea of seeing her face on the television, with "Penny Rawling, New York City Realtor" written across the screen. She had intended to be charming and articulate. She would speak warmly about all that she had learned from the Wakeling family and the trust Virginia had placed in her. She would seem like the type of person who attends the Met Gala, the type of professional a person of means might entrust with a listing.

And the fact that *he* didn't want her talking to the producers was the icing on the proverbial cake. She still couldn't believe that he'd had the gall to call her after nearly three years, only to pressure her not to speak to a television show. After the way he dumped her, he was the last person with a right to ask a single thing of her.

But the interview with the producers didn't go the way Penny had pictured. She thought it would just be a few questions about Ivan and the party that night. She didn't expect them to ask about her, let alone her relationship with *him*. Maybe I should have just told the truth, she thought, but that would have ruined the image I'm trying to project for my television appearance. I want to be seen as "Penny the Successful Realtor," not "Penny Who Got Dumped by the Guy She Was Secretly Dating Behind Her Boss's Back."

She didn't see the harm in denying the relationship, because it had nothing whatsoever to do with poor Virginia's murder. But then they had kept pressing her for answers—about her boyfriend, about the family, about those little balls of paper in the garbage can.

Penny kept replaying Laurie Moran's final question: "Did you tell Anna, Carter, or Peter—or anyone—about those notes you found? If they knew Mrs. Wakeling was going to change her will—"

After Margaret Lawson was finally finished with her renovation plans, Penny pulled up his number on her cell, still in her call list from when he had contacted her last week.

He picked up after two rings. "I'm surprised to hear from you," he said. "Is everything okay?"

"That show called me, like you said they might." She saw no reason to tell him that she was the one who had contacted them.

"I told you that you don't have to talk to them."

"Are you afraid of what I might tell them?" she asked.

"Of course not," he said. "It's just . . . no one really knew about us. Don't you think that might be a complication?"

She felt all those old resentments returning. Of course no one knew about them. He had forbidden her from telling anyone, claiming that it could complicate her work for Virginia, that it could complicate the dynamics of the family, that his personal situation was complicated enough as it was. But the situation was never actually complicated. The truth is that he had been ashamed of her. She thought that after he saw her successfully mingling with all those fancy people at the Met Ball, he would see her in a different light. He would view her, finally, as an equal.

But he had ignored her all night, and then Virginia died, and things got even worse. She just didn't matter to him.

"Is that the only thing you're hiding?" she asked now. "Our relationship?"

"I'm not hiding anything."

"I told you about those notes I found, including the ones about her will."

There was a long silence on the other end of the line. She checked her screen to make sure they hadn't been disconnected.

"I don't know what you're talking about, Penny."

Was he serious? He was actually going to deny it? "What? Do you think I'm recording you or something? My God. Please tell me that you didn't do it. Did you kill her because I told you about those notes?"

"With all due respect," he said, "you sound like a crazy person. If you tell that show some ludicrous story about whatever notes you're rambling about, I'll tell them how Ivan wanted you fired because you didn't work hard enough. That you shortcut your work to try to land a relationship with me instead. That we only went out a couple of times and you became obsessed with me. Is that really what you want?"

"Are you threatening me?" Penny demanded.

"I'm just speaking the truth. I could sue you for slander and tie you up in court for years. You might want to consider getting professional help, Penny. You sound unstable."

The line went dead. Penny stared at the screen, wondering if there was anyone she could trust.

45

The following morning, Laurie was waiting with Charlotte in a conference room at Ladyform's corporate offices when the Met's former security officer Marco Nelson walked in for his nine o'clock meeting. Charlotte introduced herself as the head of Ladyform's New York operations and introduced Laurie simply as "Laurie." Marco was about six feet two inches tall, and Laurie estimated that he probably weighed around two hundred pounds. His dark gray suit was tailored to accentuate his athletic frame. He wasn't as large as Ivan, but was certainly strong enough to have thrown Virginia Wakeling from a roof.

Charlotte began by giving Marco an overview of Ladyform's security needs: a technician to review their data systems for protection from hacking and other cyber crimes, as well as physical security for fashion shows and other industry events. Marco was prepared with glossy handouts touting the various services provided by his company, the Armstrong Group.

"Who's the Armstrong?" Charlotte asked.

Marco smiled. "There is no Armstrong. It just had a more security-oriented ring to it than the Nelson Group."

"So you're the boss of the shop?" Charlotte asked.

"Technically, but we all work as a team."

"I got your name from a former co-worker of yours at the museum," she said. "Sean Duncan?"

"Sean, he's a great guy. He was second in charge when I was there, but he deserved that promotion. He's a friend of yours?"

"No. Actually, it was Laurie who was speaking to him about another matter, relating to the museum."

Laurie took that as her cue to jump in. "Sean made it sound like a dream security job. Why did you move on from there?" she asked.

"Honestly? I'd make a lot more money protecting your fashion shows than a museum. And that's even after I give you one of the fairest rates you're going to find in the business."

"It wasn't because of the investigation into your girl-friend stealing from the museum gift shop?"

Marco looked annoyed by the question, but still seemed to view it as part of the usual vetting process by a new security client. "Did someone at the museum tell you that? That was total absolute nonsense and I would be rude if I told you what's on the tip of my tongue. I left for one reason only. I needed to start making more money."

"Your girlfriend wasn't stealing?" Laurie asked.

Nelson grimaced, probably seeing the chances of landing a new client circling down the drain. "Unfortunately, she was. But I had no idea. If she did it on nights I was working, it was probably because she thought I'd go easy on her if I caught her—which I didn't. She had a secret pocket built into her purse. Maybe I could have been more thorough, but protocol only called for a quick, visual scan of the employees' personal items. If I had started digging around and grabbing the sides of purses to search for secret compartments, I would have been violating our own procedures. No one ever would have pointed a finger at me if it weren't for the fact that we were dating. So, I got a new job, along with a new rule: no dating at work," he finished with a chuckle.

Laurie had to admit, it was as good of an explanation as he could have offered under the circumstances.

"I don't actually work for Ladyform, Mr. Nelson," she said. "I'm the producer of *Under Suspicion*. The matter I met with Sean Duncan about was the murder of Virginia Wakeling."

He shook his head as he realized the true reason for this meeting. "That's pretty dishonest, calling me down here under false pretenses."

He started to get up from his chair, but Charlotte stopped him. "I do need security. And I was impressed by your pitch, as well as your explanation for what happened at the museum."

Nelson sat back down quickly.

"A woman was killed," Laurie said, "and you were the last person to see her alive, other than her killer . . . or killers. There's a reason I wanted to speak to you." She pulled the two photographs of the Jacqueline Kennedy dress from her bag. "Look, that bracelet was there before the exhibit opened, but was gone by the time Virginia Wakeling was killed."

He studied the pictures carefully. "My ex-girlfriend was stealing jewelry from the gift shop, not from the galleries. What she did was bad, but it wasn't the same as a museum heist." He stopped suddenly and squinted, as if searching for the details of a memory that had just come back to him. "The alarm," he said. "A silent alarm got tripped in the exhibit that night. I got an alert from our Dispatch Department. I was one of the guards who responded. You think it was because this bracelet disappeared?"

"Until we know what happened to it, it certainly seems possible. Do you remember if it was still there earlier in the night?"

"A small detail like that? No, I doubt any of us would have noticed, except the curator, I suppose. That was Cynthia Vance's exhibit."

"Did she notice anything missing that night?"

"No, because that was the year she had to miss the Gala. The first time in her entire career, to my knowledge. She had mono and was out for a month. When we got to the galleries, we didn't see anyone, and nothing seemed out of place. We figured it was tripped by one of the outside vendors who were working on the cameras."

"Does Cynthia Vance still work at the museum?" Laurie asked.

"I would assume. She's the type that will stay there until God has other plans."

Laurie made a mental note to contact Cynthia Vance as soon as possible. The possibility of the bracelet being connected to Virginia's murder had never been considered, but it would be nice to have this one loose thread tied up.

"You told the police that Virginia was upset when she went up to the roof—as if she'd been arguing with someone. We've learned from a different witness that her son and son-in-law were seen arguing earlier in the temple room. Is it possible that she had a confrontation with one of them?"

"I have no idea who she was talking to. It was hard for me at the time to even explain to the police why I had the impression she'd been in a tiff of some kind. She never said that, to be clear. She just said she wanted to be alone and needed some fresh air. But she was looking back toward the party with an expression I would call a glare. I definitely had the impression that she was annoyed with someone and wanted a break. She had told me once that the roof was one of her favorite spots in the city. It never dawned on me she'd be in danger there. I warned her it would be cold out there. She said she didn't intend to stay more than a few minutes."

Laurie asked a few more questions, but it was clear that Marco had told them as much as he knew. "I really appreciate your willingness to talk to me," she said, "especially given the way we brought you here this morning."

He held up both palms. "No hard feelings. In my line of work, I understand that you do what you need to do to get the right result. And whether it's now or down the road, I do hope you'll consider me for your security needs, Ms. Pierce."

Charlotte promised that she would follow up, and Laurie believed her.

As Marco was about to leave, he turned back around. "Good luck with your show, Laurie. My biggest regret of my career is not going up to the roof with Mrs. Wakeling. I wake up sometimes in the middle of the night, picturing her falling."

46

Laurie's next stop was the Metropolitan Museum. She had called Sean Duncan, the head of security, after her interview with Marco Nelson. After initially trying to avoid anything negative about Marco, Duncan confirmed that Marco's girlfriend had used a concealed pocket within her purse to steal merchandise from the store and that the museum never had any direct evidence to implicate Marco. According to Duncan, if it had been up to him, the Security Department would have handled the matter differently, but the prior boss had been the one to suggest to Marco that it might be better for everyone if he moved on, which Marco had been considering in any event.

Duncan also confirmed that the curator of the exhibit, Cynthia Vance, was still employed at the Met and offered to put Laurie in touch with her. When Laurie explained why she was calling, Cynthia suggested that they meet right away.

Now Laurie was seated in the members' dining room of the Met, enjoying a cup of coffee and an enviable view of Central Park. Cynthia Vance smiled at her from across the table. She was probably in her early sixties, with curly auburn hair, a round face, and rhinestone-adorned glasses resting on the top of her head. Her smile was warm and broad, and she radiated a hum of energy. "The bracelet," she announced, pressing her palms together for emphasis. "I was so angry that we lost it."

"When did you notice?"

"Not until after the exhibit was over, and I still blame the mono. I was out for weeks—more than a month, actually. I mean, mono is awful for anyone, let alone at my age, and the timing literally could not have been worse. I had the exhibit all planned, thank God, and nearly all of the work had been done. I thought I just had a bad cold and was trying to power through, but two days before the opening, I woke up feeling as though I'd been hit by an eighteen-wheeler. Once my doctor said I had mono, the director of the museum gave me strict orders to stay home. They can't have one of the curators infecting hundreds of patrons. I had to oversee the rest of the work by Skype. My poor staff—I had them running around the galleries with iPads, scanning every inch so I could inspect every last detail. It's the only gala I've ever missed. I still need to find an occasion for my amazing dress—inspired by Mamie Eisenhower if you can believe it. Very retro."

"You didn't notice the bracelet missing when you got back?"

"Right. The bracelet," she said, getting herself back on track. "So, by the time I got back to work, it had been weeks since I'd seen my own exhibit. Each piece was gorgeous, and I was so proud of the work we had done to tell a compelling story about the changing role of an American first lady. But, honestly, I was catching up after missing a month of work, and perhaps wasn't overseeing the details as closely as I would have if I weren't so far behind. After the exhibit was dismantled, I was inventorying all of our pieces to return them to the lenders. And, for the life of me, I could not find that darn bracelet."

"That seems like a big thing to miss."

"Well, I certainly take it seriously. But the reality, Laurie, is that we have, literally, hundreds of thousands of items in this museum, some of them extremely small—an arrowhead, a bullet, a little charm bracelet in this instance. Things get repaired, moved, lent to other museums, and, very occasionally, misplaced. I was heartsick about it, but, fortunately, the woman from the Kennedy estate was very understanding. You see, the strand of pearls they loaned to us for the exhibit was authentic, but the charm bracelet was strictly costume jewelry—I loved the idea of pairing a classic necklace with one of the whimsical, inexpensive pieces that Jackie so often favored. She was brilliant about combining high and low fashion. So, I suppose if I had to lose something—every curator's nightmare—it could have been worse."

"You didn't go through the security footage to try to figure out when it went missing?"

"We only keep footage for a week, and by the time I realized it was missing, the exhibit had been down for longer than that. It really never dawned on me until you called that the bracelet might actually have been stolen."

"I just keep thinking about the alarm that was triggered during the gala that night."

"Which I completely understood once you laid it all out for me. But, believe me, that bracelet was quite literally one of the least valuable things a person could steal from a display here, if one were inclined to do that. And it is exactly the kind of small item that could get lost in the shuffle of dismantling a large exhibit. I don't solve mysteries for a living, but I wouldn't lose much sleep over this one."

She was right. Surely, if someone was going to risk getting caught stealing something from the largest museum in the country, they would select something more valuable than a simple bracelet that was indistinguishable from any trinket that could be picked up at the local shopping mall. Laurie could check Marco Nelson and the charm bracelet off her list of theories.

She passed on the waiter's offer of more coffee and asked for a check, but Cynthia insisted that the bill was already taken care of. "After all the support Virginia gave us over the years, it's the least I can do for someone trying to solve her murder. I had hoped that one of her children would accept the invitation to take their mother's seat on the board, but I think Anna is too busy with the family business to take up philanthropy at the same level as her mother."

"I noticed you only mentioned Anna," Laurie said.

The curator's smile grew even wider and her eyes flashed with intelligence. "Have you met the son, Carter?"

Laurie nodded. "The entire family is cooperating with our production."

"I only met you a few minutes ago, but I suspect you're observant enough to have picked up on the dynamics there."

"Anna seems driven. A natural leader. And her husband, Peter, seems like a very competent partner."

Cynthia nodded knowingly. The implication regarding Virginia's son, Carter, was clear.

"Is Carter still single?" Cynthia asked. "Virginia was always hoping he'd meet the right woman and settle down. She wanted him to have children in time for them to grow up alongside their cousins. Her own children were never close to their cousin because of a problem between Bob and his brother."

"Carter's not married," Laurie confirmed. "I didn't realize you were close enough to Virginia to have those kinds of conversations."

"We didn't socialize outside of the museum, mind you, but she was a frequent visitor and took a real interest in the work, not just the parties, like some donors. Plus she loved her family and spoke of them all the time."

"And did she speak of Ivan, too?"

"She did, and her whole face glowed with happiness. It's hard to imagine anyone wanting to harm her, but I truly hope that it was not Ivan. I think she loved him deeply. The thought of her realizing at the last second that he was going to do that—" She placed a hand over her heart.

"We're looking at all the options."

"Good luck with it. And please tell the Wakelings I say hello. Penny, too, if she's still in the picture. I was sort of hoping she might be the right woman for Carter."

The sudden mention of Virginia's assistant took Laurie by surprise. "What makes you say that?"

"Penny was around so often, I figured she was almost part of the family already."

"But were she and Carter interested in each other?"

Cynthia arched her eyebrows. "I would certainly hope so, given that I saw them kissing once."

"When was that?"

"It was—oh gee, I was already starting to feel like I was coming down with a cold, so maybe a week before the gala. Virginia was here for a special walk-through for trustees and high-level donors. Penny was with her, and her family was supposed to meet her afterward for lunch. I stepped outside to smoke a cigarette—a horrible habit, I know, plus I was sick—and there's Penny sneaking a little kiss when Carter arrived, while Virginia was still in the powder room. Come to think of it, that was the last time I saw any of them."

For the first time since Ryan came to her office talking about Ivan Gray, Laurie felt like she had discovered a new piece of information that might change the entire case.

She called Jerry as soon as she was outside: "Set up a production schedule. I think we're actually ready to start cameras rolling."

47

Laurie felt like a coach in the locker room as she stood at the whiteboard in her office, marker in hand, while Ryan, Jerry, and Grace were gathered at the conference table in front of her.

"As always, we go in with open minds, but we've got two leading suspects: Ivan Gray and Carter Wakeling." She circled both names on the board. Jerry had done phenomenal work over the past five days. They had a complete production schedule already nailed down. This team meeting was to go over final details and make sure Ryan was prepared for interviews.

"The case against Ivan is essentially the same information that led police to suspect him in the first place." Ryan's Harvard-trained legal mind was evident as he quickly listed the details: the age difference between him and Virginia, his financial motivation to seek a relationship with her, and, most important, the absence of any corroboration that Virginia had known about the half million dollars transferred from her accounts into Ivan's gym. But even though Ryan had clearly mastered the facts, Laurie could tell from his dismissive tone that he was not taking the evidence against his personal trainer seriously. She decided to keep her thoughts to herself for the time being.

"The new information we have relates to Carter," she said. Grace was taking down notes furiously, like a front-row student in the classroom. "To make this theory work, we need to lock down three new points. Ivan has always said that Virginia was planning to change her will, greatly reducing her kids' inheritance. We now have backup from Virginia's assistant, Penny."

"If only we had that interview on tape," Jerry said.

"I think Penny will come around if Ryan can get Carter to admit that they were seeing each other," Laurie said. "My guess is that's the secret Penny is trying to keep. Once that's out, she may want to tell her side of the story. And that brings us to the second new fact: Carter and Penny's relationship. And the third fact comes from Gerard Bennington: Carter and his brother-in-law, Peter, were seen arguing at the gala shortly before the murder."

As Ryan tied the three pieces of evidence together, he sounded like a prosecutor delivering a closing argument. "Virginia was going to change her will. Penny found out and told Virginia's son, Carter, who stood to lose millions. Carter pushed Peter, who was not only his brother-in-law, but also a close legal advisor to Virginia, for details and didn't get them. One, two, three. He was desperate to keep his mother from changing the will, even if it meant killing her."

They were still speculating for now about what had

happened during that third step. Did Peter confirm that the will was going to be changed? Did he refuse to intervene?

"What about the original will before Robert Wakeling died?" Laurie asked. "Do we have that from the probate court yet?" Even though it was a long shot, Laurie still wanted to compare Virginia's will to the one she and her husband had written together while he was alive.

"We should have it tomorrow," Ryan said. "I took care of it already."

She had a feeling that Ryan had not, in fact, taken care of it, but would remember to do so now.

"And are we sure about interviewing Anna and Peter together?" she asked. It had been her decision, but she was having second thoughts.

To Laurie's surprise, Ryan, who'd initially disagreed, backed up her first instinct. "I've come around on this," he said. "I think you're right."

"Should I get a tape recorder?" Jerry joked. "That might be a first."

Ryan smiled, but Laurie could tell that the comment had irked him. "You said that Mr. Bennington was very clear that the conversation between Carter and Peter was heated, enough so that Anna told them to quiet down. And you all agreed that Anna and Peter seem like a couple in complete lockstep. If we interview them separately, neither one of them will budge from whatever statement they prepared in advance. But if they're together when we tell them what we know, there's a chance something new will break."

"And Jerry, we're all set for filming tomorrow?"

They only had access to the inside of the museum for one day, so the plan was to interview Ivan, Gerard Bennington, and Marco Nelson there, in addition to getting footage of the roof itself. Marco had agreed to participate on camera after Laurie assured him there was no need to mention the circumstances of his departure from the museum.

"A hundred percent," Jerry said. "I worked with that wonderful curator, Cynthia Vance. A tiny corner of one little gallery is being painted this week. We're going to stage it with Gerard's dresses and then splice it together with footage taken of the exhibit before it opened. After some cut-and-paste magic, it will look like we were there for the real thing."

"Amazing," Laurie said.

As they were getting ready to leave, Grace offered to type up her notes and circulate them to the full team. Laurie thanked her for taking the initiative and then asked Ryan to stay behind for a second. Grace closed the door behind her. As always, she could read Laurie's mind.

"I know you think Ivan's innocent," Laurie said.

"Because he is. I've spent time with the guy. He's not a killer."

"Okay, but we're a news show. We have to be objective."

"If I recall correctly, our last case involved a woman with a connection to one of your best friends."

The show's most recent special had questioned the

evidence against Casey, who had already been convicted of killing her fiancé. Casey knew about the show because her cousin worked for Charlotte.

"True," Laurie said, "but I told her—and everyone else—from the very beginning that I would go wherever the evidence led us. We put Casey through a grueling cross-examination, as you'll recall."

"I'll take that as a compliment," he said.

"Are you prepared to do the same with Ivan Gray? If you go easy on your boxing coach, the audience will see it. It could call our entire series into question." Laurie had worked for years to earn a reputation as a credible producer with journalistic values, despite the "reality show" label used to describe *Under Suspicion*.

"I'm going to do my job, Laurie. Because you know what? When it all comes out that Carter Wakeling's guilty, I want everyone to know that we were fair."

She nodded. "Then we're on the same page." To herself she added, At least I hope so.

She had only been in her office alone for a few minutes when she found herself looking at the phone on her desk. She wanted to call Alex.

She reminded herself once again of the vow she had taken not to step back into the same cycle that had driven him away in November. He had pressed her to answer one simple question: "What am I to *you*?"

She stared at the phone, asking herself why she was so desperate to speak to him. It wasn't about the case. In fact, today's team meeting had probably been the longest she'd gone without once thinking of Alex since they first met. It wasn't about an event with Leo or Timmy. It wasn't a complaint about Brett or Ryan.

If I called, what would I want to say?

And then she realized that the topic of conversation wouldn't even matter. They could talk about politics, music, television, the snow, or the color of the sweater she was wearing today. She just wanted to hear his voice. She wanted to see him. She would even settle for sharing a phone call with him. She missed him, for no reason other than that he had been a big part of her life, and now he was gone.

She was ready.

She picked up the phone and dialed his cell phone number from memory. With each ring, she felt her heart sink further. She pictured him staring at the screen, waiting for it to go to voice mail.

You've reached Alex Buckley. Please leave a message.

Her handset was halfway back to its base when she decided that, no, they had waited long enough. She was done hitting the pause button on this part of her life.

"Alex, or should I say, 'Your Honor,' this is Laurie. Please give me a call when you have a chance."

As she hung up, she studied the framed photograph on her desk of Greg, Timmy, and her. I looked so happy then, she thought. I want to be happy that way again. Greg, you would want that for me. You would like this man. He is good and decent and he loves me—or at least, he did.

Please, don't let it be too late.

48

Jerry had not been exaggerating when he said that he and the museum had come up with a plan to make a small corner of the museum look like the sprawling "Fashion of First Ladies" exhibit. Looking at the set with a naked eye, Laurie saw a couple of dresses on mannequins in front of a green screen, with two chairs for Ryan and Ivan. But when she looked at the scene on the screen next to the cameraman, the wall behind them appeared to be part of the original exhibit. "Camera magic," as Jerry had described it.

Unlike the workout clothing she was accustomed to seeing Ivan wear, he had chosen a well-tailored dark gray suit and a conservative striped tie for his interview. For the first time, she could imagine how a cultivated woman like Virginia would find him attractive.

Ryan had already walked Ivan through the basic background of his relationship with Virginia and how they had met at an art exhibit. After just a few dinners together, they began dating regularly. When she bought him a Porsche for his birthday, they had been dating for only seven months. They picked out her engagement ring on the one-year anniversary of their first date. "I considered us engaged," he said. "She just wasn't ready to make the announcement yet."

"What became of the ring?" Ryan asked.

The question caught Laurie by surprise. She hadn't thought to ask before, and the question signaled that Ryan, as promised, was not going to go easy on his boxing coach.

"I took it back to the jeweler about a month after Virginia died. Seeing the box in my dresser drawer was a reminder of what I'd lost."

"And the jeweler gave you a refund of some kind?"

"Yes, back on my credit card. They were very understanding about it."

"But wasn't Virginia the one who actually paid your credit card bill at the time you bought the ring?"

Ivan shifted in his seat. "Yes. I know how it looks. But, honestly, it made no sense for me to keep that ring, and I knew the family wouldn't want it. It was because of their hang-ups she wasn't wearing it in the first place. And by the time I returned it, they were telling anyone who would listen that I was a killer. In my mind, I thought Virginia would want me to return it and put the money into my gym, PUNCH."

"On top of the half a million dollars she had already fronted you," Ryan said.

Laurie could tell that Ivan had assumed that the interview would be friendlier than this. "As I said before, she believed in my vision. And it turned out she was right. I could have paid her back sixfold by now."

"Virginia wasn't the first older, wealthier woman you had dated," Ryan said. It wasn't even a question. "You met many of them among your clients as a personal trainer."

"There were a few others, but nothing serious. Not like with Virginia."

"How would you describe the mood within the Wakeling family on the night of the gala?" Ryan asked.

"Cordial," he said, choosing his words carefully. "Polite, if a bit stilted. They told their mother in no uncertain terms that they did not think I should accompany her to such a high-profile event. Ironically, though, that night was probably the most comfortable I had ever seen Virginia around her family and me together. I honestly thought the ice was beginning to thaw, and then she was gone."

"What made the atmosphere less chilly that night?"

"I hate to say it, but I think it was because the family had someone else to disapprove of that night instead of me. Their cousin, Tom, had managed to score an invitation to the gala." Ivan explained Tom's place in the family tree and the bad blood between Robert Wakeling and his brother, which lasted beyond both of their deaths. "Virginia and her kids kept saying Tom never would have been allowed through the doors if not for his last name. He didn't sit with us, but he did come by a few times, obviously trying to ingratiate himself with the family. He had this crazy date with him. She was slightly drunk and was rambling on about how her grandmother—a former cabaret dancer—had a passionate love affair with a famous politician and deserved to have a dress of her own in the exhibit. Ginny said it was the most entertainment she'd gotten from that side of the Wakeling family tree in thirty-five years." He smiled sadly at the memory. "I think the family was having so much fun chuckling at Tom's expense that I seemed tame in comparison."

"But you're not actually tame, are you?"

"I don't know what you mean by that."

"Virginia Wakeling was five-foot-four and weighed a hundred and ten pounds. You could easily lift her weight over your head, couldn't you?"

"Of course, but that means nothing. Most men, and many of the women I train, would be able to lift someone as small as Virginia. And someone obviously did, because I would never, ever hurt her."

From there, Ryan returned to the subject of money, laying out a detailed comparison of Ivan's expenses in the months before Virginia's murder to his income. The implication was clear: he was living off his much wealthier girlfriend.

"Virginia told her children that she was only helping you with occasional spending money," Ryan said, "and yet she transferred approximately five hundred thousand dollars to open your business. Do you have any contracts showing an agreement with her?"

He shook his head. "It wasn't formalized. Once we were married, it would be moot. We were going to take care of it as part of a prenuptial agreement, which I was happy to sign."

"In fact," Ryan said, "you don't have any evidence at all to show that Virginia gave that money to you on her own, do you?"

"No, but there's no evidence I stole it, either, and I shouldn't have to prove my innocence. Look, was it helpful to me personally that Virginia was wealthy and generous to me? Of course. But once I fell in love with her, she could have lost everything, and I still would have wanted to marry her. I brought something today, and would like to read it with your permission."

"Go ahead," Ryan said. He looked to Laurie and she nodded. They always edited later.

"You told me once that Bob was your soul mate. At the time, I understood you were telling me not to expect anything serious or lasting. But then you told me I was your second chance at happiness, and I knew that you had opened your heart to me, where I want to stay with you always, for every breath you and I can take together. Those are the words I used when I proposed to her, because I knew she was not starting a new life with me. I was joining a life that was already long and full before I came along."

Laurie felt a lump in her throat, thinking about Alex. When I was with Greg, she thought, he felt like my soul mate. She wasn't erasing anything about her life with Greg, but maybe it was possible to get a second chance.

49

The rest of the day went off without a hitch. Even with the museum's tight time constraints, they managed to film the spot where Virginia was believed to have been thrown from the roof, plus their interviews with Gerard Bennington and Marco Nelson. Laurie was confident that Gerard's description of Carter and Peter arguing at the party, followed by Marco's description of a rattled Virginia asking for privacy, would be two of the most dramatic moments in the special.

By the time they wrapped up filming, it had been several hours since she had powered up her cell phone. She knew Timmy could always call her father in the event of an emergency, but she was still anxious to make sure that everything was all right.

She scanned the list of new voice mails. Nothing from either Timmy or Leo. Her eyes moved immediately to Alex's name on her screen. Her hand was nearly shaking when she hit the play button on his message.

Laurie, it was great to hear your voice. I'm so sorry for the delay. I was at the Capitol all day yesterday meeting

*with senators on the Judiciary Committee, and then had
a dinner with the White House aides who are preparing
me for confirmation hearings. By the time I finished, it was
too late to call, and, well, now I'm babbling.* There was
a long pause. *I'm glad you called. Give me a ring when
you're free.*

She started to put her phone back into her bag and
realized she didn't want to wait a second longer. She
found a quiet spot on the roof, away from where the gaffer
and grips were packing up the lighting and camera equipment, and redialed Alex's number.

He picked up after only half a ring. "Laurie," he said.
He sounded happy, maybe even a little nervous.

"How is the D.C. charm offensive going?" she asked.

"It's miserable. I feel as though I'm in a beauty
pageant for lawyers, as I'm marched from office to office,
delivering my carefully practiced, judicious responses
with a smile. I have a thirty-minute break in my schedule
and I'm tempted to run while no one's looking. I can't
wait to get back to my regular life tomorrow."

"So you're coming home tonight?"

"The first shuttle in the morning."

"Are you free tomorrow night?"

"I have no plans. Is this about Timmy's recital? He
mentioned it when I saw them last week at Madison
Square Garden."

"No, that's Thursday."

"The Knicks have an away game tomorrow or else I'd
invite you all there. I know how much Leo and Timmy
enjoy going."

"Nope. No sports. No recitals. I'd like to take you to dinner, just the two of us—if you're open to that."

She could almost hear him smiling on the other end of the line, and she felt her heart swell.

"That sounds like the best invitation I've received in a long time, Laurie," Alex said fervently.

50

When Laurie showed up at the studio the next morning, Grace greeted her with a whistle. "Well, look at you, Queen Moran. Are you thinking about joining Ryan in front of the camera today?"

Laurie knew that she was an attractive woman, but she wasn't the type who went for heavy makeup or fussy hair. Today, however, she had put a little more effort into her morning routine than her usual wash-and-wear bob and single coat of mascara. She also knew that the bright green wrap dress was a perfect fit and made the flecks of color in her hazel eyes pop.

"Let's just say I have plans after work," Laurie said.

Grace pressed her palms together in a small clap. "Oh, is this who I think it might be? Rhymes with Malex Duckley?"

"He would hate that you called him that."

"He loves me. Not as much as he loves you, but—"

"All right. I think that's enough gossip for now. Don't get ahead of your skis, Grace."

"Me? On skis? No thank you. Snow and I do not get along. Thank goodness that gunk finally melted."

"Where's Jerry?" Laurie asked, peering into his empty office.

"He headed up to Greenwich already to make sure the equipment got all set up." Today they were interviewing Anna Wakeling and her husband, Peter Browning, at the Wakeling family home in Greenwich, Connecticut.

All the better for me, Laurie thought. The sooner we finish, the sooner I can head back to the city for my dinner with Alex.

The driver finally came to a stop at the turn of the long U-shaped drive. Laurie and Ryan stepped out to look up at what could only be described as a mansion. The Wakeling home was a magnificent Georgian with meticulously groomed ivy creeping up the stone exterior. The estate's gardens rivaled Versailles.

"Not too shabby," Ryan whispered.

Anna Wakeling answered the door, but was distracted by something happening inside the house. "Please be careful with the floors in there." She looked annoyed when she turned to greet Laurie. "Come in. When we agreed to this, I didn't realize there'd be so many cameras. We should have just done this at the office."

"Seeing where your mother lived will give viewers a better sense of her," Laurie said. "The more viewers engage, the more likely it is we turn up new information about your mother's murder."

"And the better the ratings for your program," she said cuttingly. "Sorry, I'm just being crabby. I get it. I'm a businesswoman, too."

"Do you and Peter have any questions before we get started?" Ryan asked.

"Not a single one," she said firmly. "Ask us anything you'd like, Mr. Nichols. My husband and I are open books."

51

They filmed the interview in a brightly lit sitting room decorated in country French design. Peter and Anna sat side by side on a tufted love seat, holding hands. "This was my mother's favorite room in the house," Anna said wistfully. "She'd sit right here with a book for hours while my father worked in the den."

Ryan used a light touch during most of the interview, allowing Anna and Peter to air their grievances against their mother's younger suitor. They depicted him as uneducated, unsophisticated, and in a rush to marry their mother for money. Laurie had been worried that Ryan's belief in Ivan's innocence would skew his treatment of the show's participants, but he came across as fair—even sympathetic to their concerns about the man.

"Peter, Ivan tells us that he and your mother-in-law had discussed a prenuptial agreement. Didn't that quell some of your worries?"

"I was a legal advisor to Virginia in addition to being her son-in-law, so I really can't disclose anything Virginia said to me."

"But Ivan was not your client. Isn't it true that he went specifically to you, as a trusted advisor to Virginia, to make clear that he was willing to sign anything that would reassure the family about his intentions?"

Anna interrupted. "It's not just a matter of the prenup, which only applies in the event of a divorce. The whole point is that we were worried about him spending Mother's money while they were actually married. She bought him a sports car when she barely knew him! It was unseemly. He'd have his hand in a far larger cookie jar as her husband."

"So you think your mother was in fact planning to marry him," Ryan said.

"No, she would never. And what difference does it make now anyway?"

"My understanding is that you think Ivan killed your mother because she discovered that he was stealing money from her and that she was going to report him to the authorities. If she was truly planning to marry Ivan, doesn't that make it more believable that she actually gave him the seed money for his business?"

"I refuse to believe that she'd do something so heedless," Anna snapped.

"Why do you say it was 'heedless'? After all, Ivan's business has thrived. It's one of the most popular workout spots in Manhattan."

"Well, she couldn't have known that at the time." Anna huffed.

"Or maybe she could, if she saw a side to Ivan that you and Peter did not. Don't you think it's possible she was confident in his abilities?" Anna and Peter did not respond, but the implication was clear. If Virginia had given that money to Ivan voluntarily, he had no motive to harm her. Ryan shifted direction. "Isn't it true that your family was very concerned about your mother's finances leading up to the night of the gala?"

"I don't know if I'd say it rose to the level of *very concerned*, but, as I said, we thought she was being overly lavish with this man."

"The very day before she died, in fact, you said, 'Daddy's the one who worked for this money. He would be destroyed if he could see the way you are spending it.'" Ryan was reading from his notes. Both Anna and Penny had recounted the comment.

"It was an ugly thing to say," Anna conceded, "but it wasn't untrue."

"You also told me earlier that you were glad to have one last day together in peace after that awful argument."

She nodded sadly in agreement.

"But it wasn't entirely a day of peace in your family, was it?"

Anna and Peter exchanged a confused look.

"Isn't it true, Peter, that you and your brother-in-law, Carter, had an argument before dinner at the gala?"

Peter blinked and Laurie noticed him give his wife's hand a small squeeze.

"Anna," Ryan said, "the argument was heated enough that you walked over to hush Peter and your brother. You said they had argued enough for the day and shouldn't discuss something 'so morbid' in public. We have a witness to the conversation. It was in the temple room if that helps to jog your memory."

Anna shifted in her seat, uncrossing and recrossing her legs.

"The morbid topic was your mother's will, wasn't it?" Ryan pressed. "She was planning to change it, and the family was worried."

"That's not true," Anna finally said. "Our mother was very generous, both to her family and to the charities she supported. Nothing was going to change that."

"But that's what the conversation between Peter and Carter was about. True?"

Anna and Peter were looking at each other again, and Laurie was wondering if they had made a mistake filming them together. If Anna stood up right now, Peter would follow, and the interview would be over.

Ryan nudged one more time. "Carter went to Peter as the trusted legal advisor, asking about your mother's will. Carter knew she had plans to change it. Peter respected Virginia's confidences and said nothing. Wasn't that why they were arguing?"

Ryan had moved into new territory, speculating about the source of the argument between the two men, but Laurie could tell that their theory had been correct. She could see the worry in Peter's expression. He wanted to say more.

"He didn't *know* anything," Peter finally said. "He just kept asking me if Virginia had spoken to me about any changes. I thought the entire topic was tacky and selfish, so I kept trying to avoid it. He kept pressing, and that's when Anna intervened."

"Did you know that Carter was dating your mother's assistant, Penny Rawling, at the time?"

Their surprised expressions made clear that they had not known this fact.

"Penny used to read little notes your mother would ball up in her office garbage," Ryan said. Anna shook her head disapprovingly. "Some of the notes were about changes to her will. In many of them, you and Carter were going to inherit your mother's shares in the company, Anna, but nearly all of the other assets were going to be designated to charity."

Anna's mouth opened, but nothing came out.

"Penny told this information to Carter," Ryan revealed. "*That* was why he was pressing Peter for information."

They looked at each other again, but this time was different. They were no longer worried about the tone of Ryan's questions. They were seeing something they knew in a different light. They were scared.

"I just thought he was being paranoid," Anna said quietly. Ryan waited for her to explain. "Mom talked to him, maybe a month before she died. She was worried that he felt 'entitled.'" Anna released her husband's hand for the first time since the interview began and used air quotes to emphasize the last word. "She saw how much harder I worked. Mother told Carter, 'I'm afraid that if it weren't for the family money, you would have turned out just like your cousin, Tom.' Mind you, Tom's great, and he's doing fabulous work for the company now, but at the time, trust me: for Mom to compare Carter to our cousin was no compliment at all. Tom was in and out of different jobs, crazy girlfriends, gambling—all in the past now. So when Carter was asking Peter about Mom's will, I told him he was being paranoid. I thought Mom was just trying to get Carter to grow up a little. I don't want to believe that he—"

She paused and held Peter's hand again.

"That he what?" Ryan asked. "What do you think your brother did?"

"I have to tell them," she whispered. She waited until Peter nodded his approval, and Laurie realized that the power in their marriage might be more equal than it appeared on the surface.

"That argument I had with Mom the day before the murder? It was because Carter had asked about her will, saying he was worried she was going to change it and cut us out. It got me thinking about all the money she was spending on Ivan, so I let her know I did not approve. She made it clear that she was a grown woman who had the right to do what she wanted. But Carter wouldn't let it drop. As soon as he saw us at the gala, he wanted to know if I'd gotten assurances from our mother that she was going to keep the money within the family. And then he kept nagging Peter about it, demanding that he lecture her about the foolishness of giving the family money away. That's when I went over and told him to knock it off—we were in a public place."

"And what did your brother say?" Ryan asked.

"That we—"

Peter interrupted, and Laurie was certain that the

lawyer in him was going to cut off the conversation. Instead, he finished Anna's sentence for her.

"That we had to stop her. That we had to stop her from changing that will, *no matter what*."

Anna blinked a few times and her eyes began to water. Peter put his arm around her and waved a hand at the camera, signaling that they were done.

52

By the time Laurie got back to the city after filming, she managed to make it to Union Square Cafe ten full minutes before the time of their reservation. This was one night that she did not want to risk making Alex wait.

She was at a bar seat near the entrance when she saw him step from the backseat of his black Mercedes, not waiting for Ramon to open his door. She watched as he straightened his jacket at the curb and then checked his hair in the reflection of the glass before he walked inside.

She wondered whether it was possible he had become even more handsome in the past two and a half months, and decided it was.

She had braced herself for an awkward reunion, but as soon as they greeted each other with a quick hug and a kiss, it felt as if they'd seen each other only yesterday. In fact, it was better. It was as if they had reached an unspoken understanding that any hurdles that may have existed before would no longer stand in their way.

The hostess had their table ready, in the back, away from the windows, as Laurie had requested. Even before she had met him, Alex was already a public figure because of the acquittals he had obtained for his clients in several high-profile trials. His work on the first three *Under Suspicion* specials had broadened his celebrity. Now that his name had been submitted for the federal bench, she did not want their dinner to be interrupted by strangers asking for autographs and selfies.

"So tell me about D.C.," she said, once they were seated.

"I will. I will tell you everything—so much that you will never want to hear another word about the Senate Judiciary Committee, but I want to hear your updates first. Please tell me that I won't need to withdraw my name from consideration in order to defend you against charges of slowly poisoning the young Mr. Nichols."

The last time she and Alex had spoken, Ryan was incessantly undermining her at work and she was finding him completely insufferable. Laurie smiled. "Let's put it this way. He still plays teacher's pet with Brett, and it's impossible to underestimate the size of his ego, but at least he's not stupid."

"Wow, that is some kind of endorsement!" Alex said wryly. His eyes lit up as he smiled at her across the table.

"It's actually getting better," she said grudgingly. "He's still the worst host we've ever had, to be sure, but I think it's working out." The only other host of *Under Suspicion* had been Alex, Laurie thought, and no one could ever fill his shoes.

We're talking as though the last two months didn't exist, Laurie thought happily. Oh God, how I've missed him.

"I accept the compliment." He was browsing the menu. "Everything looks delicious. Have you been here since they reopened?"

Danny Meyer's first restaurant remained one of Laurie's favorites, but she hadn't been able to bring herself to come in since it moved to a new location. She realized now that she'd been waiting to go with Alex. "No, this is my first time back. How about you?"

"Mine, too." He put down the menu. "I was hoping to go with you."

"And here we are."

Their appetizers had been removed when Laurie finally insisted that Alex tell her all about his federal judicial confirmation process.

"The politicians exist in a completely different universe. There I was, enjoying a career as a criminal defense lawyer. I would have been happy to have kept my practice as long as clients would have me. But now that I've been thrown into this circus of judicial confirmations, each side views me as a potential Supreme Court justice someday. They're trying to figure out whether I'm a 'strict constructionist' or a 'legal realist.' I told them I'm just a lawyer who reads the law and applies it to the facts, which is what trial court judges are supposed to do. I feel like a football in a Giants-Eagles matchup."

"But is it going smoothly?" she asked. "I can't imagine a better nominee."

"Oh, *they* can, trust me. But the White House assures me that they don't foresee any problems. Meanwhile, to keep you up to date on another front, Ramon has decided to be vegan. Some diet he saw on TV. He thinks he put on too much weight over Christmas. It's a miracle he isn't trying to talk me into it."

"Maybe he can do all that yoga he was pushing on you last year," Laurie said, laughing at the memory. After Alex's blood pressure was at the borderline of high, Ramon acted as if Alex had been diagnosed with a serious heart problem.

"Don't laugh," Alex said, even though he was chuckling, too. "He was playing soothing spa sounds on the car ride down here, saying he was worried that the trip to D.C. had been too stressful for me."

"It's sweet. He loves you like family."

"I certainly feel the same way. In fact, I have to fill out these forms disclosing the names of anyone who plays a substantial role in my life, even if they're not formally family. My only biological family is Andrew, of course, but there was no question about listing Ramon."

Something about the way he was looking at her made it clear that there was someone else who belonged on that list, too, but then the waiter arrived with their entrees, and Alex switched the topic to a budding scandal coming out of the Mayor's Office. As the night continued, they talked about everything—some new restaurants they had tried, the books they were reading, the worst youthful dates they'd ever had. By the time the waiter asked once again if they needed anything else, Laurie noticed for the first time that they were the last couple in the restaurant. She looked at her watch. They had been there for nearly four hours, and those four hours had gone by too quickly, she thought.

Alex signaled for the check. The waiter looked relieved, but when he brought it over, Laurie beat Alex to it. "I invited you, remember?"

"Very well, then," Alex said. "But that means next time is on me."

"I'm looking forward to it."

"Is tomorrow too soon?"

"I feel like it's not soon enough." She could not stop smiling.

She accepted his offer of a ride back to her apartment, where Leo was watching Timmy. Ramon was clearly happy to see her and turned down the spa music multiple times to ask for updates about her and Timmy. When they were almost at Laurie's, Alex put his arm around her. The entire night had been "effortless," to use Alex's word. She was no longer studying their relationship like a project to be managed. She hadn't paused every few minutes to ask herself where this was all going.

Alex had pressed her to decide what he was to her. She finally had her answer. He wasn't simply a co-worker or a friend, a pal to her father, or a buddy to Timmy. He wasn't even just a boyfriend.

It had been Ivan Gray, of all people, who had helped her make sense of it all when he had read his proposal to Virginia: *You told me I was your second chance at happiness, and I knew that you had opened your heart to me, where I want to stay with you always, for every breath you and I can take together.*

Alex was the next chapter in her life. She was certain it was what Greg wanted for her. And now there was no doubt that it was what she wanted and needed.

53

Peter Browning opened his eyes, momentarily confused about where he was. Then he remembered that he and Anna had decided to stay overnight at the house in Greenwich after the filming yesterday. Marie was taking care of the children in the city. He knew that Anna needed some quiet time in what had been her parents' primary home. Here they could collect their thoughts about yesterday's *Under Suspicion* interview.

Now Peter could see from the light of the nightstand's clock that his wife's eyes were wide open. She was staring at the ceiling. The clock read 4:32 A.M.

He turned to face her and draped one arm across her waist.

"I'm sorry," she whispered. "Did I wake you up with all my tossing and turning?"

"No," he said, even though he was certain that he had opened his eyes because of her. Sometimes he thought they shared a telepathic connection. Even in sleep, he knew when his wife was anxious. "How long have you been up?"

"Hours. I had that terrible nightmare again." He knew which one she was talking about. She'd had it countless times since Virginia was killed, but she walked him through the familiar sequence anyway. "I saw her up on that roof, in her beautiful gown. She was looking out at the skyline over Central Park South, and snow was falling. And then she turned and looked over her shoulder, and said 'Ivan?' just the way I always picture it. But this time, it wasn't Ivan standing behind her."

She brushed a tear from her face and Peter pulled her closer. "Shhh, it was just a dream, sweetie." He didn't force her to finish her description of the nightmare. They had spent most of the previous night discussing her worries about her brother, Carter.

"What if it wasn't just a dream? I pictured the entire scene. He followed her upstairs to harangue her about the will. You saw how obsessed he was. He wouldn't let up on the subject, even at the gala. And in my dream, she was just as defiant to him as she was with me when I raised the subject the day before. But where I let the matter drop, Carter kept pushing and pushing and pushing until she told him that he hadn't earned any right to that money the way his father had. And then Carter—he just snapped. In my dream, he was standing at the ledge, looking down at her on the ground below, and he fell to his knees and sobbed."

"Except that was all your imagination, Anna. You didn't really see it."

"But I can picture it now. Should I call him before his interview?"

Carter was going to be filmed by the *Under Suspicion* crew at the Wakeling Development offices at noon.

"Let your brother take care of himself for once," Peter said. "Three years ago, your mother told him he needed to grow up, and he hasn't changed a bit. Look at how much Tom has matured in that time, while Carter continues to act like a child."

"You're absolutely right," Anna said, sounding determined. "If he did hurt our mother, maybe this show will get to the bottom of it. And then at least I'll finally know."

54

Laurie looked at her watch. It was a quarter after noon, and the conference room at Wakeling Development was filled with lighting and cameras, ready for the arrival of their star witness.

Ryan stood when the door opened, but it was Jerry, returning from his venture to search for Carter Wakeling.

"Any sign of him?" Laurie asked.

They had spent the early hours of the morning gathering footage of the Long Island City neighborhood that originally put Robert Wakeling on the map as one of New York City's most successful real estate developers. They had arrived at the Wakeling offices nearly two hours earlier to set up for the interview in this room with sweeping views of Manhattan and the East River. Carter's secretary, Emma, had shown them into the conference room, but they hadn't spotted any of the Wakeling family as of yet, and now Carter was ten minutes late for what Laurie had come to believe was the most important interview of the production. He was supposed to have arrived twenty minutes early for makeup.

Jerry shook his head. "I made a new friend in Emma, though. She says Carter was here earlier, when we first arrived, but then left to go into Manhattan to try to find his sister and Peter. Apparently Anna and Peter both called in, first thing this morning, to cancel their office meetings for the entire day. They hadn't been answering their phones when Carter had tried calling."

Laurie wasn't at all surprised that Jerry had found a way to learn the inside details of Carter's whereabouts. He had a knack for becoming gossip partners with perfect strangers.

"So he went all the way to their apartment to look for them?" Laurie asked. "That seems unusual."

"Emma thought so, too," Jerry said. "Apparently she tried reassuring him that their secretaries had just spoken to Anna and Peter personally a few hours ago, but she said she'd never seen Carter so concerned."

"Concerned for *himself*," Ryan said, swinging his chair to prop his feet at the edge of the conference table. "He's probably eager to find out what Anna and Peter said yesterday during their interview in Greenwich."

Laurie agreed. She had seen the flash of fear in Anna's eyes yesterday afternoon when she realized that her brother had an objective reason to believe that their mother was going to reduce their inheritance soon. Laurie said, "In my opinion once Anna found out about what Penny Rawling had been communicating to Carter, she finally allowed herself to entertain the possibility that her older brother had killed their mother. If I had to guess, Anna and Peter canceled their meetings today to avoid seeing Carter before his interview."

They were leaving him to fend for himself in front of the cameras.

Laurie paused, turned to the lead cameraman, and said, "Nick, go ahead and get us started with a shot of the door from that camera back there," gesturing to the camera next to Nick at the far end of the room. "That should get most of the room, correct?"

He took a look at the digital screen and gave her a thumbs-up.

"Good. I want to be rolling from the second Carter shows up. This could get interesting."

55

It was nearly one o'clock and Nick was complaining about a rumbly stomach by the time the conference room door opened without a knock. Carter Wakeling looked flustered, using his fingers to rake his tousled sandy blond hair from his eyes.

"Sorry, I got hung up in traffic on the bridge," he explained. "I'm afraid we're going to have to reschedule, Ms. Moran."

Laurie clasped her hands together, trying her best to appear sympathetic. "Midday traffic's the worst. Fortunately, I think we can be quick here, Carter. Why don't you and Ryan get started and we'll see if we can wrap it all up in a few minutes so you can get back to your work."

"I'm afraid I can't do that. Peter and Anna are out of the office today, so I have a ton of stuff to do."

Laurie looked to Jerry, who subtly shook his head. As she'd suspected, Jerry had become chummy enough with Emma the secretary to have a sense of Carter's availability for the rest of the day.

"I've had my whole crew here for three hours, Carter.

Please, just have a seat so we can check you off the list of witnesses we need on camera. We don't even need to bother with makeup or anything. They can do wonders with editing these days," she said, adding a reassuring smile.

"It's not about my appearance," he snapped. "I just can't deal with this today. As I said, we'll need to reschedule."

Laurie pressed again. "Maybe your cousin, Tom, could help cover for a short while," she suggested.

"That wouldn't be appropriate. He's not one of the corporate officers!"

His face was now flushed with anger. It reminded Laurie of the rare temper tantrums Timmy used to have as a toddler.

"We have a very tight production schedule," Laurie said firmly. "I can't guarantee we'll be able to circle back to you."

"No offense, but that's your problem, not mine."

"Except we're trying to call attention to your mother's murder in the hope of identifying her killer. I would think you'd have an interest in helping that process."

"I already know who killed my mother—Ivan Gray!"

Laurie noticed Nick adjust something on his camera. She knew he was getting all of this on film and that the release Carter had signed would allow them to use the footage.

She cleared her throat and gave a sharp look to Ryan, still seated at the end of the table, though he had at least moved his feet to the floor. It took him a beat to pick up on her hint, but when he did, he rose to stand.

"We know that Penny Rawling told you about your mother's plans to change her will," Ryan snapped.

Carter's mouth opened but he said nothing.

"You were dating your mother's assistant," Ryan continued. "You didn't want the rest of the family to know, but you were desperate to enlist Anna and Peter to stop your mother from going through with her plans."

"Is that what Peter and Anna told you?" Carter asked. "And Penny? What else did they say about me?"

He was still seething with anger, but he now looked terrified as well. Laurie could tell that the time Carter had spent wondering what others had been saying to them had put him in a paranoid state of mind. She could only imagine what his mental state must have been like three years earlier when his mother lectured him about the need to "grow up," right on the heels of his learning from Penny about his mother's plans to greatly reduce his and Anna's inheritance. She wondered if he had yelled at Virginia the way he was yelling now.

Ryan was not letting up on his interrogation. He took two steps toward Carter. Laurie hoped that he wasn't blocking the camera angle. "You had a heated argument with Peter just before dinner at the gala that night. You told Peter and Anna that you all had to stop your mother from changing her will—*no matter what.*"

"That money was no more hers than ours!" Carter hissed. "My father put his heart and soul into this company. He wanted the Wakeling name to join the ranks of the Rockefellers and the Vanderbilts. That was to be our legacy. And she was going to give it all away. Of course I thought we should stop her. It was damn stupid what she was going to do."

He was nearly out of breath when he finished ranting. The room fell silent and he suddenly looked at Nick behind the camera.

"Is that thing on?" he said, pointing at the camera. "Turn that off. Now!"

He charged directly at Nick, his arms outstretched. Laurie tried to grab him, but he was moving too quickly. Ryan, who was positioned between Carter and Nick, jumped forward to block Carter's advance.

Carter pulled back his right fist. The punch landed squarely on Ryan's left jaw. Ryan then threw an uppercut against Carter's chin. The impact jerked his head backward and threw him off balance. He stumbled toward the conference table, where Ryan pinned his arms behind him.

"Calm down, man," Ryan ordered. "You're not getting that film, and you're only making yourself look worse."

Laurie could see the tension begin to leave Carter's body as he resigned himself to the situation. Ryan slowly released his grip, keeping his hands in front of him in a protective stance until Carter backed away toward the door, rubbing his chin as he moved.

"You are *sick* if you think I would hurt my own mother," he shouted. Then he shook his finger in a rage. "You'll be hearing from our lawyers. Ivan Gray's a killer. Are you too stupid to get that?"

He turned his back and slammed the door behind him as he left.

As soon as he was gone, Laurie and Jerry rushed toward Ryan.

"Are you okay?" Laurie asked.

"Yeah, I'm fine," he said, wiggling his jaw to make certain. "I didn't see that sucker punch coming, but I clocked him pretty good after that, didn't I?"

"You sure did," Laurie said emphatically. As many times as I wouldn't have minded knocking Ryan around myself, she thought, I'm so glad that he wasn't really hurt.

The crew broke down the set in record time, and hustled out of the building.

As Nick and the rest of the crew were about to climb into their van, Ryan ran over to them. "You got it all, didn't you?" he asked eagerly. "Carter shouting at me, then punching me and my punching him back. It will be the most dramatic segment on the show."

Nick answered with a thumbs-up, then closed the door of the van.

"Awesome," Ryan said, seemingly to himself as he climbed into the SUV waiting to take Laurie, Ryan, and Jerry back to the office. "The audience is going to love that."

"It's obvious his ego emerged unscathed," Jerry whispered as he settled in the seat next to Laurie.

56

Laurie stepped back from the whiteboard and admired their handiwork. She and Jerry had been working feverishly for the last two hours.

"This has to be a record," she announced. "Is it possible?"

"More than possible." Jerry rose from the conference table and held up his right hand for a high five, which she returned. "We're done filming!"

They had storyboarded the entire episode, scene by scene. Between the glamour of the Metropolitan Museum's party of the year and the intrigue of the case, Laurie was certain they had another hit on their hands. They had also unearthed new evidence about Virginia's intention to reduce her family's inheritance and her son Carter's agitation about her plans. Still, it was in Laurie's nature to search for additional avenues of investigation.

She knew it was unrealistic to expect to solve the case every time, but she couldn't help feeling a sense of disappointment. If they stopped at this point, Ivan Gray would continue to live under suspicion, and now so would Carter Wakeling. Even poor Anna and Peter were implicated to some extent, because they never told anyone about Carter's concerns over the will. They hadn't knowingly aided a killer, but they had placed the family's reputation over the integrity of the original investigation.

"I'll get to work on a rough edit," Jerry said. "Drinks after work to celebrate?"

"Can I take a rain check for next week? I'm already booked tonight." She was seeing Alex again. The thought of it put a smile on her face. In the meantime, she had a phone call to make.

Her father picked up on the second ring.

"Hey Dad. Do you have time for me to bend your ear with a work question?"

"Always."

Laurie, Timmy, and Leo all "shared locations" with one another through their cell phones. She had already checked before calling to make sure that Leo was back from picking up Timmy from school. He'd be happy to watch his grandson for a second night in a row, and he was thrilled when he heard that he'd be doing it so Laurie could join Alex again.

"The good news is that we definitely got under Carter Wakeling's skin today. He showed up an hour late for his interview and tried to back out. When we confronted him with what we knew about his relationship with Penny and his mother's plans for the estate, he flipped his lid and took a swing at Ryan. It was a really hard punch. He was really out of control."

"Laurie, in his state of mind, he could easily turn on you!"

"I realize that. He could attack me or someone else. I saw a side to him today that was frightening and volatile. He was demanding to know what we'd been told by Anna, Peter, and Penny."

"My main worry is about you," Leo said quickly. "But I agree that the others also might be in danger."

"Dad, I can't decide what to do. On the one hand, I want to keep a lid on the developments in our investigation until the episode airs. On the other, I certainly would never forgive myself if someone got hurt because I didn't reveal a possible threat."

"Trust me on this one," Leo counseled. "Your show would take a major publicity hit if something bad happened while you sat on evidence. And the police might never cooperate with you again."

He didn't need to spell out another consideration: Laurie knew how Leo's reputation in law enforcement had helped her build good working relationships with the police. In exchange, she had a responsibility to be more forthcoming with them than other journalists might be.

"Can I make a suggestion?" Leo asked. "What if I call Johnny Hon and give him a heads-up about what you've learned? He can weigh the new information in the context of the full investigation and decide what to do from there. He seems like a trustworthy person to me."

It didn't take Laurie long to agree that the suggestion to include Detective Hon was sound. She doubted he would leak anything to other media outlets, and, ultimately, what mattered was the safety of potential witnesses. If Carter was a killer who feared imminent exposure, he could be dangerous.

"Sounds good, Dad. Let me know how it goes. And thanks."

"Happy to help. The only thing I ask in exchange is that you enjoy yourself tonight."

She hung up, knowing that it would be an easy promise to keep.

When she was off the phone, she finally had time to sort through the snail mail waiting in the in-tray on her desk from that morning. She found a brown mailing envelope addressed to her from the probate court. She ran her letter opener across the seal as she walked to her office door and asked Grace if she could check whether Ryan was free. He had been the one to request a copy of Robert Wakeling's will to compare against Virginia's. His legal experience would come in handy during the review.

Grace shook her head. "I saw him hopping onto the elevator when I went to use the copier. My guess is that he couldn't wait to tell Ivan about his impromptu boxing match with Carter Wakeling."

Laurie rolled her eyes. Ryan had done a good job of appearing objective on camera, but she worried about his loyalty to Ivan off camera.

57

Laurie returned to the conference table in her office and removed the papers from the mailing envelope. As she had expected, the envelope contained the joint will of Robert and Virginia Wakeling, which went into probate when Robert passed away.

Next, she flipped open the binder she had received from Johnny Hon and found a copy of Virginia's will, as it existed when she died. She was already familiar with Virginia's estate. She also knew the distribution of assets that had occurred when Robert passed away: half of the shares in the corporation went to Virginia, a quarter went to each child, and the remainder of the estate passed to Virginia.

What piqued Laurie's curiosity were the subsequent pages in the joint will, which addressed what would have happened in the unlikely event that both Robert and Virginia passed simultaneously.

Laurie had taken out a notebook to keep track of any discrepancies between Virginia's will and the joint will in the event that the married couple had passed together. The similarities were striking, which was not surprising to

Laurie. When she and Greg had created a will right after Timmy was born, the terms were simple: if one departed, the other inherited everything; if they happened to pass at the same time, the situation was more complicated, involving Leo and some family friends to care for Timmy. When Laurie unexpectedly found herself a widow, her lawyer took the "backup will"—the plan if both she and Greg departed together—and used it as the road map for her own individual will.

Now that she was comparing Virginia's will to the will she had signed with her husband while he was still alive, she could see that Virginia had used the same approach. Virginia's will relied on the same terms as the joint will in the event they both died together.

Laurie was doing a second scan of all the numbers when she realized there was one significant difference. In the joint will, Robert's nephew Tom would have inherited $250,000 cash in the event that both Robert and Virginia departed at the same time. Because Robert predeceased Virginia, that condition never came to pass, and Virginia inherited almost everything. But while Virginia's own will tended to cut-and-paste terms from the previous joint will, she had made one change: When she died, Tom's interest was reduced from $250,000 to $50,000.

Laurie wrote the two numbers side by side on her legal pad, wondering what the change meant. Given that Virginia was worth $200 million plus half of the value of the corporation when she was killed, the change was a small percentage of the money that was at stake. On the other hand, most people would consider either amount significant, and the 80 percent reduction to her nephew was a notable alteration. This was the only revision she had made, and it seemed obvious that she must have had a reason for it.

Laurie closed her eyes, trying to imagine what it would be like to be a person with that much wealth at stake. When she opened them, she firmly believed that if she had been Virginia, the only reason she would have reduced a nephew's inheritance—and no one else's—was if she did not trust the nephew with money. She thought again about Anna's recollection of the arguments Virginia had had with her children before she was murdered. She had told Carter that he needed to grow up, that he was still playing the field and not working hard enough at the company. According to Anna, her mother told Carter, "I'm afraid that if it weren't for the family money, you would have turned out just like your cousin, Tom."

Laurie had eliminated Tom as a suspect after confirming his alibi with Tiffany, but she wanted to be absolutely certain that she wasn't overlooking anything before finalizing their special.

She went to her desk, picked up the phone, and dialed Anna Wakeling's cell number. Anna sounded apprehensive when she answered. "What happened today? Please tell me that my brother didn't do this."

"It didn't go very well," Laurie said. "He didn't confess, but he was very defensive."

"Does he know what Peter and I told you?"

"Yes. I'm sorry, Anna, but it's part of the process we use. Are you afraid of your brother?"

"No. At least, I don't think so. I just wish I knew for certain. It's been hard enough to live without closure, but I always told myself it was just a matter of time before the police could build a case against Ivan. Now I don't know what to believe."

Laurie knew any consolation she offered would sound hollow. "All I can say is that we're doing everything we can to get at the truth. To that end, I was hoping to ask you one more question about your cousin, Tom." She explained what she had learned about the very small inheritance Tom had received from Virginia. "When your father was alive, the plan was to leave Tom a quarter of a million dollars."

"My father had a running feud with his brother, but he had a soft spot for Tom. I think he blamed his brother for Tom's lack of focus in his younger years. My mother was less sympathetic. She saw Tom as always having his hand out when it came to our family. I can't say I'm surprised that she changed what Daddy had planned. Granted, the fifty thousand dollars that Tom inherited was a great deal of money to him, given where he was three years ago, but Carter and I still felt guilty. That's why we decided to give him a job at the company when he asked. We've all moved on."

Where he was three years ago. Anna had previously mentioned Tom's lack of regular employment and penchant for gambling. "I hate to ask you this, Anna, after the questions we've also raised about Carter, but do you think there's any possibility that Tom did this?"

"No, but I said the same thing about Carter until

yesterday. My recollection is that he and his date were sneaking around the portraits gallery. That woman was a bit eccentric, but I don't see why she'd lie to the police for him. Did you talk to her?"

"I did," Laurie said. "She confirmed that she was with Tom the whole time."

"Well, at least I don't need to suspect him," Anna said sadly, still concerned about her brother. "Please promise me that if you learn something about Carter one way or the other that you'll let me know."

"I will," Laurie promised.

58

Detective Johnny Hon hung up his phone and thought about what he had just learned from Leo Farley. Anna Wakeling and her husband, Peter, had never told the police about Carter's insistence, just hours before the murder, on stopping their mother from changing her will. In fact, this was the first time anyone other than Ivan Gray had mentioned the possibility that Virginia had such plans.

If he had gotten this tip under any other circumstance, Hon would probably have arranged to reinterview all the relevant witnesses immediately. But Leo Farley had given Hon his professional opinion that he should allow his daughter, Laurie, to continue investigating on her own for now. Because she didn't work for the government, she didn't have to comply with rules like Miranda warnings and was able to persuade witnesses to disclose information they might not hand over to the police. Hon had to admit that Laurie had made a break in the case after only two weeks, after it had been sitting cold for nearly three years.

On the other hand, Hon was worried about Carter's state of mind. A man who was volatile enough to take a swing at the host of a national television program might seek retaliation—or worse—against any witnesses who could implicate him.

He tapped his fingers against his fiberboard-topped desk, weighing his options. According to Leo, Carter was at the offices of Wakeling Development as of earlier this afternoon. He Googled the address of the building in Long Island City and grabbed his coat from the back of his chair. He'd try to get a bead on Carter leaving the office and follow him from there, just in case.

59

Mommy, I'm so glad you and Daddy are home now."
Vanessa bounced onto the sofa next to Anna. This was
the third time her daughter had mentioned missing her
last night when she and Peter had stayed at the family
estate in Connecticut. Meanwhile, her big brother,
Robbie, was completely unfazed by their absence and
had hopped straight to his video games when he got
home from school.

"I missed you, too, sweetie," Anna said, giving her
daughter a quick hug. Then, in an instant, Vanessa was
running off to the kitchen again to help Kara put away the
groceries. She wished her mother and father had lived
long enough to know how kind and happy their grandchildren were.

She looked at her watch. It was five o'clock. Her
cousin, Tom, would surely still be at his desk. He was
always one of the first to arrive and the last to leave.

Sure enough, he picked up his office phone after two
rings. "Did you and Peter have fun on your 'hooky' day?"
he asked.

When she had called in this morning to clear her calendar, she had asked Tom to cover a site inspection for her on a project they were launching in Astoria. She had told him that she and Peter needed a personal day, not mentioning that she was trying to avoid Carter. Now that she was back in the city, her concerns about her brother felt like a temporary case of insanity. Ivan Gray killed her mother. She was certain of it, and she wasn't going to let some television program get into her head again.

"I wouldn't exactly call it fun," she said. "Those people from *Under Suspicion* were in the office today to interview Carter. After dealing with them yesterday, I was happy to avoid them."

"Carter looked upset this afternoon," Tom said. "I asked him what was wrong, but he huffed away to his office. I wonder if the show's producers got under his skin as well."

Anna was too drained to discuss the roller coaster of emotions she'd been experiencing since that first phone call from Laurie Moran. "He's probably angry at me for deciding it would be better for the family reputation to cooperate with the program. It's been much more intrusive than I ever imagined. They really do turn over every stone. Can you believe they were even asking me about that wacky woman you brought to the party that night?"

"Tiffany."

"That's the one. They were even asking about you."

"Weird. That female producer spoke to me one time in the office and then I never heard from her again."

"We should all be so lucky," Anna said wryly. "Anyway,

I was just calling to see if there were any problems at the site inspection today."

"Absolutely not," Tom asserted firmly.

"Thank you, Tom. Truly. Sometimes I don't know what I'd do at work without you." In truth, she thought Tom brought more to the table at Wakeling Development than her own brother, but she pushed away the thought. She was still ashamed for even entertaining the possibility of Carter being involved in their mother's murder.

"Anytime, Anna. You have nothing to worry about."

60

Penny recognized the number—the second time he had called in the last week after almost three years of silence.

"Hello?" she said, trying to sound nonchalant.

"Hi, Penny. It's Carter Wakeling." His voice was quiet, even deliberate.

Penny found herself straightening the blue blazer draped over her dress. She couldn't remember a time when Carter had addressed her so formally.

"Why are you calling me?" she asked, trying to sound impersonal.

"Did you speak with the people from *Under Suspicion*?"

She was tempted to deny it, but assumed he could learn the inside details of the production.

Choosing her words carefully, she said, "It was a quick chat. I think they wanted a few words from your mom's *former assistant*." She spoke the last two words as if they were poison.

"I know you talked about my mother's notes and her will, didn't you?"

What was she hearing in his voice? Anger at her?

"Yes, I did. There was no reason not to," Penny said. Or was there?

There was a long silence. Then Carter said, "Penny, I have to see you. Where are you? I'll pick you up."

Penny wanted to hear what Carter had to say, but she did not want to be alone with him in his car. "Let's do it this way. Meet me in an hour for a cup of coffee at Le Grainne Cafe, in Chelsea on Ninth Avenue."

Carter quickly agreed. When she ended the call, Penny realized that there had been something different in Carter's voice, as though he was trying to hold himself in control. Why? And had he possibly been the one who followed his mother up to the roof that night?

61

Laurie was at her desk, surfing the Web, when she got a text from her father: *I called Hon and filled him in. I think he appreciated being kept in the loop. Seemed to take a "wait and see" approach. Fingers crossed.*

She typed a quick *thank you!* and hit send. Dad has done enough work for my show to be credited as a consultant, she thought, but he swears the last thing he wants is to have to put up with Brett Young.

She returned her attention to her computer screen. She was looking at Tom Wakeling's Facebook posts from three years earlier. Just hours before his aunt Virginia was murdered, he had posted a selfie from the red carpet of the Met Gala. *Just hanging out with the other celebrities in my tuxedo*, read the caption.

The fact that Virginia had overridden her husband's desire to leave a more sizable inheritance to his nephew was still nagging at Laurie. Virginia had been toying with the idea of leaving everything except the company to charity, but this initial decision to reduce *only* Tom's inheritance struck her as different. It wasn't philosophical. It was personal, specific to her nephew.

Now that Laurie was learning about the "old Tom" from his previous social media posts, she was beginning to understand why Virginia might have been unwilling to trust Tom with significant amounts of money. Even from what Laurie could glean from Facebook, it seemed that Tom went to casinos in Atlantic City and Connecticut at least twice a month. She remembered Anna mentioning Tom's gambling habit. He could have been in debt from gambling. The $50,000 he inherited when his aunt died wasn't much compared to the Wakelings' worth, but it might have been enough to dig him out of a hole. And once his cousins had sole control of the corporation, they had been willing to give him a chance with a job, in which he was now a trusted insider.

Her thoughts were pulled away by the sound of her phone. Alex's name was on the screen.

"Hello, Your Honor, I'm looking forward to dinner tonight."

"Me, too. That's why I was calling. We have a seven o'clock reservation at Marea if that's acceptable to you."

Because Laurie had planned yesterday's evening, Alex had insisted on making the arrangements for tonight. "Better than acceptable." It was the restaurant where they'd had their first dinner alone.

"Should I pick you up?"

"I'm not sure where I'll be coming from. I was going to try to swing home to see Timmy if I have time, but I may leave straight from here." It was already five o'clock. "I went down the rabbit hole of a witness's old social media posts. Something's bothering me, and I just can't let it go."

"Oh boy, that doesn't sound like you at all," he said laughing. "Do you want me to push the dinner later?"

"Not at all. But let's plan to meet there." She knew this entire conversation would be yet another reminder to Alex that a relationship with her was more complicated than dating a woman without a busy career and young son.

"Sounds good," he said.

"Can't wait."

Once Laurie was off the phone, her thoughts turned back to Tom Wakeling. She told herself again that it was time to let it go. Tiffany had been absolutely certain that Tom was with her the entire night. As Anna had noted, Tiffany was eccentric but she had no reason to lie for a man she had only gone out with twice three years earlier.

And then Laurie realized that an explanation for the alarm that night might have been sitting in front of her the entire time. How many times had Ivan and the Wakeling family mentioned Tiffany's crazy stories the night of the gala? She had been rambling about her grandmother the cabaret performer, the one who supposedly had an affair with President Kennedy and, in Tiffany's view, deserved to have a dress of her own among the first ladies exhibit.

Did Tiffany have a reason to lie about being with Tom

all night, but not to protect Tom? If she had stolen the bracelet and set off the alarm, she was protecting herself. Tom might not have an alibi for the time of the murder. This was probable or at least possible.

But how do I get Tiffany to admit to that? Laurie asked herself.

She had an idea how to get Tiffany to open up. She called the number Tiffany had provided for her home. Tiffany answered on the second ring.

"Tiffany, it's Laurie Moran from *Under Suspicion*. I just wanted to thank you once again for your participation and to let you know that we'll be airing our episode on Valentine's Day. I wanted to send you a swag bag from the studio as a small token of our appreciation. What's your address so I can get it in the mail to you?"

Given the nature of Tiffany's "mobile wedding" business, Laurie was betting that she worked out of her home.

Tiffany recited an address in Queens, which Laurie immediately typed into Google maps. "It's nothing extravagant," Laurie said, making small talk as she hit *street view* on her computer to get a look at the address. "Just some souvenirs from our various shows."

"That's so nice of you."

Laurie was looking at a brick Tudor on her screen, definitely a residence. "We'll send it right out," she said. "I think I know that area of Queens. Forest Hills? A lovely neighborhood."

"It's actually my grandmother Molly's home, where she raised me. I moved back in when she needed some help, but now she's in assisted living. Anyway, it still feels like home."

Laurie thanked Tiffany for her help again. Her next call was to Charlotte.

"Hey there. I was just thinking of calling you," Charlotte said. "Time for a drink after work? I'm dying to hear about your date with Alex last night."

"It was perfect. In fact, we're going out tonight, too, so I'll have to take a rain check on drinks."

Her rain checks were adding up.

"My loss, but I'm so happy for you. You've been putting on a strong face, but I could tell you missed him."

"I don't have time to meet for a drink, but I would like to borrow you for a couple of hours if you have time. It's another favor for the show."

"The last time you recruited me worked out on my end, too. I'm hiring Marco Nelson to handle security for our spring fashion show."

"I'm so glad," Laurie said. "I felt guilty that I was wasting his time when we asked him to come to your office."

"Feel better. You did him a favor."

"Honestly, Charlotte, this job will require more than a few white lies. I essentially need you to pretend you're someone else. The witness isn't dangerous, more an airhead than a threat. I need her to answer some questions. But I totally understand if you're not comfortable getting involved."

"Don't be silly. It sounds exciting. I love helping you play Nancy Drew. Where should we meet?"

"I'll grab a cab and meet you in front of your office in ten minutes."

"Whoa, that's soon, but I can make it work."

"Sorry for the rush, but the person we need to see is definitely home right now, so we have to hurry." Laurie disconnected, wondering and hoping she'd have the truth about Tiffany in time for her dinner with Alex.

62

Alex stared at the draft document he had been carrying around for nearly two weeks now. An aide from the Senate Judiciary Committee had phoned this morning, warning that his nomination could be stalled if they did not start the necessary background check immediately. He had promised to send the document by tomorrow morning.

Every section was complete except for one question: "Please provide biographical information for any individuals who serve a role similar or comparable to those listed in parts (a) and (b), above, regardless of legal affiliation or formal definitions of family (such as intimate partners, part-time roommates, financial dependents [whether or not adopted], etc.)."

Alex rotated his chair, wiggled the mouse of his computer to wake it up, and pulled up the document on his computer.

He typed in three people: Laurie Moran, Timothy Moran, and Leo Farley. He knew the dates of birth for

Laurie and Timmy from memory and looked up Leo's online. He had only shared one dinner with Laurie after weeks of silence, but if he had to answer the question right now, he was betting on a future with the woman he loved.

63

Johnny Hon sat behind the wheel of his department-issued Impala. He was across the street from Wakeling Development's corporate offices. He had already run the plates of the cars in the reserved spots closest to the entrance. The black Range Rover with the personalized plate "WAKE2" belonged to Carter Wakeling.

He looked at his watch. It was three minutes after five. Virginia Wakeling's son hadn't struck Hon as the hardest working man when he'd gotten to know the family during the investigation. If he had to guess, Carter wouldn't stay in the office much longer.

Sure enough, he walked to his car two minutes later and started the engine. He had gained a few pounds in the almost three years since Hon had seen him last, but still looked youthful for his age. He also looked anxious.

When Carter rolled out of the parking lot, Hon followed, keeping a half block's distance.

64

Laurie gave the cabdriver the address for Charlotte's office. Not wasting any time, she immediately tapped the screen of her phone to call Sean Duncan.

She was relieved when he picked up. "I was afraid you would have left at five."

"That never seems to happen, I'm afraid."

"I have a question for you. Two of the guests at the Met Gala said they had sneaked into the American Portraits gallery on the second floor at the time Virginia Wakeling was killed."

"It's certainly possible. The guests have a hard time following the rules during that party. You wouldn't believe how many of the celebrities think it's perfectly acceptable to start smoking cigarettes—and sometimes other things—right in the middle of the party."

Laurie recalled Tiffany's description of sneaking upstairs with Tom: *We slipped up to the second floor. No one was around. It was magical. We roamed all over.*

"You said that most of the cameras were turned off

because you use that night to test and update the equipment in the closed-off sections of the museum."

"That's correct."

"One of the people who slipped upstairs said she and someone else roamed all around the entire second floor and did not encounter a single person. Is that possible?"

"Not likely. We would have had people up there working on the cameras while the equipment was turned off. Not a ton of workers, mind you. I suppose it's possible someone could have gone up there undetected, but it would have taken quite a bit of sneaking around—hiding around corners, that sort of thing."

"That's not how this woman described it. She was very clear that they were meandering around the galleries, entirely alone."

"No, if they were exploring the whole floor, they definitely would have come across multiple workers."

"Got it."

"It sounds as if you're making progress."

"I hope so." She thanked him once again before ending the call.

All along, she had been convinced that the alarm triggered the night of the murder had to be connected to it in some way. The police believed that the killer or an accomplice had set off the alarm to create a distraction while the killer followed Virginia upstairs. But Laurie had never understood why someone seeking to create a distraction would have selected a spot in the middle of the fashion exhibit, where it would be difficult to slip away.

Now it was becoming clear to her what might have happened that night.

Impulsive, eccentric Tiffany must have gone to the fashion exhibit and taken the charm bracelet from the Jackie Kennedy display, triggering the alarm. When the police arrived—not because of the theft, but because of Virginia's murder—they began asking guests to account for their whereabouts. Tiffany must have told Tom that she had stolen the bracelet and asked him to cover for her by saying they were together the entire time in the portraits gallery. That itself was a transgression of guest rules, but a "confession" to such a minor violation would protect her from suspicion if anyone noticed the theft of the bracelet.

Laurie supposed it was conceivable that Tom would have been willing to lie to protect a woman he barely knew, but he may have had a very different motive.

The cab came to a stop, and Charlotte hopped in to join her. She was prepared for the cold, bundled up in a navy-blue wrap coat.

"So what's the plan?" she asked.

Laurie spelled it all out for her on the drive to Queens.

65

Tiffany Simon was reviewing the checklist for the wedding ceremony she was planning for the following night at a fire station in Brooklyn where the groom was a firefighter. The couple was named Luke and Laura, which reminded Tiffany of how much her grandmother loved her "stories." Granny Molly was always saying that no soap opera romance could ever top Luke and Laura from *General Hospital* in the 1980s.

Tiffany had just finished putting together the script for the ceremony when her doorbell chimed. She looked through the peephole and saw a woman, probably in her late thirties, wearing an elegant navy-blue wrap coat.

"Hello?" she called out through the closed door.

"I'm looking for Molly? My name is Jane Martin. I'm a researcher for a book publisher."

Tiffany opened the door. "Molly's my grandmother. This is her home, but she's in assisted living now."

"Can I come in? I'm doing some fact-checking for a book we're publishing. We're having trouble verifying one of the author's claims. It involves your grandmother."

Tiffany stepped aside to welcome the woman into the house.

"Wow, this is incredible," "Jane Martin" said, looking around in awe, as most people did when they first entered the living room.

"Full of memories of my grandmother's amazing life," Tiffany bragged.

The walls were decorated with photographs of Grandmother Molly with various celebrities and in her cabaret performances. There were at least a dozen of her favorite costumes on display, not to mention the miniature versions worn by an assortment of dolls placed on the chairs and end tables.

"Gran would be so excited that a publisher was here to see her!"

"I wish I could say we were doing a book entirely about your grandmother, but the project in question is a presidential biography. The author has collected a series of never-before-published facts about various presidents. As you can imagine, it's not easy to verify the events years after the fact."

"I'm happy to help if I can. Is this about the affairs she had with presidents?"

"Oh, so you know about them?" "Ms. Martin" asked.

"Gran was so beautiful that men fell head over heels in love with her, even three presidents."

"Three? She must have been gorgeous!"

"Oh, she was," Tiffany crowed.

Charlotte hoped "Jane Martin's" next question would sound natural. "Did she have a favorite?"

"Jack Kennedy, of course. You can imagine why. He was gorgeous, too. At a fundraiser at the cabaret one of the hosts came over to her and said he wanted her to meet the President. One thing led to another and Gran and the President became involved. She knew of course that it would never last, but on her birthday he gave her a lovely charm bracelet. He said to Gran, 'You are my charm.' Can you imagine how she felt?

"Of course, we all know what happened. Gran never got over him, and then years later, someone got into her dressing room and stole some jewelry including the bracelet. She used to tell me how much she loved it, how it made her think of him, and how heartbreaking it was to lose it."

"She must have been very young at that time," "Ms. Martin" suggested.

"Oh yes, she was. And she was so beautiful that an Arabian prince proposed to her and so did the Duke of Wellington. And that was after three presidents."

Gran must have been very busy, Charlotte thought. "When did your grandmother marry?"

"Oh, not until she was forty, but unfortunately, my grandfather never amounted to a hill of beans. Gran raised my mother alone, and then my mother and father were killed in an automobile accident, and she raised me. I loved to listen when she told me the stories about her wonderful, exciting life. Now she is in a nursing home, and I know it won't be long before I lose her. The only thing I want is for her to be as happy as possible."

"That's a wonderful attitude, Tiffany," "Jane Martin" said.

"Thanks to Gran, I live every day of my life as though it will be my last. So, will Gran's stories be in your book?"

Charlotte felt guilty as she said, "I only collect the stories and turn them over to the writer. I'm sorry if you didn't understand that."

"If they don't use her, it may be for the best," Tiffany sighed. "The excitement might be too much for her."

"So tell me more about that bracelet from President Kennedy."

66

Carter was waiting when Penny arrived at the French bistro she had chosen for their meeting. Unlike the times that he had chosen a table at the back of the restaurant to avoid any chance of running into his family and friends, he was now seated at a window front table.

When he spotted her, he jumped up and threw his arms around her tightly. "Penny, you can't believe how much I've missed you."

All the anger and hurt Penny had felt over the years came to the surface. The waiter was at the table. "Black coffee please," Penny said.

When he was out of earshot, in a low steely voice she said, "Carter, what new game are you playing now? You have the nerve to tell me you missed me when out of the blue three years ago you dropped me and never returned my calls. You had decided I wasn't good enough to be part of the Wakeling family. You didn't give a damn about how much you hurt me. I've had plenty of time to think. The fact is I should have dropped you. Ivan told me that I didn't pay enough attention to my job when I worked for your mother. He was right. There were lots of times when I would come in late or leave early. And it was almost always to meet you."

"Penny, I'm sorry."

"You couldn't be sorry enough. Just in case it never occurred to you, you've done me a big favor. You're lazy. You complain because you're jealous of your sister. She always worked hard; you didn't."

Carter was shaking his head.

"Don't dismiss what I'm telling you," Penny said. "I've got more to say. I'm working hard at a job, and I am going to be a success at it. And I have one last thing to tell you. I have come to the conclusion that you and your family aren't good enough for me. How do you like that?"

There was a long pause. Then Carter, his voice low and clipped, said, "Now you listen to me."

Penny realized that she was fighting back tears and reached for a paper napkin to stop her mascara from running. "There is nothing you could say that I want to hear." She pushed back the chair and started to get up. Carter suddenly reached both hands across the table and grasped her wrists. She winced as he forced her back down into her seat.

"I'll start by saying that you are exactly right. I've been feeling sorry for myself all my life. In the beginning my father used to take me around when he was having meetings to discuss projects. But I was bored. I went along because I had to. I didn't like being told what I was going to do for the rest of my life. I didn't work hard at it because I didn't want it. Now, after I made a fool of myself during that TV interview, I finally faced myself. Everything you just said was true. But I'm going to change. I'm forty-one years old and I'm not going to waste another minute. For the first time I'm going to work hard at the company because it's what I want. And there's something else I really want and need.

"I've been missing you every minute of every day these past three years. I love you, Penny. I know I don't deserve it, but please give me a chance to start over with you."

Penny knew the expression on her face gave him his answer.

"Carter, I have one small problem," she said.

"What is it?"

"I can't drink my coffee when you're squeezing both of my wrists," Penny said, and they both started to laugh.

67

Laurie was waiting at the corner in Queens while Charlotte spoke to Tiffany pretending to be a book researcher. It couldn't have been more than twenty minutes, but it felt like hours before she saw Charlotte approaching her.

"How did it go?" Laurie asked. "Did she say anything about the bracelet?"

"First things first," Charlotte said. "That house is like a trip to fantasyland. Outfits the grandmother wore in her cabaret days complete with dolls dressed in her getups."

"Were you able to record her?"

Charlotte played the beginning of the recording to check the audio. It was crystal clear. Tapping on her phone, she said, "I'm emailing it to you right now."

"You're the best. What did she say about the bracelet?"

"Laurie, Gran the cabaret dancer lived in a world of her own and raised Tiffany telling her stories. It is obvious that most, if not all, of them, are made up. According to Tiffany, Granny had affairs with three presidents, an Arabian prince, the Duke of Wellington, and God knows who else."

"Did she say anything about John Kennedy?"

"Oh, he was Granny's favorite, and this is where the bracelet came in. According to Tiffany, he gave her a charm bracelet exactly like the one he gave Jackie that was on the display at the Met. Supposedly he told Granny that she was his charm. Tiffany said it was a treasured symbol of JFK's love. The bracelet was stolen along with other jewelry from her dressing room, and the loss broke Granny's heart. Now Granny is in a nursing home, very sick and still talking about the bracelet."

"Charlotte, that confirms everything. Why Tiffany might have grabbed it to give to her grandmother. And then when she realized she needed an alibi, she asked Tom Wakeling to cover for her. It's the missing piece that's been driving me crazy. I'm going to knock on Tiffany's door and try to persuade her to tell the truth."

"Maybe I should go with you."

"No, I'll be fine. It's better if I talk to her alone, and I've kept you out long enough."

A cab was coming down the street. Laurie hailed it, waited until Charlotte was in the backseat, then started walking the block to Tiffany's house.

Tiffany was clearly surprised to find Laurie on her porch. "Is this about the thank-you gift you were sending? You didn't need to bring it out here yourself."

"No, I'm afraid it's about something else, Tiffany. May I come in?"

68

When Tiffany invited her in, Laurie's first thought was that Charlotte had not exaggerated when she described the house. It was stuffed with memorabilia.

"I have to start with an apology," Laurie said. "The woman who was here wasn't a book publisher. I invented her."

Tiffany gasped, "That's awful—"

Laurie held up a hand. "I'm so sorry. I had my reasons, and I can explain them later, but this is urgent. I know you were the one who set off the alarm in the fashion exhibit the night of the gala. The last thing I'm concerned about is that charm bracelet. I'm trying to find a killer."

"How did you know—"

"I really don't have time for that right now, Tiffany, and I wish there was another way I could have done this. You thought Tom was doing a favor covering for you that night, but I am almost certain you were also covering for *him*. I believe he was the one who killed Virginia Wakeling."

Tiffany's face paled as Laurie's words took effect. "That can't be possible."

"I know. It's hard to believe."

"As for the bracelet, I knew it wasn't valuable," Tiffany said with tears in her eyes. "It was just when I saw it, I knew how thrilled Granny would be to have it."

"I understand, but this is your chance to make it right," Laurie said. "Will you confirm—to the police and on camera—that you weren't with Tom Wakeling on the second floor after all?"

"I'll get arrested. I know I will!"

"You won't. I know the detective in charge of the homicide investigation. I'm sure they'll give you immunity if you testify. Now tell me exactly how it happened."

"I was so panicked that night when I heard the commotion and knew something was going on," Tiffany babbled nervously. "I rushed back to the main party without getting caught. But by then the police had arrived, and they began asking questions. I was so scared. I told Tom what I had done. He offered to back me up with an alibi. We really *had* sneaked into the portrait gallery shortly after dinner and had a few laughs about the paintings. We hid when we heard some people coming . . . they were workers. Tom suggested we go back downstairs separately to reduce the chance of anybody noticing us. That's when I went to get the bracelet. I was so grateful when he agreed to say we had been together the whole time. In a thousand years it never occurred to me that he had another motive. Oh my God! Do you really think Tom killed that poor woman?"

"Because of you Tiffany, we are a lot closer to the truth," Laurie said. "I'll straighten things out with the police and come out tomorrow with a camera crew. In the meantime, keep your doors locked and be sure to call 911 if Tom gets in touch with you."

Tiffany's face became fearful.

"I meant, just in case," Laurie assured her. "He has no idea that I suspect him."

She thanked Tiffany warmly once again, and waited until she heard the bolt of the door turn behind her before she walked away.

69

Johnny Hon was still behind the wheel. He had followed Carter Wakeling into Manhattan, down the FDR Drive, and crosstown to Chelsea. He watched as Carter parked on 21st Street halfway between Eighth and Ninth Avenues, then walked to the cafe around the corner.

Less than a minute later a woman went into the restaurant. From his parked car Hon studied her through binoculars. With her slender carriage and classic features, he recognized Penny Rawling. Because of her midnight-black hair, white skin, and radiant blue eyes, one of the detectives had nicknamed her Snow White.

When he saw her sit down at Carter Wakeling's table, he slipped an official tag on his car and followed her in, taking a table in the far corner where he could observe them. He had interviewed each of them three years ago and did not want to make it easy for them to see his face.

Leo had told him that Penny was one of the witnesses who had provided new information that could possibly implicate Carter in his mother's death. She claimed to have told Carter that his mother was planning to reduce his inheritance substantially.

Suddenly Penny looked down and began to cry. She pulled paper napkins from a steel dispenser on the table to wipe her face. An instant later Carter leaned across the table and grabbed her wrists.

Hon could not be certain what was happening between the two from across the room, but he was more than concerned now. He was on alert. It looked to him as if Carter might be pressuring or threatening Penny as a witness. She was afraid enough to cry in public. If she continued and Carter panicked, he might go further in his efforts to silence her.

But then the two began to smile. Carter released his grip on Penny's wrists, and it was obvious that whatever was going on between them, Penny was now at ease.

Johnny Hon signaled for his check and went back to his car. His instinct told him Carter Wakeling was not a killer, but he had seen murderers who looked as innocent as choirboys. He was not going to let Carter out of his sight. If he persuaded Rawling to get in his car or a cab with him when they left the restaurant, Hon would be right behind them.

70

When she left Tiffany's house, Laurie looked at the time as she hit send on her phone.

The audio of Charlotte's meeting with Tiffany was on its way to Jerry. She then tried to call him. It was 6:45 P.M. He often worked far longer hours than this, but he had been eager to celebrate their completion of the episode's storyboard. As she listened to a fourth ring, she pictured Jerry and Grace having cocktails at Tanner Smith's, the prohibition era–themed speakeasy they tended to frequent when Laurie didn't tag along.

She waited through Jerry's familiar outgoing message, and then left a message at the tone: "Call me as soon as you get this. I know who killed Virginia. We need to meet first thing in the morning to discuss our next moves. I'll need to work on getting an immunity deal for a witness, and we need Ryan to interview at least one more person. So call me."

By the time she hung up the phone, it was already 6:48. She was supposed to meet Alex on Central Park South in twelve minutes. The ride to Queens had taken forty-five minutes. The drive back would be quicker in reverse traffic, but it would still be a crawl across the bridge.

She decided that the subway was her fastest option. The F train was almost a straight shot. Even so, she would still be late. She knew he would understand, though. Last night at dinner, they had felt completely comfortable with each other, as if they were finally on the same page. This time, they were jumping in with both feet.

She pulled Alex up on her phone and was about to send him a text message. She hadn't started typing yet when she heard footsteps behind her.

71

Tom Wakeling had been getting out of his car when he saw an unfamiliar woman leaving the house where he had picked up Tiffany for their two dates three years earlier. The stranger was wearing a navy-blue wrap coat. He had watched her walk to the corner. His pulse raced when he spotted Laurie Moran waiting for her.

The two women had a quick conversation, and then Laurie walked into Tiffany's house alone. She had been inside for more than five minutes. He had no idea what to do now.

He'd formulated a plan the second his cousin, Anna, told him that the TV show people had been asking questions about Tiffany. He had a bag of painkillers in his pocket and had planned to make Tiffany's death look like an overdose. He had a gun, too, and would use it to force her to swallow the pills. A woman like her was so eccentric, the police would write it off as yet another unfortunate casualty of the nation's opiate-addiction crisis. Now that everything was going so well in his life, he couldn't take any chance that Tiffany would retract her statement to the police. That story about being together on the second floor had spared him closer scrutiny after that horrible night on the roof with Aunt Virginia.

Now he was on the sidewalk in front of Tiffany's neighbor's house, pretending to make a phone call. A large pine tree between the two houses would shield him from view, but he was keeping an eye on Tiffany's front door with the occasional glance. He watched as Laurie said good-bye to Tiffany and began walking. He had been worried that she might spot him behind her, but she was distracted by her phone.

He was close enough to hear her voice when she spoke. "Call me as soon as you get this. I know who killed Virginia. We need to meet first thing in the morning to discuss our next moves. I'll need to work on getting an immunity deal for a witness, and we need Ryan to interview at least one more person. So call me."

Listening, Tom cursed his bad luck. Until today, he'd been on a winning streak. After the incident on the museum roof, Tiffany out of the blue had told him that she had stolen some kind of bracelet while the two of them had been apart at the gala. She swore it wasn't valuable, but the confession had confirmed his impression that she was insane. At the same time he couldn't believe his good fortune. In an instant he had an alibi for the time of the murder. The money his aunt left him turned out to be a lousy $50,000, but it was enough to pay off his gambling debts. And then, unlike his uncle Bob or aunt Virginia, his cousins had given him a chance to prove himself with a job at the company. He had turned his life around on that one awful night.

But now all the good luck had run out. If he had arrived here just a little earlier, his plan might have worked. But now he was too late. Obviously Tiffany had been pressured to change her statement, and those people at *Under Suspicion* were about to place him under their microscope. Anna had said they were relentless.

He was going to be caught, unless he could figure out a way to kill both Tiffany and Laurie Moran.

Stealthily, he walked swiftly behind Laurie. He pulled the Glock from the back of his waistband. She didn't seem to hear his steps until he was right behind her. He had the gun pointed at her when she turned.

"Keep your mouth shut and do what you're told," he whispered, holding the gun low, close to his waist, inside his open coat. "We're going to take a walk."

He did not notice the phone slip from Laurie's hand as he directed her back to Tiffany's house.

72

Laurie searched futilely for a way to escape him. He had his arm linked around hers and was leading her back toward Tiffany's house. In his free hand, he held a gun pointed directly at her side.

A stranger approached on the sidewalk, the only other person visible on the street, fiddling with his cell phone. Tom's arm tightened around hers. She wanted to cry out for help, but knew that doing so could get them both killed. She tried to implore the stranger with her eyes as they passed, but the man was distracted by his screen.

She felt all hope leave her body as the stranger continued walking into the distance.

As she expected, Tom marched her to Tiffany's front porch.

"Knock," he demanded.

She remembered the sound of the door locking behind her as she left. She had warned Tiffany to call 911 if Tom sought contact with her. As long as Tiffany didn't open the door, she would probably be safe.

She stared at Tom defiantly.

"Do it," he hissed.

She pictured her father having to tell Timmy that he had lost another parent to a gunshot. Her son would be an orphan. But if she went inside this house, Tom would kill not only her, but Tiffany, too. At least if Laurie remained here on the porch, Tiffany would be safe.

She did not move. She only hoped Timmy would know that she thought of him at the end and was trying to save a woman's life.

Tom glared at her, knocked on the door, and stepped to the side, out of sight from the peephole. Laurie heard footsteps approaching the front door. "Tiffany, no!" she yelled. "Don't—"

But she was too late. The door opened, and Tom pushed Laurie inside, his gun pointed at both of them.

73

Y ou sure I can't get you a drink while you wait?"

Alex looked at his watch. He had been sitting alone at Marea for fifteen minutes, but he had arrived early. It was only 7:05.

After the wonderful evening they'd had last night, he was certain Laurie would be here shortly.

"Sure. I'll have a Bombay Sapphire martini with olives, please."

He would catch up on emails on his phone while he waited.

74

Tom Wakeling was pacing frantically in Tiffany's living room, gesturing toward various mementos on display. Every time he waved the gun around, Laurie flinched.

"How much is this tiara worth? What about this signed photo with Frank Sinatra?"

Tiffany's eyes widened. She was shaking with terror. "I have no idea," she said. "These things meant the world to my grandmother, but I don't think they're valuable."

"What about that bracelet you stole from the museum? It has to be worth a fortune."

"It's not, I promise!" Tiffany broke into sobs. "I was telling you the truth that night. It was a cheap souvenir. I gave it to my grandmother."

"What money or *real* jewelry have you got here?" Tom demanded.

"There's two hundred dollars in my wallet. My jewelry is on the dressing table upstairs. It's all costume."

Laurie was trying to remain calm, but inside, she was even more terrified than Tiffany. She knew what Tiffany did not. He wasn't looking for money. He was on the rise at Wakeling Development. Whatever he was planning, it had nothing to do with these knickknacks. Laurie realized that he was going to stage a home invasion gone wrong. He would make it appear as if someone had ransacked the place in a search for valuables, left with a couple of mementos, and killed them both.

"Your plan won't work," Laurie muttered.

"Shut your mouth!" he snapped.

"Listen to me. There was another woman here," Laurie said. "She has a recording of Tiffany talking about the bracelet and about where she was at the time of the murder. The police will know that Tiffany lied about being with you when Virginia went to the roof. If you hurt us, they'll put two and two together."

"The tall woman in the blue coat?"

"Yes."

"Who is she?"

"Jane Martin," Laurie said, recalling the name Charlotte had planned to use for her undercover work. "She works at my television studio. She tricked Tiffany into believing she was a book publisher asking questions about her grandmother."

Laurie did not reveal that she also had a copy of the recording in her email. Tom hadn't seemed to notice when she dropped her cell phone as he grabbed her on the sidewalk. Her only hope was that someone would find it and try calling the home number stored in her phone to return it. Her father would know something was terribly wrong and send police to the spot where the phone was found. On the other hand, maybe no one would find it, or the finder would make no attempt to return it. She shook away the thought. She had to cling to any sliver of hope.

"I saw her leaving when I arrived," Tom said. "I should have stopped her the second I saw her speaking to you. Call her," he demanded, picking up the handset of a cordless phone on the end table. "Make up a story to get her to come back here with that recording. If you say one word to indicate something's wrong, I'll kill you both."

Laurie felt her hand tremble as she took the phone. She quickly scanned the other areas of the house visible from this vantage point. She did not see another handset.

This might be her only shot to save them.

75

You sure you don't want some bread or an appetizer while you wait?"

Alex thought he detected a note of pity in the waitress's voice.

He checked his watch again. 7:40 P.M. "No, I'm fine, thank you."

Once the waitress was gone, he rose from the table and maneuvered near the entrance to call Laurie from his cell phone. It rang four times and then went to voice mail. "Just checking in to see if you're on your way. Let me know if you want me to send Ramon to pick you up."

Laurie had said she might be on a tight timeline if she ran home first to see Timmy, but he had never known Laurie to be forty minutes late, let alone without a text or a phone call.

He checked his phone once again a few moments later for any new messages from her. Nothing.

If she wasn't here and hadn't contacted him, something was wrong.

This time, he didn't bother leaving his table to make the call. It was too urgent.

Leo picked up almost immediately. "Alex, shouldn't you be having an extravagant dinner with my daughter?"

"Did she go home after work to see Timmy?" Alex asked.

"No, she said she was going straight to dinner with you."

"She's not here, Leo. She must be in some kind of trouble."

76

Leo put Alex on hold to pull up Find My Friends on his cell phone. Laurie had taught him how to do this so the two of them could find Timmy—or at least his cell phone—at any moment.

A map immediately appeared on his screen, showing the location of the phones in their shared friends group.

One spot on the map was the location of Laurie's apartment, indicating that Timmy was here. Leo felt a pain in his chest when he saw a second circle on the far right side of his screen. He used his fingers to zoom into the map. According to this location tracking program, Laurie was in Queens.

He tried to keep his voice calm when he clicked back over to his call with Alex. "I checked her location with my phone. Can you think of any reason Laurie would be in Queens?"

"Queens? No. She said she had some work to do—that something was bothering her about a witness and she couldn't let it go. She was going to try to swing by the apartment to see Timmy before dinner if she had time, but she didn't say anything about leaving Manhattan."

A beeping tone interrupted their call. Leo checked his screen. He didn't recognize the number, but answered anyway. He did not want to take a chance of missing a call from Laurie.

He recognized her voice immediately. He had barely breathed a sigh of relief when his panic resurfaced. "Hi, Jane, this is Laurie Moran."

"Laurie? Where are you? What's wrong?"

"I'm sorry to bother you again when you thought you were finally free for the night. I'm here with Tiffany and she wants to go over the statement she made."

It was obvious to Leo that his daughter was speaking under someone else's direction. He also knew that his daughter was deliberate and creative. She would find a way to give him the information he needed.

"Try to use your boss's name if you're in imminent danger."

"I'm sorry to be in such a rush, but Brett is pushing us on this deadline. And don't even get me started about Charlotte. You wouldn't believe the things she has to say about the show. Can you bring the recording you made back to the house so we can go through it line by line with Tiffany? She wants to make sure she didn't mischaracterize anything about her date with Tom."

"Got it," Leo said as his blood froze.

"You remember where Tiffany lives, right?" She recited the street address slowly and clearly. It lined up with the spot on the map where her cell phone was currently located.

"We'll be right there," Leo said.

"See you soon."

Leo clicked back over to Alex's call. "She is in trouble. She is talking like someone is forcing her. I know where she is. I've got to go."

"Where is she? I'll take my own car."

Leo knew he would only be wasting time to argue. He gave the address to Alex and made him promise not to approach the house without him.

Leo's next call was to Laurie's friend Charlotte Pierce, whose number he found in Laurie's contacts on her iPad. He knew that Laurie must have used her name for a reason.

The phone was answered by someone saying "Hi, Laurie." She must have recognized Laurie's home number on her phone.

"Charlotte, it's her father, Leo." He told her quickly about the strange phone call from Laurie. "What do you know?"

"I do have that recording of her witness's statement. A woman named Tiffany Simon. She told a tall tale about the stolen bracelet. Laurie is sure that she lied about being with Tom Wakeling."

Now Laurie was calling from Tiffany's house, asking "Jane" to return to the house with the recording. There was only one explanation: Tom Wakeling was at the house, and he wanted that recording destroyed.

He would be on the lookout for police. If Leo called

911, he knew what would happen. It would turn into a hostage situation. The SWAT team would look for a clean shot through the windows, but Laurie and this woman Tiffany would be in terrible danger.

He had another plan. "Charlotte, I'm sorry to involve you in this, but you're the only person who can get him to open that door without a confrontation."

"I'll do anything for Laurie."

"I'll have a patrol car pick you up. Where are you?"

"P.J. Clarke's by Lincoln Center."

"The driver of the patrol car will take you near the house. I'll meet you there."

77

Leo glanced down the hall toward Timmy's room and was glad to see his door was closed. He wanted to make sure he could not hear the phone conversations his grandfather was having.

He called one of his friends, a captain on the force, and quickly arranged for a patrol car to pick him up in front of Laurie's building.

He went immediately to Timmy's bedroom and found him playing video games when he was supposed to be doing his homework.

"I swear I was only going to play for a few minutes," Timmy said sheepishly.

Leo tried to keep his voice calm. "I got a call from the anti-terror team and need to go in for a meeting. Can I trust you to stay right here while I'm gone?"

"I'll be okay, Grandpa."

"I won't be long." Leo knew Timmy would be fine. They were in a doorman building, and he had to get to Laurie.

He was about to close the door when Timmy stopped

him. "Everything's okay, though, right?" Beneath his bangs his eyes were so innocent, even though they had seen so much already.

"All good. Do that homework, okay?" He hated lying to his grandson, but he had no other choice.

He had a plan. Pray God, it works, he thought as he raced outside to the curb. A patrol car, its siren blaring, was rushing down the street on its way to him.

He called the commissioner's office and was put through immediately. In three terse sentences he told him what was happening. A patrol car was dispatched immediately to pick up Charlotte. Numerous units without sirens or lights would begin to make their way to a corner near Tiffany's address. From there they would form a perimeter in the neighborhood.

Leo warned, "If Wakeling guesses that we are on to him, it might cost my daughter her life."

78

Just as Laurie had suspected, Tom staged the scene at the house to resemble a robbery gone bad. Tiffany cried on the sofa while Tom knocked over lamps, tore pictures from the wall, and stuffed small mementos in a canvas shopping bag he'd found in the kitchen.

"Stop looking at me," he barked at Tiffany. "You make me nervous. And when I'm nervous, bad things happen."

Laurie knew that he was panicking and could end up shooting both of them before anyone arrived. She knew that she had to try to calm him and slow the situation down. She was sure her father had understood she was in trouble and was figuring out a way to rescue her and Tiffany. But she had to somehow make sure there was enough time for the plan to work.

Instead of confronting Tom, Laurie looked away. It had been a stroke of luck that he had not listened in on her conversation with her father. She prayed the gamble would save their lives.

But now Tom had stopped ransacking the house. The scene was sufficiently staged for his purposes. All he was waiting for was the arrival of the recording of Tiffany's statement. Once the recording was destroyed, he would shoot them and flee.

"Your aunt was wrong about you," Laurie said, seeing an opportunity to get him talking. "Once your cousins gave you a chance, you ascended quickly through the corporate ranks. Anna was telling me she didn't know what she'd do without you."

"That's all I was trying to tell my aunt that night," Tom said, his voice becoming increasingly agitated. "She should give me a chance at the company. I saw her slip away alone and go onto the elevator. It stopped at the roof. You had run off somewhere by that point," he said, pointing the gun at Tiffany. "The guard by the staircase had taken off. I used the stairs to the roof to find Aunt Virginia alone. I just wanted her to hear me out. I had tried already when dinner ended, but she blew me off. I thought once we were alone, away from the crowd, she might listen to me. All I wanted was a role in the business. I wasn't asking for my father's half—even though I felt entitled to it. I thought she'd be willing to make things right, the way Uncle Bob never did. Half that company should have been my father's."

"Carter told me how cruel she could be," Laurie said, egging him on. "She told him that he needed to grow up, and he wouldn't be anywhere without the family name."

"That's nothing. My aunt treated me like a piece of garbage. She was even colder to me than Uncle Bob. When she saw me on the roof that night, she called me a gambler with no control over my life. She said I would never have been admitted to the party except that Uncle Bob had turned the Wakeling name into something valuable."

"How awful for you," Laurie said, feigning sympathy.

"Do you know what her last words were? 'Tom, you're even more useless than your father.'"

"And then you pushed her," Laurie said.

"No, I didn't. She was trying to leave, and I reached to stop her. I wanted her to see that I was a human being with dreams and plans. She jerked away from me and fell backwards. She was just so small. It was all an accident."

It was possible that Tom had actually come to believe this version of the facts over the years, but he was lying to himself. Laurie had seen that ledge. She tried to imagine the terror Virginia must have felt when he picked her up and hoisted her over the railing.

Laurie gasped at the sound of a knock on the door.

Tom swung the gun away from Tiffany and pointed it at her. "Open it."

79

When Leo arrived, an unmarked police van was parked a few houses down from Tiffany's home. The agents, looking up from their binoculars, told Leo that the blinds at the house were tightly closed when they arrived. This meant that Wakeling probably could not see what was going on outside, but also that they could not see inside. Tersely, Leo told them what he wanted to do. With few other options, they quickly agreed to his plan.

Two officers positioned themselves at the back door. Charlotte made her way to the porch, flanked by two officers to her left, and Leo and another to her right. She was wearing a bulletproof vest beneath her blue coat.

Leo had given Charlotte a firm command: her only role was to knock on the door and then run to the end of the block, where Alex and more police were waiting.

Charlotte knocked on the door.

Leo's heart jumped at the sound of Laurie's voice inside. "Thanks for coming, Jane. This should be quick. There's not much left on my part to do," she called out through the door as Leo heard locks tumbling.

There's not much left on my part to do. The phrasing sounded strange from Laurie's lips. Leo knew his daughter. Laurie was trying to find a way to convey vital information.

There's not much left on my part to do.

Left. My part. My left. She was telling him that the threat was positioned to her left. The hinges of the door were to her right.

He then signaled that the other officers should watch what was the right side of the door frame from their perspective, where they would have the best angle.

It happened quickly.

The second the door moved, one of the officers pulled Charlotte to the side and she began to run. Leo kicked the door open the rest of the way and swerved to his right, away from the door frame. Laurie ducked low and lunged out, shots whistling over her head as Leo yanked her to the side. Tiffany screamed and dove to the floor.

The shots occurred almost instantaneously. The investigation later revealed that eight shots in all were fired by police—four from each of the two officers on the opposite side of the door. Two additional shots in Laurie's direction had been fired from Wakeling's pistol.

Both officers gave identical versions of what they had seen from their vantage point. Tom Wakeling had been standing to Laurie's left side as she opened the door. Once she leapt outside, he had swung toward the open door and aimed at Laurie.

They had no choice. Tom Wakeling was dead, but their gunfire had saved Laurie's life.

80

As Charlotte raced toward the police car, the sound of gunfire exploded behind her. She collapsed against it, gasping for breath and moaning, "Oh, dear God."

Frantic, Alex was standing there. He asked, "What happened to Laurie? Is she safe?"

Without waiting for an answer, Alex rushed down the street. Two policemen tried to stop him.

He spat out the words. "I'm here with Leo Farley."

The officers waved Alex by.

He heard a woman shouting Tiffany's name. In an instant, a sobbing Tiffany stumbled into her neighbor's embrace.

But where is Laurie?

Unspeakable relief overcame him when he spotted Laurie standing with her father. An NYPD jacket was wrapped around her shoulders.

She was alive. She was safe.

"Laurie, Laurie!" he shouted.

She turned at the sound of his voice. When he pulled her into his arms, it felt as if they were all alone.

When he finally let go, both of their faces were wet with tears.

"How did you know to come?" she whispered.

"Tell you later. My God, I love you so much."

They held each other in the street, moving only to make room for the onslaught of police cars and ambulances that were arriving.

Leo came over to them saying, "You two get out of here. You don't need any more of this. A car will take Charlotte home. The department's going to want to question you, but it'll be hours before they're ready."

Laurie looked between Alex and her father hesitantly. "Are you sure that's okay?"

"Who knows the ropes of an investigation better than your old man? I'm serious: Go. I'll make sure the powers that be know how to find you." He patted her on the back, steering her in the direction of Alex's waiting car.

"My plan was to go back to the restaurant," Alex told him. "Our table is waiting." He said gently, "Laurie, are you still up to it?"

"Absolutely!"

81

I can't believe we're here now, after what happened tonight," Laurie murmured.

"Neither can I," Alex agreed as they walked into Marea and went to the table that had been reserved for them earlier. Alex could see that Laurie was still deathly pale, but the shock that had been in her eyes and her expression was beginning to fade.

The waiter came immediately. "The tortellini is your favorite," Alex suggested. "Shall I order for you? And a glass of Chardonnay, of course."

She nodded, her head still reeling with the memory of gunshots whistling past her ears as Leo yanked her to the side.

"I was so afraid Tiffany had been murdered," she said. "I would have blamed myself."

A brief jingle sounded, announcing that Laurie had received a text. She looked hesitantly at Alex. "It's okay," he said. "See what it is."

It was from Leo. She read it aloud. *"Medics examined*

Tiffany. She's OK. A neighbor took her to her house for the night. I'm in a car heading back to your place. Just spoke to Timmy who's fine. ENJOY DINNER and don't interrupt for any more texts!"

They both laughed.

As Laurie spoke, she realized this was to be the special dinner they had planned. "I kept you waiting so long tonight."

"Just long enough to go through hell when I phoned Leo, and he learned that something was terribly wrong."

"He prevented Tom Wakeling from killing Tiffany and me." She knew she was beginning to feel better. "It turned out well for all of us. We know that Tom Wakeling was his aunt Virginia's killer. And I'm probably still in shock, but for now, I want to put it behind us. I think you and I were both looking forward to dinner tonight."

"It was for a special occasion." Alex pulled a small velvet box from his pocket and opened it. It contained an engagement ring, a beautiful solitaire enhanced by smaller diamonds on each side of it. Alex slipped down from his chair and knelt in front of Laurie as other diners began to smile.

"Laurie," he said, his voice soft but intent. "I have loved you from the first minute I met you. I will love and cherish you all the days of my life. Will you marry me?"

Laurie's smile was the answer as he reached for her hand and slipped the ring on her finger.

A smattering of applause rippled through the room as the diners nearest them observed what was going on.

Minutes later a beaming waiter came rushing to them holding a bottle of champagne.

As they toasted each other, they knew that at last they were about to begin the life together that they both wanted.

And needed.

Simon & Schuster
Proudly Presents

You Don't Own Me
AN UNDER SUSPICION NOVEL

Mary Higgins Clark
&
Alafair Burke

Now available in hardcover and eBook
wherever books are sold

Please turn the page for a preview of
You Don't Own Me . . .

Prologue

Sixty-year-old Caroline Radcliffe nearly dropped one of the saucers she was carefully stacking in the overstuffed sideboard when she heard a bellow from the den. She immediately felt guilty for turning her eye from the children for even a moment. She had been looking out the window rejoicing at the fact that now, in late March, she would be able to spend more time outdoors with the children.

As she made her way toward the cry, four-year-old Bobby scampered by, an excited giggle escaping his open mouth. In the den, she found two-year-old Mindy wailing, her blue eyes focused on the tumble of building blocks scattered around her legs.

It wasn't difficult for Caroline to see what was going on. Bobby was a sweet little boy, but he took pleasure in devising small ways to torment his baby sister. On occasion, she was tempted to warn him that girls have a way of balancing the scales eventually, but she figured they were typical siblings who would work it all out in the end.

"It's okay, Mindy sweetheart," she said soothingly. "I'll help you put them back, just the way they were."

Mindy's pout only deepened, and she pushed a

nearby stack of blocks away from her. "No more!" she cried. The next sounds out of the girl's mouth were an unmistakable request for *Mama*.

Caroline sighed, bent down, and hoisted Mindy to her hip, wrapping her arms tight around the toddler until she quieted and her quick, upset breaths returned to normal.

"That's better," Caroline said. "That's my Mindy."

Mindy's father, Dr. Martin Bell, had made it very clear that he wanted Caroline to stop "babying the kids." In his view, even picking Mindy up when she cried was "babying."

"It's simple reward and punishment," he liked to say. "Not to compare them to dogs, but—well, it's how all animals learn. She wants you to hold her. If you do it every time she pitches a fit, we'll have tears flowing day and night."

Well, for starters, Caroline didn't like comparing children with dogs. And she also knew a thing or two about raising them. She had two grown children of her own and had helped raise another six of them in her years as a nanny. The Bells were her fourth family, and, in her view, Bobby and Mindy deserved a little extra TLC. Their father worked all the time and had all his little rules for everyone in the house, including the babies. And their mother—well, their mother was clearly going through a rough patch. It was the whole reason why Caroline had a job in a house with a stay-at-home mom.

"Bobby." She had heard his footsteps charging up the staircase. "Bobby!" she called out. She had learned by now that she and the children could make plenty of noise as long as Dr. Bell was gone. "I need to have a word with you. And you know why, young man!"

Even though Caroline had a soft spot for these little ones, she wasn't a complete pushover.

Caroline placed Mindy down to greet her brother at the bottom of the stairs. With each step, Bobby's pace slowed, trying to postpone the inevitable. Mindy shifted her gaze hesitantly between Caroline and Bobby, wondering what was going to happen next.

"Cut it out," Caroline told Bobby sternly. Pointing at Mindy, she said, "You know better than that."

"I'm sorry, Mindy," he muttered.

"I'm not sure I can hear you," Caroline said.

"I'm sorry I knocked your blocks down."

Caroline kept waiting expectantly until Bobby gave his sister a reluctant hug. A still angry Mindy was having none of the apology. "You're mean, Bobby," she wailed.

The moment was interrupted by the rumble of the mechanical door rolling open beneath them. Of all the homes Caroline had worked in, this one was arguably the finest. It was a late-nineteenth-century carriage house. What once served as a horse stable had now been renovated with every modern amenity, including the ultimate Manhattan luxury—a ground-floor, private garage.

Daddy was home.

"Now maybe the two of you can pick all that mess up in the den before your father sees it."

Pop! Pop! Pop!

Caroline's scream scared the children, who both began to cry.

"Firecrackers," she said calmly, even as her racing heart told her that her first instinct had been correct. Those were clearly the sounds of gunfire. "Go upstairs until I find out who's making that racket."

When they were halfway up the stairs, she hurried to the front door and then ran down the front steps to the driveway. The dome light inside Dr. Bell's BMW was on, and the driver's side door was halfway open. Dr. Bell was slumped over the steering wheel.

Caroline continued moving until she stood outside the open car door. She saw the blood. She saw enough to know that Dr. Bell wouldn't make it.

Terrified, she rushed inside and called 911. Somehow she managed to tell the dispatcher the address. It wasn't until she hung up the phone that she thought about Kendra, upstairs in her usual groggy state.

Dear God, who is going to tell the children?

1

Five years later, Caroline was still working in that same carriage house, but so much had changed. Mindy and Bobby were no longer her little babies. They were nearly finished with the first and third grades. They rarely cried anymore, even when the subject of their father came up.

And Mrs. Bell—Kendra, as Caroline often called her now—well, she was an entirely different woman. She no longer slept away the days. She was a good mom. And she worked, which is why it would fall to Caroline to pick the children up from their twice weekly visit to their grandparents' apartment on the Upper East Side. It was a task that neither of them enjoyed. Dr. Bell's parents made their son look like a free spirit compared to them.

Caroline had made it out of the apartment and halfway to the elevator when she heard the children's grandmother call out behind her. She turned to see both grandparents standing side by side outside their door. Dr. Bell was thin, almost to the point of being gaunt. His wispy hair was combed sideways across the dome of his head. As chief of vascular surgery at prestigious Mount Sinai Medical Center, he had grown accustomed to getting his own way. Nine years into retirement the scowl he had brought to the hospital every day had not diminished in the least.

Cynthia Bell, now in her eighties, showed little sign of the beauty that had once been hers. Her long hours in the sun had left her skin wrinkled and dry. Her lips were turned down at the corners, giving the impression of a permanent pout.

"Yes?" Caroline inquired.

"Did Kendra even *try* to get that television producer interested in Martin's case?" Dr. Bell asked.

Caroline smiled politely. "It's really not for me to say who Mrs. Bell speaks to—"

"You mean *Kendra*," he said sternly. "My wife is the only Mrs. Bell. That woman is no longer married to my son, because my son was shot to death in his driveway."

Caroline continued to force a pleasant expression. Oh, how she remembered the drama that had unfolded in the living room six months earlier over the subject of that television producer. Robert and Cynthia had asked to come to the house following Mindy's after-school dance recital. They told Kendra all about *Under Suspicion*, a television show that reinvestigated cold cases. Without notifying Kendra, they had sent a letter to the studio asking them to look into Martin's unsolved murder.

The official Mrs. Bell, Cynthia, interjected. "Kendra tells us that the producer, a woman named Laurie Moran, passed on the case."

Caroline nodded, "That's exactly what happened. Kendra was at least as upset about it as you are. Now, I need to get your grandchildren home before my shift ends," she added, even though she was never one to watch a clock.

As the elevator made its way down from the Bells' penthouse apartment to the lobby, she had a feeling that the couple wasn't going to let this subject drop. She was going to hear the name Laurie Moran again.

2

Laurie Moran was doing another round of "up . . . and down . . . and up . . . and down" to the beat of eardrum-piercing techno music in a room lit like a late 1970s disco. The man in front of her let out another enthusiastic "Wooooh!" which Laurie was certain added no additional health benefits.

To her right, her friend Charlotte—the one who had suggested this morning's spin class—grinned mischievously as she wiped her brow with a small towel. Her voice couldn't overcome the music, but Laurie could read her lips: "You love it!" On her other side Linda Webster-Cennerazzo looked as exhausted as she did.

Laurie most certainly did not, in fact, love it. She felt a moment of relief when the music changed to a song she recognized, but then the perfectly tanned and toned instructor ruined it by yelling, "Turn those knobs, people! It's time for another hill!"

Laurie reached down to the frame of her stationary bike as instructed, but snuck in two quick rotations of the knob to the left instead of the right. The last thing she needed was to increase her resistance, especially if you counted the psychological type.

When the torture finally ended, she filed out with the rest of the winded students and followed Charlotte and Linda to the locker room. It was unlike any gym Laurie had ever frequented, complete with eucalyptus-soaked towels, fluffy robes, and a waterfall next to the saunas.

Laurie's beauty routine took less than ten minutes, thanks to her wash-and-wear, shoulder-length hair and a quick application of tinted moisturizer and one coat of mascara. She rested on a cedar recliner as Charlotte attended to her own finishing touches.

"I can't believe you put yourself through that agony four times a week," Laurie said.

"Neither can I," Linda said.

"And I cross-train the other three, don't forget," Charlotte added.

"Now you're just bragging," Linda said, an edge in her voice.

"Look, I finally decided I have to exercise like this, because most of the time, I'm sitting in a chair at work or going out to dinner with clients. The two of you run around plenty enough in your regular lives."

"So we do," Linda added as she headed for the shower.

Laurie also knew that it was practically in Charlotte's job description to be in tip-top shape. She was the New York head of her family company, Ladyform, one of the country's most popular makers of high-end workout attire for women. "If I come back here again, I'm going to sit in the hot tub next to that waterfall and leave the *wooooh*-ing to you."

"Laurie, suit yourself. I think you're perfect just the way you are. But you're the one who said you wanted to get in better shape before the big wedding."

"It's not going to be *big*," she protested. "And I don't know what I was thinking. Those wedding magazines pollute a woman's brain: designer dresses, thousands of flowers, and so much tulle! It's too much. I've returned to my senses."

As she thought of her impending marriage to Alex, a surge of joy swept through Laurie. She tried to keep her voice even as she concentrated on what she was saying to Charlotte. "Once Timmy's done with the school year, we'll do something small and take a family trip together."

Charlotte shook her head disapprovingly as she tucked a tube of hair gel into her black leather Prada backpack. "Laurie, trust me. Forget about a family trip. You and Alex are going on your *honeymoon*. It should be just the two of you. Toasting each other with champagne. And Leo would be happy to take care of Timmy when you're away."

Laurie noticed a woman at a locker in the next row eavesdropping and lowered her voice. "Charlotte, I had a big wedding when Greg and I were married. I just want to have a quiet wedding this time. What matters is that Alex and I are finally together. For good."

Laurie had originally met defense attorney Alex Buckley when she recruited him to serve as the host of her television show, *Under Suspicion*. He became her closest confidant at work, and then more than that outside of the office. But when he stepped back from the show to return full-time to his legal practice, Laurie hadn't been entirely sure how Alex fit into her life. She had already found a great love in Greg and, after losing him, had forged ahead by juggling the demands of her career and being a single mother. She thought she was perfectly content, until Alex finally made it clear that he wanted more from Laurie than he believed she was ready to give.

As it turned out, she realized after a three-month hiatus that she was miserably unhappy without Alex. It was she who had called and asked him to dinner. The moment she hung up the phone she knew she had made the right decision. They had been engaged now for two months. She had already become accustomed to the feel of the platinum ring with a solitaire diamond that Alex had chosen.

She honestly couldn't recall whether she had even asked Alex what *he* wanted, even once.

She tried picturing herself walking down a long aisle in an elaborate white gown, but all she could see was Greg waiting for her at the front of the church. When she pictured herself exchanging vows with Alex, she saw them somewhere outside, surrounded by flowers, or even barefoot on a beach. She wanted it to be special. And different from what she'd had before. But, again, that was what *she* wanted.

She was almost to her office door by the time she realized that her assistant, Grace Garcia, was trying to get her attention. "Earth to Laurie? You in there?"

She blinked and was back in the real world. "Sorry, I think the spin class Charlotte dragged me to made me dizzy."

Grace was looking at her with wide, dark eyes lined

in perfect cat style. Her long, black hair was pulled into a tight *I Dream of Jeannie* topknot, and she was wearing a flattering wrap dress and knee-high boots—only three-inch heels, practically flats by Grace's standards.

"Those spin addicts are a cult," Grace warned dismissively. "All that hooting and hollering. And people wearing crazy outfits like they're in the Tour de France. Girlfriend, you're in a gym on Fifth Avenue."

"It definitely wasn't for me. You were saying something when I was in la-la land?"

"Right. You had visitors waiting for you in the lobby when I got in this morning. Security told me they arrived before eight and were adamant about waiting until you arrived."

Laurie was grateful for the success of her show, but could do without some of the ancillary benefits, such as fans who wanted to "pop in" to the studio for selfies and autographs.

"Are you sure they're not fans of Ryan's?" As popular as Alex had been with viewers, apparently the current host, Ryan Nichols, was considered "crush-worthy" by the younger generation.

"They're definitely here to see you. Remember the Martin Bell case?"

"Of course." A few months earlier, Laurie had thought the case would be perfect for *Under Suspicion*—a renowned physician shot to death in his driveway while his wife and children were just yards away inside the house.

"His parents are in conference room B. They say the wife is a killer and they want you to prove it."

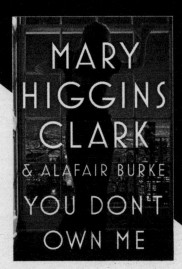